I froze just before he plunged it into my skin. My mouth went dry when dark red liquid filled his tube.

"What is that for?" I asked as he pulled away and left the room.

"Lord Nathan wants to ensure that you don't have any *diseases* from all your whoring around. He requested a full blood panel before your wedding night. Can't say I blame him, considering you'll open your legs for anyone. I should probably have my son checked, too."

I scowled. "Fuck you."

"Aren't you hungry?" He smirked. "You've barely touched your food. I'll make sure my men don't bother you."

I was hungry, but it was hard to swallow when my throat was dry with trepidation. I couldn't stop thinking about the day ahead of me. "No thank you."

"Oh, here is our guest of honor," Theodore said. I seethed with anger as Lord Nathan clumsily stumbled into the room. He reeked of alcohol and looked as tired as I felt. Wobbling toward the table, he ripped off his coat and threw it onto the chair. His eyes met mine, cold as ice and filled with an unspoken rage. I watched him slowly lower himself onto the seat, the tension in the room growing more powerful with every passing second. "Morning," his greeting echoed off the walls.

"Good morning," said Theodore.

"Good morning," I said, my voice dripping with contempt.

He eyed the robe I'd put on and frowned with disapproval. "I see you dressed for the occasion," he said sarcastically. "And it's an occasion worth dressing for, isn't it? I knew I'd get to marry you in the end."

My dry tongue ran over my cracked lips as a sinister frown crept onto my face. "Your brother thought he'd marry me," I said, defiance evident in my voice. "Killing him was far too easy. I can still hear the sickening crunch of his skull. His blood still stains the floor to this day." My anger was intense, radiating from my clenched fists and gritted teeth.

Lord Nathan's forehead creased ever so slightly, a hint of a grin at the corner of his mouth. "I must thank you for this, I suppose." His voice carried a dangerous edge that belied the nonchalant words. "I was always the spare, but his death allowed me to inherit what I truly wanted: the title and my parents' properties. And now, I'm inheriting a pretty young bride too." He sneered out the last words, his fists clenching at his sides as rage bubbled just beneath the surface.

I snapped my gaze up. "I'm not a piece of property you can own, Lord Nathan."

"Aren't you?" He was staring at me, his eyes huge,

his lips parted. "You're mine. I could haul you by the hair from your seat if I wanted."

I felt my skin crawl as he looked at me, the same angry expression his brother had worn three years ago. His eyes glinted with something malicious. He had evil intentions—that much I could tell—and I felt a powerful current of defiance rise within me. I focused all my anger and resentment into one look, refusing to succumb to his advances.

I met their stares with a silent challenge, daring them to notice my revulsion. My jaw tightened and my mouth thinned as I took a deep breath.

"Nathan, are your men settled?" asked Theodore.

"Yes," replied Lord Nathan. "They're setting up camp. I wouldn't want my queen to be threatened on her wedding day."

I growled. "It's funny," I replied. "Your men couldn't take down the castle last night. You had to use the DuPont army to get the job done. You have a lot of faith in a bunch of outcasts."

His lips curled into a sneer. "My men don't disappoint. Many of them needed something to believe in. They were angry at the monarchy. Fighting for change. Theft and murder were the only things they knew. I gave them something to fight for, and now they're dedicated to me." His voice was filled with rage, as if he were recalling an injustice inflicted upon him. He was not the victim in this scenario. He was just a powerful man who thought the world owed him everything.

"Oh, you think you're a clever man, don't you?" I snorted. "You're just as stupid as your brother was. You think you can just live your life with me as your queen. You come from a low-ranking family. No one will respect you. At least the DuPonts earned their way to the top of their empire. You had to ride Theodore's back to get what you wanted."

"I've got plenty of influence in this kingdom," he sneered. "And I've got your pretty neck."

I smirked. "I'll snap my own neck like a twig before I let you have me, then you'll have nothing."

"I'll have your royal cunt, one way or another."

I laughed. "Over my dead body."

"Stop it, both of you," said Theodore. "You're just antagonizing each other. You will put your differences aside when it comes to the union. Don't forget what's at stake, Christine. You have your men to think of."

The blunt reminder of Atticus, August, and Leo made my heart stall.

My throat tightened as I held back my rising panic. I barely managed to force out a meek, "How are they?" Atticus, August, and Leo had been taken brutally just yesterday, and I hadn't seen them since. I was filled with fear for their safety.

"Atticus is angry but will learn why this is necessary soon enough. I can beat him into submission if necessary. Augustus is useless. Pacing his cell with worry. Leo is…well… Would you like to see him? I'm a kind man. I thought it might make you more generous with your affection if you're reminded of who will suffer if you don't comply with my demands."

This felt like a trap. "I can see him?"

Theodore grinned as if he had me right where he wanted me. "We're going to make an announcement today. I want you to show the world that you're alive and thrilled to marry Lord Nathan. You're going to tell everyone you wanted to be with him all along, but August was a tyrant keeping you apart. You're going to look lovingly at your future husband and solidify this union."

I sneered. "Never."

Theodore nodded, as if he expected this answer. "Bring in the prisoner," he directed his guard, and my heart skipped a beat as he disappeared behind the large door. I held my breath as the sound of a body being dragged across the marble tile filled my ears. Someone kicked open the doors, and Leo was tossed inside the room. I gasped and got up from my seat, my fists clenched at my side as I tried to process what I was seeing. "Leo!"

He was beaten, that much was obvious. His cheek was bruised and swollen, his hair matted and caked with blood. His eyes were dilated and red from crying. His clothes were ripped, his hands and feet duct taped. He was dragged to the area right in front of me, and I fell to my knees. I was so devastated to see him beaten and bloodied that I was crying. I reached for his hand and kissed it, not caring about what Theodore would do to me for touching him.

"Leo," I sobbed.

"This is who you really want to fuck?" asked Theodore. "He's pathetic."

I ran my hand over Leo's cheek. He was hot to the touch, and streaks of red covered his skin. "He's feverish. Something is wrong."

Theodore shrugged. "He's dying. Needs antibiotics. I could give him some, you know. But only if you cooperate."

My gaze snapped to him, and I felt my hatred for the man grow. He was toying with me, trying to make me comply. And the damning truth was, I'd do anything for them. *Anything*.

"I'll do it," I gritted. Leo moaned. "But I want to

see him given the medicine. I want to be able to check on him. I want regular visits with *all* of them."

Theodore exchanged a look with Nathan. "No. I call the shots here. I'll give him the medicine and you'll have to trust me."

I pressed my forehead to Leo's. "It's going to be okay. I'll take care of you." He grimaced and his breathing became labored. I kissed his forehead and then his cheek. "I love you, Leo."

"Do we have a deal?" Theodore asked impatiently.

I gently released Leo and stood, rolling my shoulders back as I glared at him. "Fine. But I want to see proof that the medicine worked."

"If you give a convincing performance at the announcement ceremony, I'll consider it," he replied.

I clenched my jaw so tightly I almost cracked a tooth. "Deal."

Lord Nathan clapped his hands. "This is fun."

"Next week, you'll be crowned queen. We've released word that Augustus was illegitimate, and the lords that are still alive are eager to transfer power to the rightful heir. After that, the two of you will marry," Theodore said.

My throat burned with the effort of repressing the violent scream that was clawing its way up my throat. I was so enraged that my whole body was on edge. I wanted to go on a rampage, yell at Theodore for treating me this way, scream at Leo to get better, and howl in anguish at myself for getting mixed up in this situation. I knew it was over. I knew I would have to accept my reality, marry this monstrous man, and suffer the consequences. Fury and tears clashed inside me as I contemplated what I must do, but I was so filled with rage and terror that I couldn't think straight.

A heavy weight of defeat settled in my chest. I tried to look Theodore DuPont defiantly in the eyes, but instead, I hung my head and whispered, "I'll do what you want. I'm going to marry Nathan, just please, please don't hurt them. I'm sorry, Leo. I'm so sorry." Tears stung my eyes and I felt like a traitor, standing there powerless against fate. Leo's struggle became more intense as he fought against his bindings. I tenderly ran my fingers over his cheek. I lied to him, and to myself. "It's going to be okay," I murmured through quivering lips. In my heart, I knew that it wasn't true. There was no guarantee that he would be alright. But I would do all I could to make sure that he was.

Theodore sneered at Nathan. "Go and get ready, Nathan. Christine needs to look her best for the announcement," he barked, standing tall. "I'll sort out the meds for Leo's IV. I'm sure he'll feel right as rain by the time it's over." He glared at me. "Make sure you stay put while the beauty team tries to conceal all those nasty bruises of yours."

My voice cracked as I croaked, "Understood." Theodore nodded and Leo was hauled out of the room. I slumped back down into the chair, my sweat-soaked arms wrapping around myself. My stomach felt like it had been filled with rocks. Theodore and Nathan left, quietly shutting the door behind them. I was alone with three guards in the room, their gazes silently scrutinizing my every move.

For a few moments, I let Theodore's words loop around in my head. I was going to be queen.

I was going to have to marry Nathan.

I was going to have to pretend to be happy.

I was going to have to marry Nathan.

I was going to have to see him crowned king.

I was going to have to marry Nathan.

I was going to have to marry Nathan.

I needed to be calm, and I needed to think of a plan.

I was going to have to marry Nathan.

A menacing chuckle spilled from my throat, and I clamped my hand over my mouth to muffle it. If I married him, I'd paint my wedding night with his blood. There was no other way.

But could I sacrifice my men to save myself?

It was an unbearable thought. I felt my heart pounding, ready to burst from my chest at any moment. I gulped in a breath of air, desperately attempting to steady my racing heart, striving to contain the tears that threatened to pour down my face. Anger and frustration began to boil in me until I could feel madness radiating from every pore of my body.

I was going to marry Nathan.

I was going to marry Nathan.

"Lady Abernathy?" a soft voice called. "It's time to get ready."

Chapter Two

LEO

I could barely remember the days leading up to this. My body felt like it was weighed down and I could barely move a muscle. My mouth was gagged tightly with duct tape, and my eyes were wide open. Christine was standing before me, her figure shrouded in fear and despair. Through the darkness, I could make out two frightening figures behind her. All I could hear was the sound of her muffled sobs as she bravely tried to restrain her tears. I felt sick, scared, confused and terrified all at once, my mind over-whelmed with worry and concern.

The walls of the claustrophobic room were an icy white. The only source of light was a lone lightbulb, suspended by a single wire in the center of the ceiling. On one wall, there were two barred windows, shut tight and blocking out the outside world. My head felt like it was splitting open, while my feverish skin felt scorched. I felt helpless and disoriented, my fear intensifying with every moment that I spent in the isolated space.

I was desperate to remember what had happened before everything went dark. I had been bound to the bed for hours—or days? Time meant nothing anymore. Our eyes met and her mouth moved as if to say something, but no sound emerged.

I begged her with my eyes for a shred of understanding.

She nodded, her lips wobbling and tears streaming down her face.

The door opened and another figure stepped inside. His heavy footsteps echoed in the otherwise silent room, sending chills down my spine. I felt my heart pounding out of my chest as they advanced, their black eyes watching me like prey.

I recognized Theodore and Nathan. The third man was older and lankier, with a crooked nose, graying hair, and a cigarette dangling from his fingers. He had a broad face, a small jaw and unblinking eyes. I had no idea who he was, other than he wore a lab coat, but he had the demeanor of an aristocrat.

He wasn't dressed like the other guards.

I watched as he sauntered over to Christine and kissed her hand. "My lady," he said, bowing before her. She snapped her hand back in disgust.

He straightened and gave me a bored look. "His infection is gone, and I dressed his wound to the best of my ability. He'll live. For now."

So he was a doctor? And he'd healed me.

Why?

"Can I talk to him?" Christine croaked.

Theodore rubbed his chin with his thumb and forefinger. "You seemed to do so convincingly well at the press release. Even *I* believed that you were in love with Lord Nathan," he said. His tone was measured, but there was a little pride behind it. "Such a good little whore. Convincing everyone with your smiles and flirty words."

The way he spoke about Christine both confused and infuriated me. My fists clenched. I imagined throwing him to the ground, strangling him with his own intestines. The anger burned like a furnace that blackened the edges of my sanity.

Lord Nathan's lips spread into a smirk, a self-satisfied smile that said he knew she was pretending and that he took pleasure in that knowledge. "She's such a beautiful little whore. A liar, yes. But so good at using her beauty to convince the masses."

Theodore nodded. "The perfect queen. Isabelle trained her well." He then stepped aside, allowing Christine to approach me. She slowly walked closer, each step weighed with intent, until she crouched before me. Her fingers trembled as she reached for my hand. She bit her lower lip, trying to keep her composure while tears streamed down her cheeks.

"Are you okay?" she asked softly, searching my eyes for an answer.

I blinked slowly and nodded.

"Good," she said before turning to Lord Nathan with a glare of contempt. "Now get him out of these restraints."

Lord Nathan glared back at us. "He is *my* prisoner, and I will do as I please," he snapped back at her with a smirk spread across his face that sent chills through my body.

Christine stood up abruptly, every muscle in her body tense as rage filled her veins. "You aren't going to get away with this," she spat at him before rounding on Theodore, who stepped forward protectively by Lord Nathan's side. Christine continued, the anger in her tone heavy. "And you—I will *ruin* you."

Theodore merely raised his eyebrows at her outburst before turning to Lord Nathan, who simply shrugged carelessly in response—clearly unbothered by Christine's threats. He then gestured toward me with a wave of his hand. "Behave, Christine. You wouldn't want one of your lovers to die. Or perhaps I'll make you do more than tell a few lies. We want the world to believe you love Lord Nathan. Perhaps you could fuck him on the balcony—"

"No," Christine gritted.

"Then behave," Theodore snapped.

Christine slumped her shoulders, making me fume. What had she done for me? Guilt slammed into me as Theodore DuPont, Lord Nathan, and the doctor walked toward the door. "You have ten minutes," Theodore said. "We will be just outside."

Christine nodded.

Once we were alone, more tears streamed down her cheeks, carving paths through her makeup. She ripped the tape from my mouth, and the searing pain of it made me groan.

"We have to be quiet," she hissed. "They're right outside." She was biting her lip so hard that I was sure it would split open.

"Are they going to kill me?"

"No," she said. I wasn't sure why her voice was shaking so hard. "Not yet, at least."

I gazed at her with a mixture of pain, worry, and

fear. "Why are you here?" I whispered, unable to hide the emotion in my voice. "Are you okay?"

She nodded stiffly. "I'm fine, I promise," she said unconvincingly, not meeting my gaze.

I knew she was lying, but chose not to push it.

She took a deep breath, her eyes filling with tears. "But you're not. I'm so sorry, Leo."

My voice cracked like thunder as I yelled out, "I don't fucking care about me. What's going on? Why are you still here? You need to leave, Christine. You can't marry him." My whole body shook with rage, but underneath all my anger was love. A deep, powerful love that I wanted to show her with every fiber of my being. I wanted to wrap her in my arms and protect her from all the surrounding dangers. I wanted to give her the love she deserved, the kind I should have given her from the start.

Fear snaked its way through my veins, paralyzing me with dread. My selfishness was a blaring beacon, mocking me with its intensity. I was petrified—of not taking up space in her heart, of my own insignificance as just a mere man, a guard who didn't matter in the grand scheme of things. I was nothing compared to them. Nothing.

How could she ever love me the way I loved her, when she shared her heart with them?

But if I could do it all over again, I'd be brave. I'd take her. I'd fight for her. I'd take whatever sliver of affection I could.

She placed her hand over my mouth. "Shh… We have to be careful, or they won't let me see you again."

"What happened?"

"You were badly injured. You needed treatment, so I had to go along with what they asked of me."

"What did they ask? Did Lord Nathan hurt you… did he…" The words hung in the air, stirring up a cauldron of emotions. Shame and terror coiled around my heart like an anaconda, tightening with each memory of her perfect body getting violated. Acidic bile bubbled in my gut, and I shook my head, unable to face the answer to my question. I locked eyes with her, both of us knowing the truth: no matter how far we went, she and I would be tethered together forever by Lord Geralt's heinous crime.

"No. No, Leo. I just had to tell the world I wanted Lord Nathan to be my husband. I had to renounce August." She looked away, as if ashamed.

"You did what you had to do," I rasped. "I don't deserve it—"

"I would do *anything* for you, Leo. Anything. I love you."

"Christine," I said, disbelief coursing through me. It

didn't matter how many times she claimed to love me, I couldn't believe someone as perfect and precious as her truly felt that way about me. "Thank you." I wanted to declare my love for her, too, but something held me back.

She shook her head, her eyes welling with tears. "I did what I had to do."

I looked down. "I know. I know."

She spat out her words, her face contorted in rage. "They didn't just want my words. They wanted me to make it convincing. So I had to kiss him. Let him hold my hand. I was disgusted with myself." Her tears cascaded down her face. She furiously swatted at them. "I'm sorry. You're sick and I'm here sobbing like an idiot."

"Why are you apologizing to me? I'm the one that failed you."

She shook her head. "I trained to defend myself. I should have been stronger. I should have saved us."

"No, I was the one who should have protected you. I don't deserve to live—"

"Stop, Leo." She grabbed my face, her fingers digging into me. "I love you. I will always love you. I should have done more. I'm so sorry."

"You did what you had to do. You did everything.

More than I deserve. I'm just so sorry that you had to do any of it."

"Stop saying that. Stop blaming yourself. Please."

"Christine, you must leave him. Run. You can't do this. Please. Please just leave."

She shook her head. "I can't. He has all of you."

"You should have left before it got to this point."

She gave me a brutal smile. "You're always trying to get rid of me."

I let out a sigh. "And I always fail."

"Yeah."

"So what now?" I asked.

"They threatened to hurt you. They told me that if I didn't go along with this, you would die." She shook her head. "I had to save you. I couldn't let you die, Leo. Now, they're going to ask me to do more. I'm…scared of what I'll be forced to do. I'm scared of the conse-quences of defending myself."

She had saved me. How many more times would she *have* to save me?

She leaned her head on my shoulder and cried. "I love you, too," I whispered, the bravest words I'd ever said. "I'm not sure when I fell for you, but it's been slow and steady. I fell little by little, each moment chipping away at my heart." I squeezed her tighter. "I fell for you when I watched you smell roses in the royal garden." Her head tilted up, and she brushed hair out of her face. "And again when you danced with Augustus at an event." When she blinked back tears, I kissed away the wetness on her cheek. "You always bit your pen in the library while you studied," I said, pressing my lips to her ear. "I fell harder when you fought with me. When I saw how strong you'd become. And I'll love you when there isn't air in my lungs. When you find a way out of this damn castle and leave for good."

"I will never leave you," she snapped. "I'll find a way out of this. I swear."

It wasn't what I wanted to hear, but a small part of me triumphed. It was selfish and wrong. I didn't want to be like Augustus, who took her love for granted, or Atticus, who stole her heart without remorse. I wanted to do what was best for Christine, even if it meant never getting a future with her.

She pushed away from me and gave me a weak smile. "Let's focus on the positives."

"Which are?" I asked.

"Well, you're alive."

I sighed. "And you're going to marry that...that bastard."

She bit her lip, trying not to cry again. "I will get rid of him, Leo. For us. I will."

"I don't want you to risk yourself, Christine. It's not safe."

She shook her head. "I will. I will take care of it. You can't get rid of me that easily."

"I wouldn't want to," I whispered.

She smiled at me. "I'm glad to hear that, because I'm not going anywhere."

Two guards walked in, and I knew my time was up. I had to let her go, at least for now. "Go," I said, trying to rein in my emotions.

She nodded, looking me directly in the eye. "I love you, Leo."

"I love you, too."

She knelt back down and planted a soft kiss on my lips. "I'm not finished with you. I'm going to get you back."

"I'll be here."

Chapter Three

"A formal coronation is necessary," Theodore DuPont said. I stood in his new bedchamber, glaring at him. He was making himself right at home in the destroyed castle. Once again I was summoned, and once again a guard stood with a gun at my back. "The ceremony will help your people accept you as queen. Everyone loves royal festivities, and seeing it will make them follow you. I always thought it was a mistake that Augustus prioritized his wedding to you over the coronation. If his people had seen him crowned as king publicly, perhaps it wouldn't have been so easy for them to be swayed otherwise."

Lord Nathan nodded. "The sooner she is queen, the

better. I want to move quickly to solidify our position. The surviving lords need to swear their allegiance to her today."

Theodore grinned. "I agree. I've summoned them for a meeting."

I lifted my chin up and glared at them. "They won't bow before me," I said, my voice rough.

"Of course they will," Theodore replied. "They have nothing, and you're next in line for the throne. We've proven that Augustus isn't the rightful heir. Once the lords bless your ascension to the throne, we can plan the coronation. By the end of the day, you'll have the title. And by the end of the week, the entire world will have to recognize it."

I scowled at him. "Aren't you afraid?"

His face hardened. "No," he growled. "What should I be afraid of?"

"If I ascend to the throne, I'll have an entire army at my disposal to do as I please. I could order them to massacre you in a single breath."

Theodore and Lord Nathan shared a determined glance before roaring with laughter. "If you think that you can succeed," my fiancé sneered. "Our forces have your castle surrounded. Nobody within these walls is loyal to you. You've convinced the world that you desire this marriage, but don't forget that we've imprisoned your men. Just one word from us and they'll each have matching bullets in their skulls."

Theodore shifted on his feet. "You might have the title, Christine. But never forget who truly has the power."

I felt my face contort with rage as I spoke. "Is that so?"

Theodore raised an eyebrow in challenge.

"I'm assuming you have more threats and demands to throw my way, or you wouldn't have summoned me here. So what kind of 'duties' are you expecting me to perform now?" I was thinking of Atticus, August, and Leo. I just wanted to know what I had to do to keep them alive.

Theodore grinned, like he had been expecting this reaction. "I need you to be the obedient queen in front of the lords. Give them the impression that all of this was your plan from the very beginning." My hands clenched into fists, and I swallowed a lump in my throat, knowing I had no choice but to obey.

"You want me to be the scapegoat."

Lord Nathan shook his head. "I want you to be the mastermind. The lords need to believe that you want this. It'll make them more compliant."

I resisted the urge to roll my eyes. "Isn't fear of death enough of a motivation? You killed half the castle. Many of them died during your raid. We don't need to lie to them to get them to bow. Just fill the room with your armed guards."

"To a certain extent, yes," Theodore said. "I don't want anyone thinking they can stand against us. So, you'll play your part this morning. I want you to ask for my help. Ask for my protection."

"So essentially, I'll be the queen in name, but you'll be the king in reality," I said, my voice dripping with venom.

Theodore DuPont nodded. "Be good and I'll let you see Atticus. I think he's spent enough time in his cell. I need my son's help, and he needs to see that this is best for all of us."

My ears perked up. "You'll let me see him? What's the catch?"

Lord Nathan spat his words, his face reddening in rage. "I'll be damned if I let my betrothed behave like a common whore and be bedding someone else. Keep your filthy hands off of Atticus, if you know what's good for you. I won't allow you to make the same mistake as my predecessors and have an illegitimate child running my kingdom." His anger was unexpected, and I noticed him glaring at my stomach like it offended him.

Theodore arched his brow. "That mistake is the

reason you'll be king, Lord Nathan. I suggest you watch your tone."

Lord Nathan sucked in a breath of air before straightening. "I'm sorry, I appreciate the trust you've placed in me, but I won't just sit by and watch her gallivanting around with other men. Your son might have been fine sharing her, but I'm not. What kind of man allows that to happen? He was weak and—"

Theodore's eyes blazed with fury. "Do not talk about my son. I suggest you remember your place here."

"You were threatening to kill him just days ago," I interjected.

Theodore's eyes darted to me, his lip curling up as his nostrils flared. "I've said that I want him to see reason. If he spends a few days reflecting in his cell, he'll come to realize the error of his ways. Maybe he can't help his attraction to you, but he will realize this is best. My son is the future of the DuPont empire."

Lord Nathan scoffed. "And *I'm* the future king. I won't share my prize."

I felt sick to my stomach. I was nothing more than a possession.

"As long as you remember who handed her over and keep your end of the deal," Theodore snapped back.

Lord Nathan's eyes narrowed. "We'll see how long your son takes to realize that this is where his future lies. Perhaps once I've had Christine in my bed, he'll know his place. Though that hasn't stopped him before. Disgusting."

It made me sick for everyone to talk about my sex life like it was something to be ashamed of. I loved Augustus, Atticus, and Leo equally. It wasn't wrong.

"We'll see how long your kinghood lasts if you don't learn your place," Theodore growled. "You're new to the position, and you're making too many enemies. I'd be careful not to step over the line."

Lord Nathan sniffed. "You'll be the one to watch your step, Theodore. I don't share. End of story. Your son was spineless, but Christine..." He paused to walk closer to me. I flinched when he lifted his hand up to stroke my cheek. It took everything I had not to break his arm. "Christine needs a firm hand. Someone that ties her up so she doesn't wander. Someone willing to break her." He paused to look at Theodore. "I thought your son was ruthless, but he couldn't even control this harmless creature. You focus on Atticus and keep him away from *my* bride."

"I'll make sure he realizes how important it is to stay away from Christine, if you give my family the respect we deserve. You couldn't have taken down this castle without us. Remember that."

Lord Nathan smirked. "And you couldn't have taken it without me, either. I laid the groundwork."

Theodore's spine straightened. "And I held the sword. You should leave."

Lord Nathan glared at both of us. "I have work to do. I'll see you both at the meeting with the lords."

My jaw clenched tight, my eyes firmly averted from the leering men in the room. My voice was a hiss as I spat, "You'll never break me." Lord Nathan's face darkened with anger before he spun on his heel and stormed out of the room, leaving an oppressive silence hanging heavy in his wake.

I looked at Theodore. "He's a liability," I said. "Are you sure that's the puppet you want on the throne?"

Theodore sat in his velvet chair and crossed his legs. "He's easily manipulated and resourceful. Convinced an army of misfits to follow his lead and took down two houses."

I took a step closer to him. "But he's also greedy and untrustworthy. Wouldn't it make more sense for me to marry someone else? Someone you can trust… perhaps…someone in the family."

Theodore arched his brow. "You're suggesting Atticus."

"You'd have a son for a king."

"There's one problem with that, Christine. My son is not loyal to me, he's loyal to *you*."

"And what if I asked him to be loyal to you?"

Theodore's dark eyes flickered with an icy glint as he spoke. "He'd sacrifice anything for you. I couldn't even dare tell him of my plans to side with Lord Nathan, as he was too preoccupied with getting you out of harm's way. Blindly devoted to you since the day you met. I'd be a fool to think he wouldn't go above to protect you. I cannot let my son be your king." His gaze hardened into a burning fury. "I *will not* let my son be *your* king."

I gritted my teeth. "So why are you even using me if I'm such a liability?"

"Because you're a liability easily controlled by her emotions," he said, his face blank. "If I can control you, I'll keep Augustus and Leo alive for as long as necessary. I'll hold them over your head for the rest of your miserable life. You have a weakness, and I plan to exploit it."

I shook my head. "You're despicable."

He shrugged, his eyes cold and expression unreadable. "I am what I am. I suggest you play your part. It'll be over soon if you do what I say." His voice lowered, and he leaned forward, his expression turning menacing. His gaze bore into me as he hissed, "Remember that the moment you take your place on the throne, the lives of your loved ones hang in the balance. One move out of line and they'll feel the full brunt of my wrath."

I looked him straight in the eye and asked, "Would you kill your own son?"

His bitter laughter filled the room. "Which one? I have two." He paused, slowly licking his lips.

"The one you actually care about."

He shook his head slowly. "Of course not. He's my heir. My job would be a lot harder if you only loved him. But luckily for me, you went and fell for three men. I have plenty of options to keep you under my thumb."

I took another step closer to him. "This would be so much easier if you let me marry Atticus. You'd have everything you ever wanted. He'd be king."

"I had to put an end to your relationship with my son. You may have fooled him, but I know the truth. Your morals are as shallow as a puddle, and I can't let my son's life be ruined by someone who takes pleasure in cheap thrills. Atticus may be taken in by your facade again, but he will never be able to trust you. He'd do anything you desired, and that would destroy him, and I cannot allow that."

I stammered. "You don't know that."

He sneered. "I know my son better than anyone

else. You? You're his downfall, and I won't just let you have him without a fight. I won't sit back and watch you tear apart everything he's worked for, everything that makes him a powerful DuPont. One day, my son will find someone to match his needs: an obedient woman who will do everything he says without question. He'll marry her, start a family with her, and he won't have to worry about her betraying him. The truth is, Christine, you don't deserve my son. You're not reliable or subservient. Sure, you look nice and have a fancy title, but I'd rather manipulate and force you to marry someone you loathe than watch you break my son's heart."

"You surprise me, Theodore," I croaked.

"What do you mean?"

"I didn't think you were capable of caring for anyone. But you're doing this because you love him—because you don't think I'm good enough." I took a deep breath and squared my shoulders, my voice firmed. "I was willing to spend my life with Atticus. It would have been unconventional but still *real*. I would have been there for him, by his side, and loved him till the end. He's more than just my lover, he's family. And I would have done anything for my family." I swallowed, a theory swirling around my mind. "But your worry about Atticus isn't the only reason you don't think I'm worthy, right? Is it because I remind you of *her*?"

He scoffed. "Who?"

I smirked. "Isabelle. You loved her, didn't you? She was the woman you couldn't control, the woman you couldn't tame. She fucked you, but she didn't choose you. And that was a hit to your pride."

"You have no idea what you're talking about," he spat.

"I don't have to know it all. It's written all over your face, Theodore. You loved her, didn't you? And she refused you."

He gritted his teeth. "I would have given her everything, but she stayed with a king that didn't even love her."

"She didn't pick *you*," I snapped. "And you're mad that in my own way, I've picked Atticus."

He looked at me, his face hard and devoid of emotion. "You're just a fleeting thought in his mind. A bad memory that will fade away with time." He pointed to the door. "Get out of my sight, or I'll have the guards throw you out. I don't have time for this."

I glared at him. "Careful barking orders, Theodore. Soon, I'll be your queen."

He narrowed his eyes. "You're my queen. But you're not my equal, and I'll treat you as such."

I gazed at Theodore's brash features. "You'll regret treating me like this," I threatened.

He laughed. "My queen, I regret everything, but I've never let my regrets stop me. I don't expect you to either."

Chapter Four

LEO

My body ached from the punches and kicks I'd endured. Blood still trickled from my broken nose and seeped from the gash in my head. One of the DuPont men beat the shit out of me when I tried to escape at meal time. It was worth it, though. I had to try. My pain only deepened as I thought of Christine staying because of me—because of us.

Atticus stopped his pacing, his face twisted in worry. "Tell me again what you discussed," he said.

Our shared dungeon cell seemed to close in around us. It was strange that they kept us together, unless it was part of the plan. It made it easier for them to monitor us this way. Theodore DuPont would do anything to keep an eye on his son, even if it meant hidden cameras in the dungeon.

"She said she's staying," I said, each word dripping with guilt and fear. "She won't leave while we're locked up." I swallowed hard, realizing there was nothing we could do now to change her mind.

"Stubborn girl," Augustus groaned. He had dried blood on his neck, and his skin was pale. "The thought of Lord Nathan putting his hands on her makes me want to punch something. I should have known better. We should have never come back."

I clenched my teeth.

We were caught in the middle of a battle between father and son. It was a DuPont war and we were the casualties.

I looked at Atticus. He was doing the best out of all of us physically, but emotionally he was a storm of aggression and shame. He kept staring at the door, as if ready to pounce on the first person he saw. There was dirt covering his clothes, making him look a little less refined. A little more rugged. "If something happens to her…" My voice trailed off. What could I do? I was a prisoner in a dungeon.

Atticus winced.

"I'll kill him," Augustus said. "If Nathan harms a

hair on Christine's head, I'll kill him…even if it means my own life." He looked out of the bars, a faraway look in his eyes. It was strange hearing him sound so blood-thirsty.

I shifted, my body racked with pain, and I groaned. Everything hurt, but it wasn't just the physical part that bothered me. The DuPont men had proven they were capable of torture and murder. Death was the only way out for us.

"We have to keep her safe," Augustus continued. "No matter what happens to us, she has to live."

I nodded my agreement.

"I'm sick to my stomach, worrying about her," Augustus said. "I hate this. What if he hurts her? What if we don't save her *again?*"

"I'm not going to let him hurt her. He'll have to break me first," I said with a growl.

"You've got a sore ass from going after him today. If you keep being a mindless hero, you're going to end up dead. We need an actual plan," Atticus said, his tone stern.

"I'm not a hero," I said. "I'm a soldier."

"My father won't keep me in here forever," Atticus said. "I run too much of the business, and a lot of our contacts are loyal to me." His brow furrowed. "It's only a matter of time before someone comes looking for me."

The dungeon door clanged and our attention snapped toward the sound. Two DuPont men walked in carrying a plate of food, but it wasn't scones and tea. The food was a slimy mix of worms and bugs. They slid the plate through the bars, and I closed my eyes. I couldn't do it. I couldn't eat——not a fucking *worm*.

I heard the soft clink of metal against metal and opened my eyes. Augustus had moved around the metal plates on the tray and was picking through the bugs, pulling out the worms and tossing them on the floor. Then he devoured the rest. He was shoveling it in like he hadn't eaten in days. I watched in horror as he finished the plate and reached for another.

A part of me was impressed by his endurance and adaptability. The other part was disgusted.

"Never thought I'd see a king eating slop," Atticus said.

"I've eaten a stripper's ass before. This is nothing in comparison," Augustus replied crudely.

"I can't wait for a real meal," Atticus replied bitterly. "Surely, my father will get me out of here soon."

"What about us?" Augustus sneered.

"Frankly, I don't give a damn about us," I replied. "I just want Christine to be safe."

"Exactly," Atticus added. "Once I get out of here, I'm going to free her."

I ached for Christine, imagining her in the lovely white dress I had always adored, the one that exposed her porcelain skin. Her blonde tresses spilled over her back, and her azure eyes glared at me, full of reproach. I'd give anything to have one more glimpse of her, yet I knew I would never be deserving of her love. She was from a high-ranking family. She went to the best schools. Wore the best clothes. Had a prince and a criminal mastermind at her disposal.

I was just a soldier. Someone with no money. No prospects. Just a heart that beat for her.

Augustus rinsed his mouth and spit into a puddle at his feet. "I'm not going to sit here and rot," he said before wiping his hand on his pants.

Atticus snarled, "I'll find a way to free her. No matter the cost, I will get her back." His voice was thick with determination and a possessive, jealous anger.

"You have to save her," Augustus whispered. "Christine is the only reason for existing. They can take away our freedom, or even our lives, as long as she is safe and happy." His words were a broken promise, a surrender to the helplessness he felt. "I can't let her die again. And knowing she's with Lord Nathan is almost worse than death."

I was enveloped in a sorrowful, paralyzing silence. The thought of Christine and my own careless stupidity weighed heavily on my mind. I cursed Atticus for making me face my emotions, and I despised myself more for not being able to seize the few remaining pieces of her love. I had allowed her to believe that I didn't care when all I wanted was her. I wanted to take back every mistake, but all I had left were regrets. She admitted her love for me, and I was thankful for even a chance to right my wrongs. But I couldn't stop feeling like I was undeserving.

I didn't save her three years ago, and I couldn't save her now.

"I wonder what they plan to do with us?" Augustus asked.

A chorus of despair rose from Atticus's throat. "My father delights in watching people suffer; it's how he holds his power. This is entirely my fault. I should have been more vigilant, all my attention devoted to Christine and our family business, and yet I failed to recognize the machinations of my own father. He has been plotting this for months, and I'm too late to stop it."

I swallowed the lump in my throat and whispered, "When we get out of here, he'll wish he never came between us." I couldn't bear the thought of Atticus going down for this. I should have known better. I could have put up more of a fight. I could have done something different. I should have tried harder, but instead, I just let it all go.

"He's ruthless," Atticus said in a tired voice. He reluctantly glanced at each of us, struggling to hide his own despair. "The man made me watch him kill someone when I was barely in grade school." There was a hushed silence that seemed to last an eternity until he continued. "I knew he was a terrible man, but I never expected this."

"I'm prepared for whatever the outcome is," I replied.

"I'm not afraid to die. I'm afraid they'll kill her spirit," Augustus added. "You never told me how they got you. The moment I was summoned, some man in a hood captured me. But how did they sneak up on you? Christine is a murdering machine. I can't help but feel like she could have escaped."

I exchanged a look with Atticus. I didn't really want to talk about all of us being in bed together.

"We were asleep," Atticus grunted. "And she was determined to save you."

"Asleep? One of you should have stayed awake to keep watch. And you definitely shouldn't have come looking for me," Augustus snapped.

"Yes, well, we were very tired. And you know damn

well, when Christine is determined, there's nothing that will get in her way," I said, sounding defensive. I knew I fucked up. I should have dragged her out of this damn castle, kicking and screaming.

"Tired?" Augustus asked. "Why?"

Atticus raised his eyebrows, challenging me to admit why we were so worn out we hadn't noticed the attack.

"We were with Christine. What do you think?" I replied, feeling sick to my stomach. I was having the best sex of my life while Theodore and Nathan were scheming.

Augustus's face lit up in astonishment. "You finally did it!"

Atticus cut him off. "He had a bit of assistance."

Augustus glanced between us, aghast. "You two? Together? Damn. How the hell can I compete with that?"

Atticus stood tall, attempting to look menacing. "Leo loves playing on a team. I'm sure he'd be more than happy to join you sometime. Unfortunately, I can't really get into the incest thing." A cheeky grin spread across his face. "But hey, if Christine wanted to give me a blowjob while you and Leo…"

"Okay, enough," Augustus shrieked. "I'm still processing the fact that we're brothers. Let's not talk about the moral complexities of an orgy together. Leo, man, I had no idea." He turned his attention to me, his expression full of disbelief. "I never thought you'd actually go through with it."

"What do you mean by that?" I huffed.

"You haven't been too keen on the whole sharing thing," he pointed out.

"I still am not," I snapped back. "And neither were you!"

"But you sure were sharing that night," Atticus cut in, a glint in his eye.

"What on earth are you talking about?" My voice rose in anger as a flush of embarrassment spread across my cheeks.

"You were enjoying it when I stroked your dick, got hard as a rock in my palm." Augustus gaped at the both of us. "And we both fucked her," he added, a sly smile appearing on his face.

"Oh, fuck off!" I exclaimed. He was seriously pissing me off. I didn't want to talk about this; it was just another thing I was ashamed about. I wished our first time was different. More intimate. Less…Atticus.

"Good times, indeed," he said, an amused gleam reflecting in his eyes.

My gaze bore into him as I spat, "I'll cut your dick off and shove it down your throat if you don't shut the fuck up."

His grin stretched wider as he drawled, "If you're this sensitive about it, next time I'll just bind your wrists while I have my way with her. Have you ever been tied up, Leo? It can be quite fun. I know you like to watch me eat her out." The thought of Atticus between her legs made me insane, burning with jealousy and anger. He watched me for a moment before speaking again, this time his tone softer. "She fucking loves you, you know. It's the only reason I put up with you."

"I love her too," I whispered. "But maybe I don't love her enough. If I loved her, I wouldn't have let anything get in the way of that."

Atticus scrutinized me with a calculating gaze, as if attempting to read my mind. "You love her plenty enough. And you'll do whatever it takes to get her back," he said with a hint of challenge in his voice.

I clenched my fists and met his eyes without flinching, determined not to show any sign of weakness. "You're right. I'm not giving up," I growled.

The intensity in the room was obvious as I moved closer to him, my gaze locked with his. With a deep breath, I let my gaze drift down to his lips as I murmured, "I can't give up. I need to make things right for Christine."

The air around us seemed to crackle with electricity as I reached out and rested my hand on his arm. He glanced down and grabbed my fingers fiercely before releasing them just as quickly. His voice was barely above a whisper as he said, "We'll find a way out of here, and you'll have your chance to make things right."

"The two of you have some intense sexual tension, and I did not have that on my dying-in-a-dungeon bingo card," Augustus said while peering at us.

I scoffed and pulled back, shocked at myself. "We do not. We both love Christine. And if we don't get out of here, then we'll die before I get the chance to show her just how much."

"I'm not going to die," Atticus growled. "I have to live for Christine. For my family business. For everything I've worked so hard to build."

Atticus was right. Even though we were in pretty bad shape physically, the main thing was our freedom. If we worked together, I was sure we could all survive this.

The silence stretched for a moment, and I thought about everything. My mother was probably worried sick. I didn't even know how many of my men had died in the attack. My thoughts weighed heavily on my soul, and I couldn't stop obsessing over how trapped we were.

"Atticus," I whispered, barely recognizing my own voice. Tears rolled down my cheeks as I considered the consequences of my own foolishness. "If you get out, can you tell my mother I'm sorry? I didn't want them to get involved in this mess I created. Please, just let her know that I regret everything," I pleaded.

His somber gaze bore into me as he responded in a hushed whisper, "Anything else?"

I cleared my throat. "There's money in a jar in the kitchen. Tell her to get as far away from here as possible and not to look back. I only have a couple thousand dollars saved up, but she needs to go. I don't want anything to happen to her or my sister."

Atticus nodded. "I'll see what I can do."

More time passed. We mostly remained silent, waiting for something to happen. Waiting to hear word about Christine. It wasn't until two guards approached our cell that we all perked up.

"Atticus DuPont?"

Atticus looked up at the guard. "Yes, that's me."

The other guard unlocked our cell. "Hardly recognized you under all that blood and dirt. Time to go. Your father wants you to get cleaned up for the meeting."

"What meeting?"

The guard looked at us, then back at Atticus. "The lords are bowing to Lady Abernathy today. He wants you there when the lords swear their allegiance to her."

Atticus looked at me and Augustus. "Of course," he choked out. This felt like a trap or something worse, but if he was getting out of this damn cell, then that meant he had more opportunities to flee.

He looked at me and said softly. "Be ready."

Chapter Five

CHRISTINE

My legs quivered under me as I walked up the stone steps to the throne, my muscles tight with tension. The throne room was covered in silver, the walls shining in it. And the throne, made of white stone, glowed brightly.

When I reached the top step, I steadied my spine and looked at all the eyes that watched me. At first glance, it looked like an assembly of nobles and courtiers, but as I took a closer look, I saw that most were too young to be in the court. Many wore suits like the DuPont guards. The criminal empire had their people littered all over the room in case anyone dared to challenge me.

The court fell silent as I took my seat on the throne. The soft silk of my dress rubbed against my legs, reminding me of how vulnerable I was in this moment. Other than that small sound, you could have heard a pin drop on the stone floor in front of me as my chest rose and fell with each breath.

I pushed my hair behind my ears, keeping my eyes on the middle distance. I didn't want to meet any of their eyes.

Underneath the hush of whispers, I heard something else: the thin, high squeal of steel against steel. My eyes flew to the far corner of the room, where one of the lords spoke over everyone else. "She shouldn't sit on the throne," he said, his voice carrying over the hushed conversations. He pulled out a sword and aimed it at me. "We haven't bowed yet. She hasn't been sworn in as queen."

Lord Nathan strolled through the door, his beady eyes locked on the brave lord. "Then I suggest you hurry up and bow, Iris," he bellowed, his voice as loud as a gunshot.

He wore his full ceremonial uniform—black robes and a cape that shimmered with silver thread. His sword was strapped to his side, and he had a dagger tucked into his belt. He looked every inch the terrifying tyrant that he was.

Lord Nathan raised his hand and everyone immediately went silent.

He turned to face me. "Queen Christine."

I twisted my fingers together in my lap. "Yes."

He looked me up and down, and it was as if I could see his brain working. He had a plan. I could see it in his eyes. "You prepared a speech, yes?"

In the corner of the room, I noted Theodore DuPont settling against the wall, watching how Lord Nathan handled me. And beside him…

A small gasp escaped my lips. "Atticus?" I whispered in shock.

Atticus had bruises and cuts all over his face, and his shoulders were tense. He locked eyes with me and jerked his head, giving me a slight, almost imperceptible nod. I could see the anguish and pain in his eyes.

My heart swelled, and I wanted more than anything to go to him. But I couldn't, not yet. This had to be done first.

Lord Nathan marched up the platform toward me as he glowered, his mouth a thin line. Once at my side, he hunched forward like a hawk ready to pounce. His eyes widened as they encountered my own before they contracted into dark slits. His fingers dug into my thigh as I shifted and tried to break his hold. The grip only tightened, and I became paralyzed by his fearsome presence. He lowered his head, his voice slicing like a blade, "Pay attention."

Taking a deep breath, I swallowed deeply. "I'm sorry, what was the question again?"

"Your speech," he growled in my ear.

"The speech?" I shrilled a little too loudly. "Oh. Yes. I prepared a speech." I rummaged around in the papers on a small table beside us and pulled it into my lap. Theodore DuPont had it delivered only an hour ago. I planned to just read it and get this over with. "I'm going to read you the speech I prepared," I said breathily, my hands shaking. I cleared my throat. "The House of Rose has been an important figurehead in the kingdom for decades. My father dutifully served King Frederick until his death, and I was raised in his care…" My voice cracked. King Frederick didn't care for me. He didn't like me at all. I cleared my throat. "The House of Rose was next in line for the throne, and after the truth about Augustus—"

A man with fierce green eyes spoke up, cutting me off. He had a thick, bushy beard and looked like he belonged on a pirate ship. "Is she reading a speech you wrote, Lord Nathan?" he asked. I looked up at the man and frowned. I'd seen him before but couldn't remember his name. "I'm assuming you want us all to believe this takeover was her idea," he continued, "but not all of us were hiding the night DuPont's men attacked. We know the truth. No amount of makeup will hide the cuts and bruises on her skin."

I looked around and let out a sigh.

"Finish your speech, Christine," Lord Nathan instructed, ignoring him.

I cleared my throat and read on. "As queen, I—" Someone grumbled something unintelligible that I couldn't understand. I lost my place.

"Finish your speech, Christine," Lord Nathan repeated, his voice low and dangerous. I wanted to kick him, shove him away. "Christine," he warned.

I sucked in a deep breath. "As queen, I pledge to make the kingdom of Aldrich the strongest it's ever been. Along with my chosen betrothed—"

The court erupted into whispers. They were quiet, but I could hear their anger.

Lord Nathan rolled his eyes and turned back to the court. "You," he said, pointing to one of the lords. "What is your name? I try to know everyone in court, but you must not be important enough to remember."

The man who earlier challenged Lord Nathan could not bring himself to look at him. His eyes shifted from side to side as if he were in discomfort, and he mumbled his name. "Lord Samuel Strange."

"Samuel," Nathan said, forgoing his official title.

"Bow to your queen. We all know this is a formality, so I suggest we follow through with it. The lords of the court must accept her and swear their allegiance so that we can have the formal coronation. Bow."

I breathed in deeply.

Lord Samuel didn't move, didn't bow.

"I said bow to your queen," Lord Nathan bellowed, his face reddening with fury.

Lord Samuel flinched, but still he stayed where he was. "Forgive me, Lady Abernathy. I would bow for you under different circumstances, but we both know the schemes going on here today."

Nathan marched down the three steps and was across the room in seconds. He yanked Samuel by his robes, pulling him up so his boots dangled an inch from the floor.

I shot to my feet. My heart raced and sweat dotted my brow as I tried to think of something, anything I could do to stop this. I stared out of the corner of my eye at Atticus, who held his hands up, palms out, as if he was begging me not to interfere—begging me to stay alive.

Nathan dropped the lord and gripped his sword with both hands. I gasped as he raised his blade high and swung it down hard. The blade bit into Samuel's neck and sliced through muscle, sinew and bones, bringing with it a rain of blood that spattered onto the stone floor. Samuel's head toppled to the ground, and the rest of his body followed it a moment later.

I'd expected screams of terror or even a few gasps. But no one said a word. No one moved. A brave man died, and everyone refused to join him. Lord Nathan pulled out a handkerchief and wiped his face before turning to address the crowd. "Does anyone else want to challenge me?" He looked from one person to the next. "Do you want to be next on the chopping block?" He lowered his sword, holding it between himself and the crowd.

Nathan took a step toward a frowning man, his boots splashing into the pool of blood. He raised his sword. "Make way. I have things to do," he said.

The lords parted, creating a narrow path, and Nathan turned to me. "Get to it," he said with a flick of his wrist.

I took a deep breath and nodded. "Okay," I said, turning to the crowd. My voice held no emotion and my eyes were empty. "I thank you all for coming today." I held my head high and tried to look like a queen.

Theodore DuPont wanted me to read his speech and move forward with the proceedings, but I had other plans. I crushed the paper in my fist and glared at everyone. "A strong queen is what this kingdom needs.

A leader who will fight for her people, who will stand up for what is right, and who will do what needs to be done." I looked directly at Theodore. "That is what I plan to be. And it starts today."

I could hear my heartbeat thump in my ears. I glanced over the crowd. Their faces were unreadable, the tension thick in the air. I narrowed my eyes. "Lord Nathan so graciously showed us all what's at stake here. Bend the knee or suffer the consequences."

I didn't want them to bow to me because they feared Lord Nathan. I wanted them to bow because they trusted me to take down Theodore DuPont. I stepped down and looked at Lord Nathan, who seemed oblivious to the double meaning in my speech. He smiled at me and licked his lip.

"Bow," I ordered him.

He raised an eyebrow at me. "What?"

"Bow for me," I demanded.

Lord Nathan's face darkened. "This was not—"

"You are a lord, are you not?"

"Yes," he gritted.

"Then *bow*, Lord Nathan."

He hesitated. This was an important moment. The lords needed to see how powerful I was—what I was capable of. "Fine."

He scowled and bowed for only a moment before standing up.

One by one, everyone else followed suit. Old men kneeled, their knees cracking as they did. DuPont's men were the last to bow. It felt like hours as I waited for them to do it. They kept their eyes on me, weighing me.

I'd done something.

I'd made everyone bow.

And Theodore? He stood taller.

"All hail Queen Christine!"

The crowd cheered, but I knew it wasn't for me. It was for the show. I hadn't earned their respect yet. They didn't want to be next on the chopping block, and I couldn't blame them.

I held my head high as the DuPont guards escorted me out of the throne room, and when I passed Theodore and Atticus, I paused to speak to them.

"Sorry I didn't stick to the script," I said, my eyes burning with fury.

Theodore looked at his son, then back at me. "You're trying to get yourself killed, Your Majesty."

I laughed. "If I'm going to die, I'd like to be the one doing the killing."

Theodore shook his head. "This is a dangerous game."

"It's not a game," I said. "I'm not playing any

games. You know full well what I plan to do. I will find your men, and I will use their heads for my throne. I will make a kingdom out of their bones, and I will walk over their skulls."

He straightened his spine. "Then it is your lovers that will pay the price."

I took a step closer, my eyes fluttering to Atticus. "You're the only one who will pay the price. And it will be a price you can't afford."

"You're just like Isabelle," he hissed.

"And you're still the man who couldn't tame her. Couldn't claim her. That's the real problem here. You'd rather unleash Lord Nathan on this kingdom than admit you still have feelings for her. That you couldn't have the woman you truly wanted." I took a step closer. "And it kills you to know that I'd give everything I have to your son. It's eating you up inside to know that there is *nothing* I wouldn't do for him. You're jealous. Because he's smarter. More powerful. And can make the sacrifices you weren't man enough to do."

"Enough," Theodore snapped. "I was going to let Atticus stay out of his cage, but it seems you need to be reminded what's at stake here."

"Christine," Atticus spoke, "Little Monster."

My breath hitched at the endearing nickname. "Yes, Atticus?"

"Behave. For now. Please."

"I love you," I whispered as a guard wrapped their arm around my waist and pulled me toward the door.

"Put her in the dungeon for now. We don't need her again until the coronation. Maybe she needs some perspective," Theodore said.

I tossed my head back and laughed. They were leading me right to my men. The closer I was to them, the better.

With all my might, I ripped myself from the guard's grasp and dove into Atticus's awaiting arms. I pressed my lips against his with a fierce hunger, a deep-seated desire, an unquenchable thirst for the love that I had been longing for. When I finally broke away, I looked him in the eyes and whispered with a shaking voice, "I love you, Atticus. I have always loved you."

He tightly grasped my hand and placed a kiss upon it. "I love you, Christine," he declared with a sorrowful voice.

I grinned wickedly, attempting to mask the pain of being dragged away. "Be cautious, Theodore," I hissed. "Sleep with one eye open."

Theodore's face contorted in fury, his eyes ablaze with hatred. "You'll soon be lulled to sleep by the cries of your lovers," he threatened viciously. I thrashed once more as he shouted. "You'll kill them all if you don't submit."

I was pushed, roughly, into the hallway. My lips stretched into a wide grin, feeling the cool metal of the key in my hand. Atticus had slipped it to me at the last minute, and I knew with complete certainty I'd be able to use it in the dungeons.

I had done it. After all the obstacles, all the frustrations, I had gathered my courage and taken hold of my destiny. I had proven that I was worthy of freedom—and of love. That I could stand up and fight for what I wanted.

My fingers closed more tightly around the key, relishing in its promise of a new life. All I had to do now was get my men and leave, leave this place behind for good. My plan was perfect and my heart was filled with a confidence that never wavered. I knew that, no matter what awaited me on the other side, I would be triumphant.

Chapter Six

CHRISTINE

The DuPont guards ominously escorted me down the cold and forbidding staircase to the dark depths of the dungeon. I'd been only a few times before, and the dank, stagnant air was still as putrid as ever, its heaviness clinging to my skin like a cloying fog.

The clicking sound of my heels echoed off the stone walls like a funeral dirge, and I could see the cobwebs in the eerie silvery light that shone through the narrow windows. I quivered as I felt their heavy stares burrowing into my back, my dress clinging to me like a shroud.

The guards stopped abruptly and gestured to the

cell on my left, its black iron bars glinting maliciously in the dim light. I looked up and saw a tiny black camera staring at me from above the doorway, and I held my breath, my heart pounding in anticipation.

I quickly looked around for Leo and Augustus in some of the other cells, but there was no one here but me. One of them roughly pushed me into the cell with a cruel laugh, and I stumbled inside, feeling dread fill me as I heard the door slam shut behind me.

The key Atticus had given me was still heavy in my palm, since the overeager guards were too arrogant to check me for weapons. I walked around the tiny cell, counting my steps. I had only gone halfway around when I heard the guards dragging someone down the hall. I listened carefully as the rusted gate to the cell next to me was yanked open, and a groaning person was tossed inside.

"Long live the king, eh?" one of the guards said with a cruel laugh. "Enjoy your night with the queen, Augustus. It'll be your last."

The two guards slammed the door shut and locked it. A wall separated me and the next cell, so it was hard to see, but I could hear him shuffling around in the darkness.

"Hello?" I murmured, my voice barely audible.

"Christine?"

My heart leapt in my chest as August's voice pierced the silent cell, and I pressed my face against the icy concrete wall separating us. A chill ran down my spine as I remembered the terror that had brought me to this place.

"Christine, is that you? Are you okay?" he asked again, his voice echoing off the stone walls. I heard the clinking of metal and scraping of boots on the floor, and I shuddered.

"August?" I croaked. "Is that really you?"

"Love," he breathed. "Oh God, I never thought I'd be able to hear your voice again." Tears pricked at my eyes as I felt his presence in the darkness and reached out to touch the chilly brick.

"You're safe," I said, my voice trembling. "Oh thank God, August, you're alive."

"By some miracle," he said, and I could hear a smile in his voice. A small laugh escaped my lips, and I closed my eyes. "Are they hurting you?"

"No," I replied. "Where's Leo? Is he with you?"

"A guard came to take him away a little while ago," he said. "I was so worried when they left me here all alone. Then Theodore summoned me. He had some questions about a lord."

My stomach churned as thoughts of Leo raced through my head. I needed to get him back before we escaped this living nightmare. *No one gets left behind.* I had to be strong.

"When did they take him?"

"Maybe two hours ago. It's hard to tell time in this place. What's going on? Why are you here?" he asked. I could hear the tension and fear in his voice, but he tried to keep his tone light and steady. I opened my mouth to reply but stopped when I heard someone approaching.

"Christine?" August called.

"August, we'll talk later. Just be strong." Theodore was going to punish me for not following his orders. I just needed to save Augustus and get us both out of here before they killed him.

"Christine, tell me what's happening," he said, his voice bordering on hysterics. "Are they torturing you? Are they hurting you?"

I didn't have time to answer as I heard the iron bars of his cell door scraping open, and I quickly stood up.

"Hello, Augustus. My name is Cian Beasley," I heard the new person say. "I'm so sorry we have to meet under such dire circumstances, but Theodore DuPont likes to use me when he has a lesson he wants to teach."

"What kind of lesson could you possibly teach me?" August snapped.

I heard something thud on the ground, and I bit my lip. "Do you prefer losing your toes or fingers first?"

A low, cold laugh. "You wouldn't dare." I didn't want to leave August in the cell with that psycho, but I needed this Cian Beasley to be distracted so I could take him out.

"Oh, believe me, I would," Cian said with a small chuckle.

A moment later, I heard the sound of flesh hitting flesh, and August cried out. I gasped and felt the hair on my arms stand on end.

August groaned as Cian continued his torture, his voice filling with rage. "Fuck you, asshole," August yelled.

"I'm teaching you," he said, his voice mocking and cruel. "And right now, the lesson is how to count to ten."

I heard him land a hard hit, and August whimpered. "One," Cian said with a snicker. I heard a dull thud and I felt my stomach twist as I imagined August's flesh splitting open. "Two."

No more.

I surged forward and used the key Atticus had given me to unlock my cage, then quickly moved next door. August was on the ground and Cian was hovering over him. Cian was a towering man with bulging muscles, dark hair, and sharp blue eyes. He was wearing an expensive-looking business suit, and his teeth were bright white as he smiled at me, looking pleased to see me.

"Hello there," he said, licking his lips. "I was wondering what was taking the queen so long. They said you were resourceful and I should be on my guard. It's been a while since I've met a proper challenge."

"You're going to regret this," I said, my voice steady and even.

"I'm not," he replied, puffing his chest out proudly. "I'm actually helping him learn a lesson. It'll give him something to think about when he's alone in that cell every night."

"What lesson is that?" I asked. I glanced at the bruised and battered August lying on the floor, and my heart broke. His face was crusted with blood, and his right eye was swollen shut. I shuddered as I thought about what he'd been through.

"The lesson is that Theodore DuPont is in charge," he replied with a cruel laugh.

I straightened my spine. "I think it's time you learned a lesson, too," I said.

He raised a brow. "And what lesson would that be?"

I smirked. "How to bow."

I lunged forward and barely dodged his first swing,

then I gripped his left hand and twisted his arm until the cane fell from his hand. I kicked it off to the side and felt the rush of adrenaline pumping through my veins. His face was twisted into a snarl, and he tried to kick me in the ribs.

I punched him in the groin, and he grunted as he doubled over, then I flipped him forward so he was lying on his face. Slowly, I pressed my foot against his back as I reached down to grab his left hand. He struggled to get up, and I pressed my foot against his neck, keeping him in place.

"I hope you're not enjoying this as much as I am," I whispered into his ear, then I yanked his arm as hard as I could. He let out a strangled cry of pain. "Do you enjoy your job, Cian?"

"You're not a queen," he choked.

"Christine, stop," August said. "Don't do this. We don't have time to kill him right now. We have to get out of here." He stood up and staggered slightly but, with a quick shake of his head, was ready to go.

"Yes, we should get out of here," I said, my voice firm. "Cian is going to help us."

I felt him shake beneath me, and I cracked a smile. "Is that what you think?" he spat.

"You are going to answer my questions and help us escape." I pressed my foot on his back until he was almost out of breath, then I reached for the sword strapped to his hip. "Do you understand me?"

"No one escapes the DuPonts," he growled. "No one."

"Do you understand me?" I repeated. "I'm going to give you some time to think about it."

"I'm fine," August snapped. "Let's just go."

"We're not going anywhere without a plan," I added, then I leaned down to whisper in Cian's ear. "You have two options. Choose now or suffer the consequences."

"Fine. I'll help you," he said, his voice thick with disgust.

"Good. Let's—"

"But you have to get the hell off me first," he shouted.

I smiled and stepped back, then I took my foot off his neck. "Get up." He got up and I kept his sword pointed at his chest. "Tell me where Leo is."

"He's on his way back here. I was supposed to start torturing him after finishing with Augustus. Mr. DuPont wanted you to hear it all."

I nodded. "How many guards are escorting him?"

"Four," Cian spat.

Easy enough. I could take them down.

"And what about Atticus?"

Cian let out a bitter laugh. "I'm not sure. His father is probably making him fuck a whore so he can get you out of his system. Not sure what's so special about your pussy, but apparently you've got that man's dick in a vise grip."

"Shut up," I snapped.

I looked at August, who nodded. Before we could get out of here, we had to take down the four guards escorting Leo, and they were headed this way now.

"Collect all his weapons, August. I'm going to need them."

He nodded and went through a duffel bag on the ground while I rotated the sword I'd stolen in my fist.

August paused. "I'm not…like Atticus or Leo," he murmured while pulling out a hammer. "I can't fight." The shame in his tone made me pause.

"What kind of weak fucking king can't fight?" Cian asked.

I rotated the hilt of the sword and hit him in the side of the head with it, knocking the torturing asshole out.

"I watched you beat the shit out of that guy freshman year for touching my ass in the hallway. You can fight. And you've always fought for me, August."

The concern on his face softened for a moment. I knew he could do this. He always stepped up for me.

The sound of a door opening and boots stomping downstairs made us both go still. "You ready?" he asked me while gripping the hammer.

"Let the fun begin," I replied before kicking open the door to the cell and sprinting toward the group of men.

I whipped out the sharpened blade in my hand as I charged forward, finding Leo in the center ring of DuPont guards. He was ashen but alive. His eyes met mine for a split second before he darted to the side. The moment he moved, I screamed a guttural battle cry, and the guards' bodies locked in place, shock and confusion on their faces. It took a moment, but one raised their gun and aimed at me.

With blazing speed, I evaded their gunfire and charged toward the nearest one, swiping my sword across his throat and shoving him to the ground.

August bellowed as he swung his hammer with violent force, smashing the second guard. As if driven by an unseen power and rage, I used the sword to tear through the Kevlar vest of the third guard before knocking him out with a hard kick to the back of his head.

Their bullets rained around us, narrowly missing me. With one last swipe of my blade, I pierced the fourth guard's flesh, and he roared in agony as I cut into him. August raised the hammer in his grip and slammed it down on his skull, killing him almost instantly.

I took a few seconds to catch my breath and glanced at my arm where a bullet grazed it. "I'm okay," I said to August, despite the searing pain. "Just one more."

I flexed my fingers around the hilt of my sword and glanced at Leo, his body tense. A DuPont guard held a dagger to his throat, a sneer marring his face. He shifted his attention between August and me, the dagger never leaving Leo's neck.

"I'll kill him! I'll do it," the guard growled.

My eyes hardened and I moved before either August or Leo had time to blink. My blade glided through the air like a feather and pierced the guard's eye socket in an instant. Blood sprayed over Leo, and the guard fell in a heap, his cry of agony ringing in my ears.

August let out a strangled sound of horror, but we didn't have time to waste. I quickly scanned both my men for injuries and then spun on my heel toward the stairs.

"We need to get out of here," Leo said with urgency, picking up a gun from the dead man's hand.

I nodded. "Lord Nathan has this place surrounded with his men," I said grimly.

"I can navigate us through the storm tunnels,"

August said. "They lead a few miles out of the city and are complex. People get lost in them all the time; it would be easy to lose them."

"And you know the way?" Leo asked.

August paled but nodded. "Mostly."

"Then let's go," I snapped.

Leo and August struggled to keep up with my quick pace as we climbed the stairs leading out of the dungeon. At the top, a large guard was sleeping in a chair, completely unaware of what had transpired below us.

Leo looked at him for a moment before retrieving a dagger and slicing the man's neck in one swift motion. A gush of blood coated his hands, and I tightened my grip on Cian's sword, ready to face whatever danger awaited us outside the castle walls.

"Atticus is still in there," Leo said, worry creasing his brows.

My lips curved into a smile as I nodded at them both. "We'll find him on our way out."

And with that, we plunged into the darkness of the unknown.

Chapter Seven

LEO

I limped behind Christine, exhausted but on high alert. The castle was a flurry of activity, and the entrance to the tunnels out of here was in the west wing—opposite from where we were.

"Stay close," she whispered.

Christine stood under the golden lights, an angelic sight in her snow-white gown. It was sprayed with carnage, a macabre masterpiece of her last victim's life. Her curls were stained with blood, clumped and tangled in their own version of a crown. Dirt streaked her makeup, her smeared cheeks a testament to her weary yet unyielding will. Her high heels seemed to pinch her feet, yet she stood strong with a deadly gaze, a brutal beauty that could not be matched.

I wanted to kiss her then. I wanted to wrap my arms around her and hold her close, to feel her chest rise and fall with every breath.

But I couldn't. Not here. Not now.

I wanted to fuck her, to feel her heat and her body against mine. I wanted to feel the flesh and blood of the woman I loved, to taste her lips and her sweat.

And I wanted her to feel the same for me.

We traveled through the empty hallway, our hearts pounding in unison as we crept past rooms. We moved silently, our steps light as a feather to avoid detection.

Our ears were peeled for any sound of danger. A few minutes passed before we heard two guards arguing with each other down the hall. We ducked behind a pillar and listened to them.

"I swear to God, if those guards can't find that asshole Atticus, the boss is going to have our heads," one of them said, and I felt Christine tense beside me.

"Atticus is smart. He's probably long gone," the other one said with a laugh.

"Maybe he went down to the dungeon to fuck the queen," the first one said. "Can't say I blame him. She must have a pussy made of gold to keep his interests."

If they couldn't find Atticus, then that meant he

escaped his father. Christine looked at us and nodded, likely coming to the same conclusion as me.

"Maybe I should go down to the basement and take a turn, too. I hear she has an insatiable appetite. Think she'd suck my cock and kneel before me?"

Christine gave a devilish smirk and stepped out from behind the pillar. Her long dress rustled around her as she strode toward the guards. "You're gonna have to do better than that if you want to impress me," she declared in a sultry voice before swiftly slicing through one of their throats. The guard dropped to the ground, his blood spilling onto the floor and staining the wall of the castle.

Augustus dove behind me as the other guard took aim with his gun, but Christine had already moved toward him. With a swift flick of her wrist, she severed his head from his body in a neat arc. She looked up at me, her blue eyes blazing with excitement. All these men had guns, but they had no idea how to use them. I was sure seeing Christine drenched in blood was enough to shock them and give her an advantage.

The sound of boots running toward us down the hall made us both look. "Let's get out of here," she whispered in a low voice, her sword still dripping with the guards' blood.

We charged through the castle as fast as we possibly

could, our footsteps echoing off the cold marble floors. Fear pounded through my veins, but I was determined to escape alive. Christine was focused on finding Atticus, and it seemed like nothing could stop her from completing her mission.

I followed Christine's lead down into the maze of hallways ahead of us. I knew this castle like the back of my hand, and every turn, I expected to see more men.

An eerie silence hung in the air, and I could feel my heart pounding in my chest. Suddenly there was a loud shout around the corner.

"More guards ahead!" Christine's warning ricocheted off the walls as we barreled down the hall. The guards were closing in, and I knew we had seconds to spare. But once we turned the corner, all of us came skidding to a stop, our eyes wide in surprise.

Atticus was a few steps away, and I watched in awe as he snapped a guard's neck with precision and grace.

Christine surged forward, a battle cry ringing through the air as she raced toward the second guard. But before she could reach him, Atticus moved with a speed and agility that made him seem almost preternatural, his hand already reaching for the guard's throat. The guard had no time to react before Atticus lunged forward and grabbed him in an iron grip, snatching the gun he had been carrying and throwing it away with an effortless flick of his wrist.

Atticus kept his grip tight on the man even as Christine attacked the third guard, her strikes swift and precise as she blocked each one of his defensive moves. She shifted her weight as if dancing to some unheard rhythm, and her foot connected with the guard's chest, sending him flying back several feet before he finally crumpled to the ground.

"Christine!" Atticus yelled as another man ran up behind her.

Augustus had been standing off to the side, watching the fight with a look of admiration and amazement on his face. He snapped out of it as soon as he heard Atticus's voice, and without hesitation, he ran forward and started hitting one of them with his hammer. He brought it down hard with each swing, the metal ringing against bone as he ruthlessly pummeled his enemy until there was nothing left but a lifeless body lying at Augustus's feet.

I aimed my gun at the last man once I had a clear shot and took him out. I wanted to fight more, but my wound was already hurting badly, and one wrong move would rip open the stitches. I was no use to them if they had to carry me out of here.

Atticus crossed to her with a feral smile and

wrapped her in a passionate embrace. Her cheeks blushed at the suddenness of his touch, and I could feel my stomach flip. Despite the oppressive atmosphere that hung over us, Christine seemed oddly settled in his arms. They were both covered in blood, looking like harbingers of death clinging to one another. It was a brutal, gruesome, passionate sight.

"We don't have time for this," Augustus said, his tone shaky and tinged with fear. Atticus pulled back and planted one last fierce kiss on Christine's lips before releasing her. "There's always time for that later, Little Monster," he said with a chuckle before turning his gaze to me.

"The tunnel entrance is this way," I said and gestured down the hall. We moved quickly but cautiously through the shadows and avoided detection from the guards searching for us. We reached the entrance to the tunnel as the guards' shouts reverberated around us.

"There's no going back," I said as we all stopped, our breath heavy in the silence that followed my words. The tunnel entrance was dark and covered by a warped wooden door that Atticus had pried open with his bloody hands. Cobwebs coated the walls.

"Let's go," Christine finally spoke up, and Atticus

pulled her in for one last brutal kiss that left her cheeks flushed.

"I love you, Little Monster," he said before we all turned and leapt into the abyss of darkness that was the tunnel ahead of us. Our footsteps echoed off the stone walls as we made our way through it, desperately trying to stay one step ahead of our pursuers. I knew that if we could just make it out alive, I'd make it up to Christine. I'd give her whatever her heart desired.

The tunnels were dark and ominous, and I knew we had to be careful. My eyelids dropped with fatigue as we ran, my muscles burning with fatigue. Christine's eyes were wide and alert, her face turned up to survey the dark path.

Augustus was silent but his chest heaved with each breath, and I knew he was keeping pace with us. Atticus, however, barely looked tired at all. He was calm and collected, his hands clutching his gun with a menacing aura that told me he was prepared to fight. I was reminded again of how lethal he was, and it sent a cold chill through my body.

When the tunnel split in two, Augustus pointed to the left. "This way."

"Are you sure?" Atticus asked.

"Positive."

The only light was from the vents above, casting

moonlight through iron bars. This place was a massive maze and Augustus was probably the only person that knew how to navigate it. We continued to run, the miles stretching, and we all were tired.

"Just a little farther," Augustus grunted.

"Christine!" I heard Atticus shout, and my heart nearly stopped when I heard the sound of gunshots echoing down the tunnel.

"Get down!" Atticus bellowed, and I tackled Christine to the ground, dragging Augustus with us. I tried to cover my head as gunshots rang off the walls around us.

"Fuck!" Atticus shouted as more shots fired in quick succession. I saw Atticus crouched on the ground, his arms shielding his head. Christine's body was tense, but she was still by my side.

"We need to get out of here, Atticus," she said quietly, and I could hear the sound of exhaustion in her voice.

"We can't go back the way we came. This is the only way out," Augustus said.

"Well, then let's go," Atticus said, picking Christine up off the ground and pulling her along with him.

"No, wait," Augustus said, his eyes wide as if he were weighing the options in his head. Suddenly a loud roar echoed down the tunnel, and I knew there was a pack of guards streaming down the hall we were previously in.

"Let's split up!" one of them shouted, and half turned toward our tunnel.

They were gaining on us.

Christine's eyes locked on mine for a moment, and she read the worry in my face before she shifted her attention to Atticus. A bullet pierced the air and we all ducked. Another one hit the concrete beside my head. "Give me your gun," she said, and I watched as he pulled it from its holster. She cocked it and chambered a bullet before turning her attention to a guard running toward us.

She aimed and the bullet landed in his thigh. His legs folded and I heard his neck snap a moment later as he fell to the ground. Christine was stunning. She leapt into the air, and in a graceful arch, she planted a bullet in each of the other running guards' foreheads, one after another, with such precision that I had trouble believing she could have aimed so quickly. It was a spectacular feat of athletic prowess and martial mastery that left me stunned and terrified.

She landed and let out a shaky breath. "Are you guys okay?" she asked, turning to face Augustus and me. Our eyes fell on the bloody massacre around us, and I could see the horror in Augustus's face.

"That was incredible, Little Monster," Atticus praised her.

"It's time to go," she said, her voice trembling.

We kept running down the tunnel as Augustus guided us down another split. We went left, then right, then left again until the sound of trees bending against the wind and bugs chirping filled our ears. Moonlight glowed at the mouth of the tunnel, and we all skidded to a halt once the cool, fresh air hit our cheeks. The tunnels led outside of the city, and it would take a while for guards to navigate the winding, confusing tunnels.

"We made it," Augustus said, relief in his tone.

"We made it," Christine echoed.

"Now we need to hide," Atticus said, his tone lethal.

Augustus let out a brutal laugh. "I killed a man with a hammer back there." He thrust his thumb over his shoulder in disbelief. "Beat his skull in. Can you believe it?"

Christine gave him a bright smile. "You did good."

I wanted her to smile at me.

"Where should we go?" I asked.

Atticus surveyed the area. "We're in abandoned territory, and we're going to need supplies. There's a small camping ground north of here. We could find a cabin for the night."

"As long as there is a shower, I'm game. I smell like death," Augustus complained.

We all smelled terrible. I wanted a warm bed and some food.

With our new objective in mind, we set out into the night.

Augustus was on Christine's heels, his eyes wide and alert. "You were amazing back there, Christine," he said, his voice laced with awe.

We walked in silence at first, but the damage we had experienced began to sink into each of us. My bones ached and I knew the wound the doctor had sewn shut was probably open by now. We needed medical supplies. I could feel the exhaustion in my muscles. I was so close to collapsing, and I could hardly keep my eyes open.

We walked.

And walked.

And *walked*.

I was so fucking worn down.

Atticus seemed to be feeling it too. He pulled me to the side and pointed to a small cabin that had been abandoned years ago. "Let me take the first watch. You guys get some sleep."

I didn't argue and Augustus practically collapsed on the floor of the cabin.

I was on the ground before I knew what had happened. I pushed my back to the wall, and my eyes fluttered. I knew that I needed rest. I could feel every ache in my body as I relaxed. My eyelids were heavy.

We survived.

Barely.

And now, I needed to take every fucking second I could with Christine.

Now, I needed to earn her heart.

Chapter Eight

CHRISTINE

The room dripped in fear and desperation, the walls encased in sickly crimson liquid that felt like a thick, gooey web. I writhed and struggled, trying desperately to free myself from the serpent-like vines that held me captive. My screams could barely be heard over the sound of my own heart pounding in my ears. Tears streamed down my face, mixing with the sweat and blood that coated my skin.

Amidst the chaos, I heard voices, a distant echo of familiar faces.

"Christine! Christine, oh my God! What has he done to you?"

But I couldn't answer them. My thoughts were fractured and broken like glass, each memory shattering before I could grasp it. I *couldn't see, I couldn't hear, and any movement caused an unbear-able pain to surge through my veins. I was trapped in an eerie still-ness, surrounded by an impenetrable darkness and confusion.*

Suddenly a shadow appeared on the wall before me—a figure draped in black with a menacing air about it. I opened my mouth to speak and felt something stop me from doing so—I realized I was bound, tightly restrained by the vines that dug deep into my flesh. But before I could do anything to resist them, I felt a sharp jab penetrate my side. A searing pain raced through me like an electric shock, and all the terror evaporated away as my entire body went limp. My head rolled to the side and there it was—a bony hand with talons like a predatory bird—something so familiar yet so far away that it didn't even seem real.

"Long live the Bloody Queen," the creature rasped.

"Long live the Bloody Queen."

"Long live the Bloody Queen."

"Long live…"

A creeping feeling of numbness surrounded me as everything faded away. Darkness shrouded my vision and stillness filled the air until eventually I succumbed to the confusion and drifted away.

"Christine! Baby, wake up."

My eyes fluttered open and slick sweat dripped down my head. I blinked a couple of times, and vivid green eyes came into focus.

"Leo?" I whispered.

I looked around the cabin and saw that we were alone.

"You were having a nightmare." He brushed a blonde strand of hair out of my eyes and placed his large hands on either side of my head. "Thank God you woke up."

"What happened? Where are we?" I tried to sit up, but he held me down.

"We're in the cabin. Augustus and Atticus went to meet a contact to get some money and supplies. We can't stay here long. I'm trying to get you to sleep again, but you're too restless."

He was right. My muscles were tense, my scalp itched, and my legs ached from the long hours of running.

"I can't sleep. I'm too tired to sleep."

Leo looked at me with sympathetic eyes. He'd cleaned up since the last time I'd seen him. When we arrived, he fell asleep against the wall, and I used the hose outside to wash the blood from my skin. He must have done the same. I'd stayed up for a while, numb and disassociated from all the kills. Atticus and August tried to get me to talk, but I was too strung out to process everything. Our clothes were ruined, so both of us sat naked on the bed.

I nodded. "I'm exhausted, physically and mentally. How much longer will we stay here?"

"Couple of hours at most. They sent teams of guards looking for us."

I sat up, but once again, Leo pushed me back down into the mattress. "Leo," I breathed. "We have to get ready to move. Who is August and Atticus meeting with? I should have gone with them. It's dangerous—"

"They're fine. Atticus knows them. We're going to get far away from here…"

"Leo. I don't like that they left—"

"They didn't want to wake you. You need to rest. Your feet are covered in blisters. Relax. They'll be safe."

"But they shouldn't have—"

"Christine. Please stop worrying. You need to sleep. You're exhausted."

I bit my tongue and Leo's eyes softened.

"It's not my intention to control what you do or say, but I just want you to be safe. I couldn't stand it if something happened to you. I'd—" He broke off and looked away. "I'd never forgive myself."

My heart ached and I reached out to touch his cheek. "Leo, are you okay?"

He nodded. "You saved me and brought me here. You didn't have to do that. You protected me in that damn place. If you hadn't, I wouldn't be alive."

"Leo. Of course I would save you."

"But who saves *you*, Christine?" he asked, his piercing eyes burning a hole right through my soul.

"You all do. Every day," I whispered, and it was the truth. Things had happened so quickly, but they were my reason to fight—to love again.

He nodded but his eyes were distant, his expression pained. I could feel a deep sorrow emanating from him, which made my heart ache. I wanted to mend the broken pieces of his heart and take away all the hurt he had endured. I gently took his hand, threading my fingers with his, and brushed a soft kiss against his knuckles.

"Christine, I should have told you how deeply I loved you long before now." His voice was so low and raw it sent shivers down my spine.

"It's alright," I murmured, my voice barely a whisper. "You didn't have to tell me anything, because I already knew."

I leaned closer, pressing my lips against his as if to transfer all the emotions inside of me into him. He moaned softly and tightened his hold around me, encasing me in a cocoon of warmth and safety.

"I don't deserve you," he breathed against my hair.

"Leo," I said softly. "You were there for me when I was vulnerable and scared, when there was no one else who would help me. You saved me from the darkest parts of myself, and you will always have my gratitude."

I closed my eyes, reveling in the moment as the sound of Leo's beating heart and the rustle of leaves outside filled my ears.

"Our first time together wasn't exactly what I envisioned," he said softly, a hint of a smile on his lips.

The memory of that night sent heat surging through me as I blushed in embarrassment, but looking back now, I was thankful for Atticus's intervention.

"You probably wouldn't have done it without Atticus forcing you," I said with a laugh.

Leo didn't find my words funny. "I wanted you, Christine," he whispered. "I wanted to touch you. Take you. *Taste* you."

He hesitantly peered up from under his thick, dark eyelashes and lowered the rough blanket wrapped around my body. Licking my lips, I watched him take in my bare body inch by inch. He ran a finger over my collarbone and up to my lips, tracing the outline of them before whispering in my ear. "Are you wet right now, baby? For *me*? For *only me*?"

My eyes glazed over as I stared at his raging hard-on. His thick, engorged shaft was spilling pre-cum onto his thighs. I wanted to taste him. His foreskin was peeled back, showcasing the bulging, pulsing tip in all its glory. The veins protruded in all directions, seemingly reaching for me. Leo's cock looked like it was carved from marble, and its deep crimson color matched the flush of his skin.

I stopped staring at his cock to look back into his eyes. The intensity of his gaze made me feel both vulnerable and sexy.

"I love the way you look at my dick, baby. Like it's a treat meant only for you," he said as he grazed my neck with his lips. His hands moved around me, exploring every inch of my skin. His hands were everywhere. His touch, his kiss, and the way he loved me with every fiber of his being were all perfect.

I reached up and touched his face, sending him into a flurry of kisses that expressed how much he loved and needed me. Our tongues danced together and he let out a small grunt, his eyes bloodshot as he looked at me.

"Christine…you are so…" He sank lower and slowly spread my legs apart, taking in the sight of my glistening wetness. "You are so perfect. I need to devour you," he murmured as his fingers spread me, sending tremors of bliss throughout my body. He paused and leaned closer to drag his tongue up to my clit. My fingers curled in his long blond hair. I had to shut my eyes and bite my lips to suppress the cries that were begging to escape. He explored me with his tongue a few times more before plunging it deep inside, thrusting fiercely.

I arched off the bed at the invasion. I could feel his hot mouth. His wet tongue. The groans of pleasure vibrating against my sex.

He then licked and teased my clit, driving me to the brink of ecstasy with each pass of his tongue, sending electricity through my veins. My toes curled up, and I was so close, yet so far from achieving release. He held me back from the edge, refusing to let me go, enjoying the power he held over me.

"Please," I whimpered, my body quivering in anticipation. His lips curled into a devious smirk, knowing exactly what he was doing.

"What was that?" he purred, as he covered my pussy with his mouth and slipped a finger inside of me. I could barely contain my screams of pleasure. "Did you just beg me to stop?"

"No," I panted, shaking beneath him as he increased his tempo. "I asked you to please *not* stop."

He licked my clit and fingered me with precision, commanding me to succumb to his touch and pushing me even closer to climax without letting me go over the edge yet. I could feel his control over my body and my pleasure, and I felt a rush of excitement.

"Fuck, baby. You taste so good," he groaned.

He sucked and licked to the rhythm of my shaking body, coaxing a few more swells of ecstasy from me. I was desperate for release, and I arched my back, lifting my hips higher to give him more access to my pussy. I needed him inside of me, I needed to feel him around me, and I needed to hear him come undone.

"Please, please, oh God," I begged, but he was lost to the bliss of my body. Savoring me. Teasing me. He pulled away from me and sat up. I could see the lust and desire in his eyes. He stared at me and I reached out to him, begging him to take me and give me what I so desperately needed. He shook his head and climbed up my body, pushing me back into the mattress, as if to say it wasn't my time yet.

He pinned me to the bed, his strong hands restraining my wrists. I winced as he pressed into me, the pleasure and pain intertwining and scorching my skin. His grip tightened as he moved, sending delicious shudders down my spine. I gasped in ecstasy when he surged inside of me, claiming me and making me his own with one single thrust.

My fingers dragged down his chest, down his abs, and when I hit the raised skin from his injury, I lifted slightly to look. The stitches on his stomach were angry and red. "Are you okay?" I asked before brushing my fingers over it once more.

"I could be bleeding out and I'd still find the energy to fuck you, Christine," he rasped.

That was the hottest thing he'd ever said. I loved the desperation in his tone. How he couldn't wait another single moment to be inside of me.

"Do you like this?" he growled, his face contorted in a feral expression. I nodded, unable to find the words to express my arousal. He leaned in closer, his breath hot on my neck. "Let me tell you something, Christine. I'm going to steal whatever scraps of your heart you have for me. I'm going to take—" He paused to thrust and let out a growl. "Every bit of you I can."

He moved with increasing intensity, pushing me to the brink of pleasure with each thrust. The sounds of our slapping skin filled the room, and the hard fuck made every bone in my body bounce. I screamed out his name and begged for more. I needed to feel how much he wanted me. Needed to know that this was real —that he was mine.

His face softened and he looked into my eyes before biting his lip. "Christine," he muttered, "you are so beautiful."

I stroked his cheek and smiled up at him. "Fuck me, Leo. Show me how much you want me."

His movements grew frantic as he quickened his pace, taking me on a wild ride of pleasure that left me dazed and breathless.

I tensed up and moaned his name as I let go with a loud shudder. My orgasm was bold and heavy, rocking my entire body with little zaps of pleasure that flooded my body. He held me close, both of us panting from the intensity of it.

"I love you," he whispered in my ear, his voice trembling. "I will always love you."

He was covered in bruises, and the stitches in his side were barely hanging on, but he didn't seem to care. This was raw passion. Fucking. Loving. Everything in between.

I ran my fingers over his face, tracing his green eyes and curling my hand around his full, kissable lips.

"I'm not done with you yet," he groaned before pulling back and flipping me over onto my stomach. He wrapped my blonde hair around his fist and forced me up on all fours. In an instant, he was surging inside of me once more, and the passion turned rougher. Harder.

More intense. He fucked me like we'd never been apart, like we needed every inch of each other to survive. I felt his cock twitch inside of me, and I reached down to stroke my clit. With each pump of his hips into mine, I grew closer and closer to another orgasm. He was unrelenting. Demanding. Possessive. I needed him. I wanted him. There was nothing I could do to stop this ride he was leading me on. I was completely *his*.

A low and demanding growl rumbled in my ear. "Come for me, now." With each firm, possessive thrust, he drove me closer and closer to the edge. His voice was raw and insistent, filled with urgent longing, and I wanted him to find his release too. I wanted to feel every inch of him shatter into me, claiming me in his own intimate way. His body begged for me to take all of him, so I did, pushing us both over the edge.

I arched my back, feeling an even more intense orgasm than before. My whole body shuddered and I quivered, losing all control of my senses. Our bodies collided and created a sensation that damn near broke me.

He slammed into me, his hand bruising my flesh. His guttural cry vibrated against my skin as he thrust into me harder, digging his fingers into my hips. I bit down on my lip to stifle a scream of pleasure as I felt him swell and pulse inside me. He clung to me, his nails scratching my skin, pushing me to the brink of madness. He growled in pleasure and shivered as he spilled inside me, his cries echoing in my ears.

We collapsed into each other, breathing heavily as our chests heaved. We lay in bed, just holding one another, completely naked, utterly exposed and vulnerable.

It wouldn't be long until we had to face the outside world again. I knew that our time alone together was precious and fleeting. I wanted so desperately to lie in his arms forever, to never let go, to stop time and make everything in the real world disappear, to create a world where Leo would always be mine and I would always be his.

"I'm done holding back, Christine," he whispered. "I want this. I want us."

"So do I," I responded.

"I'm done trying to fight this. I'm done letting doubt hold me back. I want forever with you."

He kissed me softly, then moved to the opposite side of the bed. He pulled the covers up over us, our naked bodies still pressed against each other. I glanced over at him, admiring my handiwork, and as I watched him sleep, I knew that this was an entirely different man from the Leo who pushed me away. He was stronger. A survivor. I could see it in his eyes, in his body language, and even in the way he held me. He was a man essential to my happiness, and I knew, without a doubt, that he would never let me go.

No matter what happened or how things turned out, I would never regret choosing all three of them. We had been given a second chance, and I intended to make the most of it.

Chapter Nine

CHRISTINE

Calloused hands caressed my cheek, and I opened my eyes to a naked Leo nestled beside me. His emerald eyes were filled with a sinful satisfaction, and I could feel the intensity radiating from his body as I took him in.

I inched up and leaned forward, pulling Leo into a passionate kiss. "I think I need you to fuck me again," I whispered.

A light chuckle echoed from the corner of the room, beckoning me to look. Atticus was sitting in a wooden chair, his tired eyes filled with amusement as he looked toward me. August was by his side, sipping on coffee.

"You're back. I'm angry that you left us," I said before stealing the blanket from Leo and wrapping it around me, creating a barrier that barely concealed our simmering desire.

I rose to my feet and sauntered toward them both. My intent was clear—to kiss August—but Atticus reached out and pulled me into his lap. His muscular arms clung around me possessively as he nuzzled my neck.

"I was so worried about you, Little Monster." He roamed my skin with his hands, as if checking me for injuries.

"I'm okay. How are you? How are all of you?"

August cleared his throat. "I have some cuts and bruises I need you to kiss better. There's one on my co–"

"We're fine," Atticus said, cutting him off. "I'm so fucking sorry, Christine. I had no idea my father was planning that."

I stroked his cheek. "It's okay. We're all going to be okay now."

"We got you some clothes and toiletries. Also got cash, a car, and a place to stay for a little while," he murmured against my ear. A shiver ran through me as I felt his breath on my skin.

"Who did you see?" I breathed, leaning in closer to him.

"Hudson. He said he's proud of you, by the way."

A smile curled at the corners of my mouth as I looked back into his eyes. "He was probably lying. Hudson isn't impressed by anyone."

"I'm impressed by you," he purred seductively. Atticus's lips lingered on my neck. Leo stepped closer, brushing his knuckles up against my bare arm. He set a cup of coffee down in front of me, then tenderly kissed the top of my head.

August cleared his throat, drawing my attention away from the others. "My mother had a safe house off the coast. It's a day's drive, but far enough away that we can come up with a game plan. It's also off the grid. Only a handful of people know about it."

"Are you sure she didn't tell Theodore about it? I'm worried they were closer than we thought," I whispered.

August sighed. "She didn't tell him. I'm certain of it. Only Adonis and me know about it."

I could feel the tension in the room too thick to cut with a knife. All I could think about were the possibilities if we did leave for the safe house—a place of our own to explore and discover ourselves. I looked up slowly from my cup and finally spoke. "Sounds perfect. When do we leave?"

Leo opened his mouth, his voice forming a harsh command.

"Now. Get dressed. The longer we stay here, the more danger we are in."

I reluctantly uncoiled from Atticus's arms and stood up. Scanning the room, I noticed the clothes and shoes that had been gathered for me, their fabric rolled into neat bundles at the foot of the bed. I moved toward them and picked them up. They were slightly too large for me, but that didn't matter. I wanted to be able to move freely, unrestricted by tightness.

Once dressed, I grabbed a gun from on the bedside table. It was cold, heavy, and familiar in my hands. Its metal handle nestled comfortably against my skin as I tucked it into my waistband—it felt right to be back in my element again.

"Let's roll," Leo growled. The ominous black SUV loomed outside. Atticus opened the driver's door, and Leo clambered in the passenger seat. August and I climbed in the back.

"Fill me in," I said, my voice quivering with worry. "How many points of entry? How many neighbors? I need to be...prepared."

August nodded curtly. "It's a safe house, built and maintained by my mother. State of the art security system, fully stocked. It's an old house on a remote island, only one way on and off, making it easy to survey. Leo's mother and sister are already there. Atticus arranged for them to go there."

Leo shot Atticus a glance before turning back to face me.

"And who else?" I asked hesitantly.

"That's it," August responded grimly. "Adonis escaped during the raid and went to stay with his daughter in Kenzington. Broke his arm while fleeing though."

My heart plummeted at his words. Atticus and Leo exchanged a worried glance before driving onto a dirt road, away from the castle and all its dangers.

Atticus hesitated, almost terrified of what he had to say. "My father is livid," he choked out. "He told everyone that August has kidnapped you, and the entire court is on edge. Since the lords swore their allegiance to you yesterday, the entire kingdom is on the lookout for their queen."

I spun toward August, my heart racing as I took in his expression. "Oh my God. Are you alright?"

August grabbed me and brought me into a tight embrace, his hand protectively wrapped around my waist. "It's fine." He smiled, trying to comfort me. "I'm used to being the villain anyways. And plus, snatching the queen has its perks."

My insides tingled as I pressed a light kiss onto his cheek. "Perks?" I whispered, relishing in the closeness of us.

A slight grin graced his lips as he proposed a plan. "Oh, yes. For example, we have a long car ride to the coast, and I'm going to make these two assholes listen to me get you off a dozen times."

I wanted to be thrilled by that idea, but my eyes flashed to Leo, who was gripping the armrest so hard his knuckles were white. I could see the battle waging in his expression—his hesitation was palpable, yet his desire was undeniable. This had to be a trial for him, accepting our group dynamic, yet I wasn't about to back down. I uncoiled from my seat and leaned into him, whispering in his ear. "Are you up for it, Leo?"

I could see his pulse racing beneath his skin. His muscles tensed and relaxed. He let out a slow breath and turned toward me, his eyes glinting with lust. "Yes, my queen," he hissed.

"Good." I smiled, feeling relieved as I settled back into my seat.

A deep growl erupted from Leo's throat. I caught his gaze, and instantly it was all I could do not to rip his clothes off him and fuck him. I wanted to show him what he meant to me and how much I wanted him. How I could never let go.

Leo's eyes darted to the back seat, to August. "Anyway," August said, pulling me close and kissing my neck. "There are no neighbors on our safe house island."

I rested my head on August's shoulder and let the feeling of being safe wash over me. "I never thought we'd get out of there," I whispered.

August squeezed my knee. "We'll get through this. I'm just glad you didn't have to go through with the marriage to Lord Nathan. He didn't...hurt you, did he?"

Atticus looked at me through the rearview mirror, and Leo turned in his seat, his eyes boring into mine. "No," I whispered. "He didn't."

"What happened?" August asked.

I gnawed on my lip. "Lord Nathan is providing Theodore DuPont with an army, but they are unskilled. They're working together, but I don't think that's why your father wanted me to marry him, Atticus."

"What are you thinking, Little Monster?"

August held me tighter. "He kept comparing me to Isabelle. Said I wasn't good enough for you. Called me a wh-whore. He's projecting all of his issues with August's mother onto me."

August lightened the tension with a shudder. "It's *so*

gross to think about our parents banging. Our families have always been friends, but I never thought…"

Atticus let out a sigh. "My father isn't used to not getting what he wants. And it's no surprise King Frederick wasn't good to Isabelle. He doesn't want me to pine after a woman who doesn't want me back."

"But I do want you!" I exclaimed. "I just want…all of you."

August kissed my neck. "You have all of us, love."

"Good. Because I'm not going anywhere. Can you understand that?"

August pushed his fingers into my hair and pulled my head back, kissing me with such intensity I was left breathless. "I'm going to show you how much I understand that."

I let out a small laugh and rested my head on his chest. It was going to be a long ride to the coast.

The salty air permeated the vehicle, and Leo watched the passing world outside his window. Atticus drove while August snored in the back seat.

I closed my eyes and sighed, trying to rid myself of the weariness I felt. I was so tired and overwhelmed by everything. At least we'd have time to process it all at the safe house.

I opened my eyes and looked out the window, watching as the landscape slowly changed from open plains to a small town.

August had been asleep for the majority of the ride, and I was grateful for that; we had all been exhausted from the last few days.

"What have you been thinking about, Little Monster?" Atticus questioned me before taking the exit off of the highway.

"Too much," I said under my breath. August shifted in his sleep and pulled me closer against him. "Is it wrong that I'm happy right now despite what happened?"

"Never," Leo murmured quietly in agreement.

"We're together, we're safe—for now—and we have time," I said softly.

August slowly woke with a yawn before saying, "Shit. I was supposed to finger fuck you through this entire car ride, and here I am sleeping." His fingers tenderly ghosted over my thigh before settling there possessively as if to emphasize his point.

I pressed my lips to his forehead, watching as his eyelids fluttered closed. "You needed the rest. We all need it."

Leo yawned and looked up at August. "Is this the right exit?" he murmured.

August leaned forward and squinted into the night. His sharp features softened as he smiled and pointed at an old road sign. "I think so. If we take a left here, it'll take us to the bridge that leads to the house. It's a long drive, though," he finished in a low voice that sent shivers up my spine.

He turned his gaze back to me and winked before brushing his lips against mine and pressing them close to my ear. "I have you all to myself for at least the next hour, so I'm going to make sure you scream for me," he whispered with a husky laugh.

My heart fluttered with anticipation, knowing that in the fleeting privacy of the car, we were able to express what we had been feeling for months now. All of us. Together. I smiled back at him and replied, "That sounds lovely."

August's hands drifted around my waist and softly caressed my inner thigh, slowly inching higher and higher with each stroke until I was begging him to stop teasing me. He laughed devilishly as he gave me one final nip before trailing his fingers up my sides to my shoulders.

My heart dropped when I heard August's quietly spoken statement: "I like teasing you."

"Well, I don't like being teased," I quipped back, tightening my grip on my thigh in a vain attempt to contain my building desire.

August continued, his voice low and raspy—I swear he could make me come with just his words. "I'm almost there, love. It's going to be worth it."

My cheeks flushed immediately; I think he knew how much I wanted him, too. "You'd better make me scream," I demanded in a hushed voice, my gaze flicking over to Leo, who looked angry in the passenger seat.

The sensation of August's fingers ghosting over my inner thigh made my stomach clench. "That's the plan, love." The look in his eyes had me panting.

I winked at him as I felt a smile tugging at the corners of my lips. "You're not the only one who can tease."

August chuckled, barely audibly, as his fingers brushed against my core, causing me to gasp. When Leo stirred slightly, my gaze darted away from August— our intimate moment ending just as quickly as it had begun. Leo looked…hurt.

August's gaze flicked up to meet Leo's, a daring challenge in his eyes.

"Fuck," Leo muttered.

"August, you better stop teasing her and make her

come, or I'll show you how it's done," Atticus groaned possessively.

I opened my mouth to say something, but a single syllable was all I could manage before August pushed his finger under the waistband of my yoga pants and beneath the lace edge of my panties. I gasped, my breath fogging the window next to me as I lifted my hips in invitation. August's finger slid inside of me, and I felt my pussy clench around him.

He paused, moving his gaze back to Leo. His lips curved up into a smirk. "Hey, Leo," he whispered, pushing his finger deeper inside me and sending sparks of pleasure across my skin. "I want you to watch. Give you something to aspire to."

His words hung in the air as I moaned, pressing my face against the window pane and arching my body toward him. "You like that?" he breathed, not bothering to take his eyes off Leo.

My body softened, wilting into August's touch. He leaned toward me, his lips gently brushing mine and setting my skin on fire. He brushed his fingers inside me again, teasing my nerve endings and bringing me to the edge of release. I gasped, pushing my breast out of my bra and teasing down my flat stomach with the tips of my fingers.

"Christ," Leo groaned, looking at August's handiwork.

August's fingers pushed deeper and I cried out, my hips bucking against him. His fingers worked relentlessly, faster and faster as I lost track of time.

"I'm going to come if you keep that up," I begged, panting heavily as pleasure coursed through me.

August laughed softly before pressing a gentle kiss on the side of my neck. "I love dirty girls who come in their panties."

The thrill of being so close to Leo and Atticus sent shivers down my spine. Every part of me wanted to be watched; I wanted everyone to know intimately how I felt for August. If we were going to do this, we needed to dive in headfirst, no more holding back.

"August!" I screamed, my toes curling and my breaths coming in short little gasps. The SUV jolted to a stop and the interior lit up, the sudden brightness blinding me momentarily. August pulled away from me and as my eyes regained focus, I saw August's hands hanging loosely in his lap and his head cradled by the headrest. His gaze was a steady smolder, like an unspoken challenge. I felt my heart thump wildly against my chest, urging me on. My entire body quivered with anticipation.

The driver's side door flew open, and Atticus

violently yanked August out of the seat. I looked beyond the rear window for oncoming cars, but there were none. We were on a long bridge with the swirling ocean surrounding us. "Let me show you how she really likes it, brother," Atticus purred.

Atticus grabbed me with such force, lifting me out of the backseat and slamming me against the side of the car. His lips connected with mine, his tongue pushing its way in. His long fingers dug into my hair, pulling my head so he could take what he wanted from me. I gasped for breath, but he had me pinned down so strongly, his whole body pressing against mine. He would not let go until he was completely satisfied.

"I missed you so much, Little Monster. Was so fucking worried about you."

My fingers trembled as I reached for the zipper of his pants. His breathing quickened as I grazed his dick. I traced a line around it with my fingertips, teasing and tantalizing until I felt him twitch in pleasure.

"You want it, don't you?" Atticus growled low in my ear, the intensity of his breathing tickling my neck. "You want my cock, Little Monster? Want to feel it pulsing inside your hot cunt?"

I fought to steady myself, my body aching for him to take control and claim me as his own. I nodded my head in answer, barely able to find my voice as he pulled me closer.

His hand wrapped around my waist, squeezing possessively and pulling me tight against him. He then jerked my pants and panties off, and I kicked them away. I spread my legs around him as he lifted me off my feet. Without warning, he thrust himself inside me, pushing into me with an intense force that sent shivers through my entire body.

"Do it," I begged in a whisper, writhing against him and biting down on my lip in pleasure.

Atticus thrust inside of me once more, and I cried out. He pushed deeper inside of me, slamming into my walls again and again. I stretched my hands out, trying to find something to hold onto and grip. I grabbed the side of the car and squeezed, trying to bite back my screams.

Atticus growled deep in my ear as he thrust into me. His tight grip was on my hair and his other hand roaming over my body. I felt every inch of him, and I never wanted to forget this moment. His breathy whispers were husky with desire, and a thrill ran through me as he fucked me hard.

"I love you, Little Monster. No one will ever hurt you again." He paused to lean in closer. "I'll kill them all, Christine. All for you."

August stood transfixed, his desire for me radiating off him like heat. Leo stood outside, too, and the air around us was heavy with sensuality, where each moment stretched out to feel like an eternity.

"This is dangerous," I whispered, trying to break the tension and excite Atticus further.

"It's worth it," he whispered possessively in my ear and continued pounding into me with increased intensity.

"Oh, God," I cried. I was so close. "Harder!"

My body quaked as Atticus's whispers caressed my ear lobe. "You belong to us, and we fucking love that. You're a dirty girl, Little Monster," he growled.

His hands reached around and held me tightly against him, his cock pumping relentlessly inside me. His grip on my hips tightened as he showed me no mercy, thrusting deeper than ever before.

"Please, Atticus," I moaned, my body quivering in anticipation of the impending orgasm.

"Not until me," he commanded, his voice full of alpha possessiveness.

I begged and pleaded for him to let me come, but he denied me again and again, exploiting my pleasure and withholding his own.

"Say my name," he ordered.

I gasped his name in a feverish pitch. My breath

hitched as he edged closer, every breath of his a sweet whisper so near my lips. His fingers were entangled in my hair, and I wanted more. His blazing gaze roved over me, setting my body afire, and I begged him to take me.

"Atticus," I sobbed. "Yes! Yes, I'm yours! Please, come inside of me."

He answered with a possessive hard kiss that curled my toes. His rhythm increased and each thrust drove me higher and higher until I was screaming. Every swell of bliss washed over me as I grasped him tight, not wanting the moment to end. His groans filled the air until his final shudder, and he pressed his sweaty forehead against mine.

August looked on with envy, and Atticus only growled out a warning for him to stay away. "You can have a turn later."

August laughed, but the bitter jealousy was still there in his voice. "Deal."

"And what about you, Leo?" I asked, the pleasure-filled haze clearing my mind as I looked at him.

To my horror, Leo frowned. "We need to get going. It's not safe to stay here."

His words made my pulse steady and my stomach drop.

No. I pushed him too far.

"Leo…"

He spun around and marched back to the passenger side of the car. I let out a breath. Maybe it was too much too soon. Maybe I was expecting too much from them. I was suddenly conscious of the fact that I was standing there, in the middle of a bridge, with no pants on. I wrapped my arms around myself. "I'm cold," I mumbled.

"Let's go, Little Monster," Atticus said. "Leo will come around."

I got dressed and the four of us got back into the SUV, and I watched as we drove down the long and dark bridge toward the safe house.

Leo sat in the front seat with a frown on his face.

I'd gone too far. This was reckless and stupid. We'd just been through a traumatic ordeal, and I was getting fucked in the middle of a bridge.

"Don't look so sad, love," August whispered in my ear. "You did nothing wrong."

"I don't think he's mad at me," I said. "He's just… I don't know."

"Just give him time," Atticus said. "We are all a little on edge."

"A little?" I snorted.

"You're beautiful," August said. "And you're ours. If

he can't handle that, then he's not the man you think he is."

I wanted to say something, but the words caught in my throat. I would need to show him what we had. We'd been through so much, and I wasn't going to give up now.

Leo was silent for the rest of the ride, and I wondered what was going through his mind.

Chapter Ten

LEO

An irrepressible rage blazed through my veins as I watched Christine get fucked by Atticus. I wanted to rush him, to tear him away from her, but I was rooted to the spot. My chest felt like it was searing with molten lava, and my head was in a whirl. I remembered what it felt like to have her in my bed, and how warm her pussy had been around my dick only a few short hours ago. God, how desperately I wanted her for myself. A possessive fury gripped me; all I could think was that she belonged to me, and only me.

We pulled up to the safe house, and I immediately got out. I didn't want to be trapped in that damn SUV any longer, smelling sex on her skin, watching the guys put that blissed-out look on her face. Atticus got out and stomped after me, leaving Christine and Augustus in the car.

He wrapped his hand around my wrist, and I tried to jerk out of his hold. "Fuck off."

"No, you fuck off," he growled. "You don't get to play nice when it suits you. August and I gave you time alone with Christine last night, even though all of us were missing her. You think I wanted to walk away? You think I didn't want to check every inch of her body to make sure that bastard didn't hurt her?"

My jaw clenched and my hands flexed as I glared into his eyes. I wanted to wrap my fingers around his throat, squeezing until his puny life was extinguished. But it wouldn't be enough. It wouldn't make Christine want him any less.

"You don't get to decide what she does with her heart or her body. You get what I give you, and that's it. Stop making her feel bad about it, or I'll remove you from the equation. And if you ever think about taking her away from me, I'll make sure you regret it." He leaned closer and smirked. "I can do things to her that you can only dream of," he whispered into my ear, and I felt the shudder of revulsion run through my body as he stepped back from me. "Behave."

He started to say something, but I cut him off with

a wave of my hand. "Just stay out of it," I growled, my eyes narrowing into slits as I spoke.

He snarled and looked away. "We both want what's best for her. But I think only I know how to get there."

"What's your deal?" I asked. "Why even bother with me?"

"You make her feel safe," he growled, his voice tight with suppressed rage. "You make her smile, and you make her beg. You're good for her, even if it's something I can't stand to see." His eyes were blazing with jealousy.

"So you admit it," I smirked. "You're jealous of me. Doesn't it bother you that she enjoys being with me so much?"

"Of course it does," he spat, his fists clenched at his sides. "But I'm not a coward, and I will deal with it. I know her better than any of you." Possessive hunger flashed in his gaze, and I felt a shiver run through me.

"Are the two of you about to fuck, or can we go inside?" Augustus asked while opening the door. "Christine is tired and I need a proper shower."

We took a step apart and Augustus got out of the car, quickly followed behind by Christine. She gave me a cautious look that made me feel bad for being such an ass. I was supposed to change. I was supposed to move past this. "You okay?" she asked.

No. No, I wasn't. But I had to be. I didn't want to be the reason she cried. I didn't almost die in that fucking castle just to fuck up my second chance. "I'll work through it."

She nodded.

The safe house was a two-story white home with pale green shutters. Behind it, I could see a sandy beach, and even though it was dark, the moon illuminated the waves crashing along the shore.

With the front door lit up, the house looked inviting. The white siding was chipping in some places, and the windows were covered in dust. The grass needed to be mowed, and the tree in the front yard was a monstrous beast, looming over the house like a giant that had no idea what to do with itself.

The safe house was surrounded by a high white picket fence, and the windows showed light behind them. They looked like eyes, watching me.

"This isn't what I expected," I murmured while nodding up at the house. I was eager to see my mother and sister, but it was late.

"What's that supposed to mean?" Augustus asked.

"It's…homey. I imagined a mansion by the sea," I explained. Isabelle was ostentatious. This was…cozy. The salty breeze carried across the beach, and I could smell the ocean and damp earth.

We started to walk up to the front door, and I fought the urge to throw my arm around Christine's shoulders. Augustus and Atticus walked in front of us, and Christine gave me a nervous little half smile. We walked through the narrow entryway, and Augustus and Atticus started discussing something in low voices.

Once in the living room, Christine sat down in a blue armchair, her face heavy with exhaustion.

"Leo?!" My mother's high-pitched voice sounded. Footsteps pounded on the hardwood floor, and I turned just as my mother ran to me with open arms.

My mother was a petite woman with light gray hair and sky blue eyes, and she always smelled like roses. She was like an angel, her soft voice sweet and delicate. She was wearing a light blue dress that complemented her fair skin, and a thin gold necklace with a pretty diamond heart dangled from her neck. She gave me a tight hug and squeezed me with all her might. "I missed you so much."

"I missed you too," I said into her hair. She pulled away, her hands on my cheeks, and brushed a tear from my eye with her thumb.

"You're back," she said, with a smile that seemed to light up the whole room. "I was so afraid when I heard about the attack. Are you okay?"

"I'm fine," I said, and my mother brought her hand

to her lips to cover a small sob. "I'm okay, Mom. No need to worry."

"A mother *always* worries, Leo."

"Where is Daphne?" I asked.

"Asleep. She needed the rest."

She turned to face Augustus and Atticus, then forced a tight smile. "Augustus, Atticus. Thank you so much. I can never repay you."

Augustus and Atticus nodded, but they looked uncomfortable—probably because they were both getting Christine off just an hour ago. We'd just come in the door, and already she was thanking them. I could see them standing awkwardly, wondering when they could get out of there.

"Hello, Mrs. Winthrop," Augustus said. He'd met my mother a handful of times, and she always made him nervous. He didn't know what to do with someone genuinely nice.

"Hello, Augustus. It's nice to see you…sober."

He cringed.

"And you," she said while beaming at Atticus. "I can never thank you enough for getting us out of the city the way you did. I was nervous when that man—Hudson—showed up at our doorstep, but he turned out to be lovely."

"Of course, Mrs. Winthrop. Leo is our close friend. His family is our family," Atticus replied.

"Thank you for everything you did for us," my mother said, walking over to him. She hugged him and he stiffened, not responding right away. "Please, call me Vivian."

"Of course," he said, giving a little cough.

"Why does he get to call her Vivian?" Augustus pouted under his breath.

"Has everything been okay since you arrived?" Atticus asked, shoving his hands into his pockets.

"Oh, yes. I spent the day dusting. The house is well stocked but needed a deep clean."

"I'm happy to hear it," Atticus said, looking into my mother's eyes. He seemed to do that a lot, look people in the eye when he spoke to them. As if he wanted to make sure that the person he was talking to was actually there.

My mother looked around the living room, and her eyes landed on Christine. "Oh, Christine!! I didn't see you sitting there, sweet girl."

My mother rushed over to her and practically lifted her out of the chair for a hug. My mother always adored her.

"Hello, Mrs. Winthrop," she said, her cheeks flushed.

"I've told you a dozen times, call me Vivian." She hugged Christine tighter before pulling away. "Oh, I've missed you. My poor Leo was so sad when you went overseas. It makes me happy to see you here." She paused and backed away, her eyes wide. "Oh, I suppose it's not proper to greet the queen with a hug." To Christine's apparent horror, my mother then bowed awkwardly.

"Please don't do that," Christine said. "It's not…I mean, I'm not…"

"You're a queen, dearie. You've got to own it."

My mother hugged Christine once more and then gave us a tour of the rest of the house. There was a hallway on the first floor, lined with closed doors. The living room was at the end with an open kitchen and dining room next to it.

She led us upstairs and we followed her into a large, nice bedroom that was directly across from the staircase. The windows overlooked the beach and the ocean, and I could smell the salt.

Augustus wound his arm around Christine's waist and planted a kiss on her temple. I could feel the jealousy bubbling up inside of me and had to fight the urge to rip his arm off. "We'll take the master bedroom," Augustus declared.

My mother's eyes narrowed as she studied Augustus.

She had a begrudging fondness for him, but she always felt that he was too entitled, and I would agree with her. Despite her disapproval, she never vocalized her thoughts that Christine was too good for him.

"Okay," Christine replied, her voice quivering slightly in the silence.

"And I'll take the room downstairs," I jumped in, eager to change the direction of the conversation. I wanted access to the ground floor in case we needed to flee in a hurry.

"Okay, dear," my mother said, patting my hand before turning to Atticus.

"I'll stay in this room." Atticus motioned to a bedroom across from theirs.

My mom surveyed all of us with a hard look before softening and squeezing my hand briefly. "You're all probably exhausted. I'll let you get settled," she said with a slight smile before heading off to check on Daphne and allow us time to rest.

Once she was gone, Atticus closed the distance between him and Christine to give her a goodnight kiss. I had to squeeze my eyes shut so I didn't punch him in the jaw. "Goodnight, Little Monster. Tomorrow, you're in *my* bed."

"Goodnight," she whispered tenderly.

Augustus, Christine and I made our way to the

master bedroom and opened the door. I could smell the ocean again. It was a spacious, beautiful bedroom with a stunning window. It overlooked the yard and beach, and I could see the rocky shore and the rippling water.

"I'm going to take a shower," she said before eyeing me.

"Sounds good." My lame response made me realize that maybe she wanted me to kiss her goodnight, too. Fuck, why did this have to be so hard?

Christine slipped into the bathroom and turned on the shower, likely eager for some space to process everything. She always needed moments alone with her thoughts when it all got too overwhelming.

"You can sleep in our bed if you'd like, Shadow," Augustus whispered in my ear.

"I'd rather sleep on the beach," I replied, deadpan.

He smirked. "Oh, so you only do group activities with *Atticus* then, hmm?"

I frowned, not wanting to hurt him. "I've cleaned up your vomit too many times," I replied, my voice low and gruff. The memories of his wilder days still lingered in my thoughts, too vivid for me to forget.

Augustus pressed his palm to his chest and smirked again. "You're not fucking me," he said. "We'd be tag teaming."

"You sound jealous," I joked, trying to lighten the mood. But his gaze was still hard as he looked at me.

"Well, maybe I am," he replied, his voice rising a little. "Am I not good enough? You watched me fuck plenty of women when I was at the royal academy."

My cheeks flamed and I shook my head. "Those were faceless whores I had to watch to make sure they didn't murder you. Why do you care?" *Would I have watched him with Christine?* a small voice whispered inside me, but I couldn't bring myself to answer.

"So you admit it, you don't want to tag team with me now?" He pouted a bit.

"So you admit it, you're being ridiculous right now?" I said, echoing him sarcastically.

Augustus's gaze sharpened, and then he yelled, "Stop answering me with questions."

I raised my chin stubbornly in reply. "Stop getting mad at me," I snapped back. We glared at each other for what felt like an eternity, and then both of us seemed to deflate at the same time—it was clear that neither of us wanted to fight.

"I'm sorry, Shadow," Augustus said, sitting down on the bed. This apology surprised me. "This whole situation is fucking with me. I'm worried, you know? What if she decides she only wants threesomes, then I'm out of the running."

"I don't think that's going to happen," I replied, sitting down next to him and grabbing his shoulder. "To be honest, you're handling it a lot better than I am."

"I don't feel like I am. I'm just… When I realized that Christine and I have a future together, my life changed."

"Is that a bad thing?"

"No, but…I don't know, I'm still me." He paused and started to look anxious. "I'm still a fuckup. Still the least responsible and tolerable person in the group. But I want to be more. I *need* to be more. Do you think she'll want to keep being with me? What if I'm not enough?"

"I don't know what to tell you, Augustus. Because deep down, I hope you fuck it up so I'll have less competition."

"Fuck. You could have at least lied to me," he said with a frown.

"You're not my king anymore. I don't have to lie."

He smiled. "I guess it levels the playing field a bit, huh?"

"Now Atticus has the leg up. Are you sure you don't want to have a threesome? I think we could really rock her world." I shoved him, but I was smiling.

"Shadow, I'm worried," he admitted. "What if Christine gets overwhelmed with all of this? What if she decides she doesn't want any of us?"

"She wouldn't," I replied, even though I wasn't entirely sure. "Why do you keep calling me shadow?"

Augustus preened. "You've always been my shadow. Following me. Watching me. Protecting me. Not to mention, you've got a bit of a voyeur thing going on lately. Lingering on the sidelines. I feel like the nickname fits."

I gritted my teeth. "You're pissing me off."

He was about to say something else, but Christine emerged from the bathroom, wrapped in a towel. She sat down on the bed next to me and put her hand on my thigh. She smelled like vanilla and something tropical. Her hair was wet and hung in ringlets down her back. Droplets of water clung to her neck and trailed down her shoulder. The sight of her made my stomach flip. There was something sexy about how she held herself. She moved with the confidence of a queen, but there was also the hint of a girl who was learning something different about herself every day.

"What are the two of you talking about?" she asked. Christine was still self-conscious around me and Augustus, and it was entirely my fault. But she'd gotten used to Atticus. Maybe acceptance was working in his favor.

"Leo is going to stay in here with us. So he can keep an eye on you," Augustus informed her, the corner of his mouth ticked up. Asshole.

Christine looked at him, then at me and then back at him. She was trying to process how to react, but I didn't give her a choice. I grabbed her in a hug and started kissing her neck. Her eyes fluttered closed. The skin on her neck and shoulders was soft to the touch, warm, alive. Goose bumps spread along my body as my hand traced down her neck and shoulder to her collarbone. The towel slipped and I felt the soft skin of her breasts.

"I'm sorry," I whispered. "I'm working on it."

"We're all working on it," Augustus added. I'd almost forgotten he was there.

"Okay," Christine replied, her eyes misty.

I eased her into the middle of the bed—because fuck if I wanted to wake up to Augustus Jr. poking me in the back. And I took off my shirt and got in beside her.

"We're totally having a threesome one of these days. I'm going to be better than Atticus, Leo," Augustus said. He took off his clothes and climbed into bed with us. He wrapped his arms around Christine and, with the edges of his fingers, tickled my arm.

"Hands to yourself, Augustus," I hissed.

"I'm totally asking Atty Daddy how he got you to do a threesome. I've never given a blow job, but I bet I'm great at it."

Christine busted out laughing.

"No."

"But—"

"Stop, Augustus. Go to sleep."

I lay in bed for a while thinking about everything. Navigating my feelings for Christine was difficult. At first, I never thought I'd be good enough. Now, I was jealous as fuck of the other men in her life. When I overcame one hurdle, I was met with another. It was killing me.

I just had to step up. I had to get out of my own head.

I just didn't know how.

Chapter Eleven

CHRISTINE

My eyes flickered open and a familiar warmth enveloped me. August's arm was draped over my waist, a heavy hand between my thighs. Atticus's voice broke the stillness, and my gaze shifted to him. His smile was soft in the darkness, yet something else lingered behind his expression that made me squirm.

"You look well rested," he uttered, his eyes traveling over the position we were in.

I cleared my throat, my pulse swelling with a mix of thrill and panic. "What time is it?"

"Early." Atticus stepped closer to the bed, his gaze locked on me. "Want to walk on the beach?"

I nodded and eased out of August's hold, my skin prickling in anticipation as I imagined their reactions when they awoke to find each other in bed alone together. Leo would be horrified, August triumphant.

"Wash up and I'll meet you downstairs," Atticus whispered before exiting the room.

The beach was quiet, save for the flow of the tide. The dew on the grass poking out of the sand glittered in the sunlight, and I sighed at the peaceful scene. The sea breeze blew through my hair, awakening the senses. The salt-heavy air stung my nostrils, and the scent of seaweed and kelp filled my lungs.

"I love it here. I can't imagine anything more perfect than waking up to the sound of breaking waves," I said. The sand was cool on my skin, but the sun was warm. The wind was gentle but strong, tugging on my clothes, my hair, my pulse.

My breath caught as he drew me into his arms, his expression tender as his lips brushed my forehead. "You are perfect," he whispered, then his voice grew hoarse. "I wanted to make sure you're okay, Little Monster."

My heart raced as I leaned against his shoulder. "It's really happening," I murmured, taking in his strong arms around me, his scent of musk and spice inflaming my senses. "We are here together, Leo is—" A sharp laugh escaped my lips, imagining Leo's bewilderment when he discovered I left him in bed with August. "All thanks to you," I said breathlessly, gazing up into Atticus's somber face.

His lips opened and he stared at me, his eyes a brilliant shade of midnight that were burning with a deep hunger. "What?" he asked softly, lifting his hand to brush my cheek tenderly.

I shivered and swallowed hard, heat flooding my body as his gaze consumed me. "You are so good to me," I whispered in awe.

The air became heavy with tension, and Atticus's expression changed to one of regret and guilt. "It's all my fault what happened at the castle," he murmured, his fingers threading through my hair. "My father…"

"No," I said firmly, pulling away slightly so I could meet his eyes. The intensity of his gaze made me tremble as our gazes locked. "You are not responsible for what your father did."

His hold on me tightened, my curves pressed against his hard chest. His fingertips dug into my flesh, and I gasped.

I slowly pulled away, my hands still resting on him. My eyes met his and I felt a shiver travel up my spine. He looked so broken, so vulnerable. I wanted to take away his pain and make him forget about the world, about the fear and hatred that had been plaguing us both.

"I was worried you'd blame me," he said softly. His voice was like a balm to my broken spirit, and I could feel the urge to protect him rising up inside me. "I suppose I've been giving you space out of fear. I couldn't hold myself back on the bridge, but…it feels wrong to touch you when I haven't gotten rid of our enemies. I'm scared that I'm not deserving."

"My Monster never shows fear," I replied, lifting one hand to cup his cheek. "And you definitely don't need to fear me."

He closed his eyes as if he were in pain. "I fear you the most." He squeezed me again and I almost forgot about the danger we left behind.

I pulled away, keeping my hands on his chest and rising on my toes to meet his eyes. "Why?"

The corners of his lips curled into a sad smile as he exhaled deeply. "Because I'd hate to see the sort of things I'd do for you," he said after a few moments of silence. His words felt like a promise and a threat at the same time. "I control the world, and you control me." His expression softened for an instant before it hardened again. "I love you, and I will end my father for what he's done."

My pulse raced as I looked at him in disbelief. The

love that swelled inside me was overwhelming, but so was the dread of what would come next. Atticus had taken me in when nobody else cared, and he had saved me from my own darkness time and time again, but now our roles seemed to be reversed as he needed saving from his own demons.

"Atticus…I know that's…hard," I whispered, my words barely above a whisper. "But you can't blame yourself—"

"And I don't," he said firmly, yet his voice was strained. He lowered his gaze before meeting my eyes again. "But I can't have you getting hurt because of him. He went against you, and I will always choose you over *him*." Atticus hesitated before finally speaking again. "I cannot have him hurt you."

I swallowed hard, my blood racing wildly. "I can take care of myself," I replied, my voice barely a whisper as I tried to suppress the emotions bubbling inside.

His forehead gently touched mine as he continued, "I know that, but it is my duty to protect you. I will always choose you over him. Over everyone."

My chest tightened at his words, and my hands trembled uncontrollably. His love for me was unmistakable. At that moment, there was nothing more that I wanted than to feel his lips on mine and to take away his pain. He looked deep into my eyes and sighed. "I worry about you with every breath I take, and it will always be my job to end any threat against you."

"I think I've proven how capable I am. It doesn't have to be you to kill him," I replied as my lungs swelled with pride. "We're in this together."

"I know. I might need to leave for a little while, Christine—"

"No. You can't."

"I need to kill my father. I need to do it while I know you're safe."

I shook my head. "Absolutely not, Atticus. We stay together."

"As soon as I can, I'll return." His tone was full of steel determination and regret.

A spark of fear ignited in the pit of my stomach. I was about to speak when, suddenly, something soft brushed against my cheek. He was kissing me. I froze, my heart beating wildly as he lifted me off the ground and pressed me against him, his hands traveling down my back and his mouth slanting over mine. My eyes fluttered closed and it became impossible to think.

The water lapping at the shore calmed my racing mind, the warmth in my body radiating outward as thrill coursed through my veins. His tongue was steady, his touch just as firm as his embrace. He was distracting me with a kiss, and it was working.

I pulled back, glancing toward the water. "We have to talk about this."

"No," he said, his voice a low growl. "We don't."

I opened my mouth, but the words were stuck in my throat. My eyes pleaded with him, but he didn't give me the chance to object.

He kissed me again, his fingers gripping my hair, his mouth moving gently against mine. His tongue brushed against my lip, and I opened my mouth to permit him entrance.

"Please let me do this, Atticus," I gasped, my chest heaving. "Let me prove that I can help you."

He shook his head and pulled me close, wrapping his arms around me. "You are helping me," he whispered. "It's my job to take care of you."

I swallowed hard and raised my hands to his chest, grasping the soft fabric of his shirt. "You don't have to do this alone," I said. "Please don't shut me out, remember?"

He pulled away, but I held him close, stepping back until we were both on the same footing. His eyes glistened with emotion, and his lips were swollen from our kiss. "You know I don't want to, but I need to," he replied. "I need to do this alone." His hands found my waist and he pulled me close again, lowering his head until his lips were a mere inch from mine.

"Why does this feel like goodbye?" I croaked.

"It's not goodbye," he whispered. "You'll see me again soon."

"Not soon enough," I whispered, leaning forward.

"I love you, Christine," he said.

I was too mad at him to say it back. His mouth covered mine in another kiss. It was so soft, so gentle, and I clung to him as the kiss deepened and his arms wrapped around my waist.

I pressed my palms against his chest, but he held me against him, kissing me until all the fear inside me melted away, replaced with a deep longing that pulsed through my body. My blood rushed in my ears, and I couldn't bring myself to think of anything but him.

We eased onto the ground, the sand digging into my back as he tore at my clothes. The urgency in his kiss matched the wild beating of my heart.

His hands tangled in my hair as he pushed me down into the sand and buried his lips in my neck, kissing me with a frenzied passion that made my head swim.

He inched lower, his tongue a hot trail against my skin, and my body hummed in anticipation as he slid a hand behind my back. I bit my lip as his teeth grazed the sensitive area where my neck joined my shoulder.

I growled, pulling his shirt off his body and exploring him hungrily with my hands. His low groan filled the air as he arched his back, his mouth quickly ravaging my neck. He licked and teased my skin, sending shivers coursing through me with every movement of his tongue. I gasped as he ran a cold finger down my arm, and I leaned into him, my skin desperate for his touch. Our fingers intertwined and he pressed our joined hands against his chest. I closed my eyes as his lips sought mine, our tongues tangling in a passionate dance.

He slipped a hand around my hip, pulling me closer to him so that I could feel every inch of our bodies pressed together. His mouth moved from my lips to my neck and then to my ear, where he whispered my name between desperate kisses. I wanted to be consumed by him, to be taken away by the fire of our love. I cried out as he trailed kisses down my throat, his hands roaming all over me as we melted together.

"Atticus, you're not leaving us here."

"Be quiet and let me make you feel good, Little Monster."

I shoved him hard. "You don't get to say goodbye to me, Atticus. You don't get to fuck me, then leave and *die*."

He growled slowly and stared at me with an unfathomable expression. His words cut through the oppressive air like a blade. "I'm not going to die, Christine." His grip tightened, his large body caging me in his arms. "But if something ever happens to me, I need you to promise me you'll run away with Leo and August."

I shook my head determinedly, my voice wavering. "No, Atticus. I'm never leaving you."

"If I die," he continued in a gruff voice, refusing to listen to me, "I need you to run. Promise me that."

Despair and agony threatened to overwhelm my senses. "No… Don't talk like that."

"Do you love me?" The intensity of his question nearly burned through my soul as tears rolled down my face. I nodded slowly, my heart brimming with adoration for him. His arms tightened around me, and he kissed my neck before speaking, his voice barely above a whisper. "Then promise me, Little Monster. Promise me you'll leave if it ever comes down to it."

I stood up. "I'm not promising you shit, Atticus. Because this is ridiculous."

He scrambled to stand up, and I pushed his chest hard and started storming off, but before I could get very far, he picked me up and tossed me back on the sand. "Promise me," he growled.

"No," I spat. I shoved Atticus in the chest again and

sneered, my fury barely contained. "You don't get to demand anything of me," I seethed.

He held me down, his strength overpowering my own. His face was eerily close to mine, his eyes smoldering with desire and rage. "Promise me," he growled again.

My eyes narrowed as I glared up at him, unwilling to back down. "Never," I spat.

In one swift movement, he positioned himself between my thighs, desire radiating from every pore of his body. A growl rumbled from his lips as his hands curled around my hips, pulling me tightly against him. "Say it."

His touch sent explosions of pleasure tearing through my veins, making it more and more difficult to push him away. I shook my head frantically and bit back a sob, my body vibrating beneath him. "No!" I cried out.

He silenced my protests by pressing an urgent kiss to my neck, sucking hard enough to leave a mark. His teeth grazed against my skin as he moved his lips around my throat and collarbone, sending ripples of pleasure through me. "Say it," he demanded again between fervent kisses. He took off his pants and tossed them to the side.

My eyes fluttered closed as I gave in to the pleasure,

seeking solace in the way he touched me. My hands ran through his hair as I yelled out in protest, wanting him to claim me the way he wanted to. "Please, Atticus… don't do this," I begged breathlessly as he settled between my thighs.

"Say it," he commanded again as his thumb ran circles around my swollen clit, massaging it gently into submission.

I shook my head fervently as a moan escaped my lips, my body betraying me with its desperate craving for him. "No!" I cried out again as his length filled me completely, pushing himself deeper into my core with every thrust of his hips.

He roughly grabbed a handful of my hair and bit down on my shoulder harshly before pulling away and growling in my ear, "Say it!"

His thrusts were relentless, his grip on me tightening as I screamed hoarsely, my head spinning and my eyes closing. My heart was thundering in my chest as I felt his lips press against my neck and heard him whisper my name.

"Atticus," I muttered.

"Tell me you'll run away," he gritted out.

"I'll run," I panted.

"Promise me."

"I promise I'll run away," I breathed heavily.

"You're mine," he snarled, his lips still hovering around the crook of my neck. "Mine to keep safe. Mine to defend."

"It's not your job to protect me, Atticus."

His movements were wild, his hips colliding with mine as I felt the sensation take over me, and my limbs shook uncontrollably. My grip on him tightened as I clawed at his back, the pain giving way to the pleasure that shot through me like electricity. He bit down on the tender skin of my neck, a guttural scream erupting from him. "It has always been my job to protect you," he growled. "You are so fucking captivating. So fucking perfect."

A moan of ecstasy escaped my mouth as I shuddered and my walls clenched around him. He moved with me, grunting as his own orgasm drove him wild. A sudden surge of pleasure and emotion coursed through me. My tears mixed with sweat from his forehead as my mouth found his.

He stayed inside me, our breathing gradually slowing down as we lay in the sand. I ran my fingers through his hair and felt the sand chill my skin. His soft lips caressed my neck as he murmured, "I love you." My body tensed at the same time as my heart filled, and I returned his sentiment without hesitation.

Anxiety filled my chest. Atticus's rules were still

hanging over us like a guillotine. He lay next to me in the sand, our eyes searching the clouds.

"Atticus?" I whispered.

"Yeah, Little Monster."

My voice quivered with fury as I spat out my words, "I lied." His eyes widened in shock, but before he could utter a response, my fist connected with the side of his temple. He groaned, eyes unfocused, and I felt a pang of regret when I saw his sticky cum still between my legs.

He was not going to leave me—not today. If I had to tie him up, that's what I would do. Every breath I took was jagged and strained as the raging fire burned within my veins. He hadn't trusted me, he had tried to abandon me, and worst of all, he had brought me here to say goodbye. All these emotions boiled within me, and all I wanted was to take my fingernails and claw at his face until it bled. My lips trembled as my tears threatened to fall, yet determination filled me—he deserved it for how he had wronged me.

I stood there, rage and sorrow clouding my eyes. "I'm going to keep you safe, Atticus," my voice threatened. "And make you regret trying to leave."

Chapter Twelve

LEO

Earlier this morning, I heard loud thumps on the back deck, and I rushed to the door to find Christine dragging Atticus's limp body inside.

My mother ran downstairs, her eyes filled with fear. She reached for her cup of coffee and took a sip, not taking her eyes off Atticus.

I was too baffled to answer at first. I felt a migraine coming on as I shook my head and pinched the bridge of my nose. All I knew was that Atticus had done something so serious that it had driven Christine to madness. She marched upstairs for a long hot shower and slammed the door shut behind her, leaving everyone else dazed and confused.

Atticus was now bound to the chair, his skin cut and bruised from Christine's relentless rope. His dark, disheveled hair was caked in wet sand, making him look like a creature of the night. His face had turned a nasty shade of purple, indicating that she had dealt him a heavy blow.

Now, I was left with Atticus and no fucking clue what to do with him.

My sister sat at the kitchen table, eyeing Atticus warily. "Did Christine really knock him out?"

My jaw tensed as I thought of my sister. She was such a fragile creature, her delicate frame almost too soft for this world. The only reminder of our mother's beauty were her tresses of red and her deep blue eyes.

I glanced at my mother. She seemed unsure of everything and, in her yellow dress, was a stark contrast to the criminal boss tied up.

"She really did," I said softly, as if I was almost afraid to break the silence that hung between us. "She said she'd let me know what happened later."

My mother nodded, a cautious smile playing on her lips. "I'm sure it's nothing to worry about."

Maybe she was right. After all, she had this habit of

brushing away the hardships of life. When my father left, she pretended like he would return even after a year had passed. But the truth was he never came back.

Atticus stirred from his slumber, his eyes gradually blinking as he took in our assembled family. He appeared about to burst with anger, his brow furrowing as he grimaced in pain.

"Would you like some tea? Just put a pot on," Mother said softly with a beaming smile, gesturing to the electric kettle while leaning forward.

Atticus glowered at her, his nostrils flaring. "Where is Christine?"

I stepped in before she could respond. "Upstairs. Showering. She looked really mad at you. What happened?"

He valiantly tried to break free from his bonds, his expression tightening as he spat out his words. "She's being intolerable," he uttered through gritted teeth.

My mother's tinkling laughter filled the room as she replied, "A woman is rarely unreasonable, Atticus. Men just don't know how to reason."

He seemed to calm slightly at this, a hint of understanding glimmering in his eyes as he regarded my sister. "This is Daphne, I presume?" Daphne coughed and nodded her head meekly, always so shy around strangers. "I'd shake your hand"—he gestured futilely with his arms bound behind him—"but…"

My family eyed us warily as I spoke, their eyes shifting between Atticus and me. I felt their unspoken questions in the air—what had I gotten myself into now?

Daphne was the first to take the opportunity to escape, scurrying out of the kitchen like a rat on fire. My mother kissed me on the forehead before shooting Atticus a wary look. "Behave," she warned before making her own exit onto the patio.

Atticus turned his gaze toward me, lips almost trembling as he spoke. "Are you going to untie me?" he asked, his voice barely above a whisper.

"Nope," I replied, leaning against the counter with a smirk. "Sucks to be controlled, doesn't it?"

A deep rumble of anger reverberated through his chest as he glared at me. "Somebody needs to control you," he grumbled. "You're too wild, Leo. You need a firm hand like Christine." He paused for a moment before continuing, smugness oozing from every word. "You thrive when someone else tells you what to do."

My jaw clenched and my tongue burned with the desire to protest his accusations when Augustus strutted into the kitchen, wearing only low-hanging boxers. "Did I just walk into some kinky fuckery? If so, can I watch?"

My frustration bubbled up, and I spun on my heel with a heavy sigh. "Did you see Christine?"

Augustus's brow furrowed. "She went into the shower, muttering something about killing Atticus over and over again. Now her ramblings make sense."

I gave a curt nod, my mouth a grim line. I glanced at Atticus struggling against his bindings, then back at Augustus. His gaze scanned Atticus from head to toe, studying the scrapes and bruises scattered across his body. "You got knocked the fuck out, man." He shook his head. "Lucky she didn't drown you in the sand."

Atticus's voice was hoarse and broken. "I was just trying to protect her. Protect all of you."

I suddenly realized what was going on.

My eyes narrowed. "You were planning to leave," I said slowly. "You thought since we were safe here, you'd get to be some kind of hero and kill off your father and Nathan." Augustus's face twisted in confusion, and before he could say something, I stepped in front of Atticus, blocking him from view. My whisper was full of exasperation as I spoke. "You can't do this alone."

Atticus's voice rumbled like thunder as he addressed us. "Like hell I can't. What's the use of risking all of your lives? This is my problem, *my* father to deal with. As long as he is alive, Christine is in danger."

I shook my head in disbelief; the thought of him

leaving felt like a betrayal. "We don't have to go back. We could go anywhere," I offered, hoping for a different outcome than the one that seemed inevitable.

"You're fucking crazy," Augustus blurted. His eyes were wide with anxiety, but his expression ultimately betrayed some sort of hope. "How can you even think about leaving us? I'm with Leo—let's pack up and go."

Atticus clenched his jaw and shut his eyes, trying his best to contain his tears. He shook his head. "With the little amount of money Hudson gave me, where would we even go? We need more than what I have."

I fixed my gaze on him. "I have money. I have a savings account that I've been putting aside just in case."

"And then what?"

Augustus spoke up, his voice soft yet stern. "Then we figure it the fuck out."

Atticus shook his head. "It's not enough."

"Are you scared?" I asked.

A hint of color stained Atticus's cheeks as he jutted out his chin in defiance. He adamantly shook his head, his voice trembling with rage and resignation. "No. I'm not scared."

I swallowed hard, my heart clenching in sadness. "Then what is it?"

"You don't get it! I bled for that empire. Killed, stole, and broke bones for the DuPont name. I grew his fortune. I made everyone in Aldrich fear the DuPonts."

The scars on his body were a testament to his loyalty to the DuPont empire. There was no denying the carnage he inflicted on behalf of the name, the lives he stole and the bones he broke.

My own heart ached with the emotion that contorted his face. "So it's not about Christine?" I choked out, tears threatening to fall.

He screamed in agony and fought against his restraints. "Of course it's about Christine! Everything I've ever fucking done has been for her. Taking over the DuPonts was supposed to give her security, protection, a damned luxurious life!" His eyes turned feral as he leaned closer to me, and I could almost feel his warmth despite the air between us.

"She doesn't need everything," I muttered. "She needs you."

He shook his head. "I'm not enough, Leo. Can't you see? It's not *enough*."

My heart sank at his words. Wasn't this what I had been feeling all this time? Our differences in wealth and position were now invisible. With all the bullshit removed, we were simply three men, each driven by our love for Christine. She held us in her grasp, and we would have given up anything for her.

Atticus sat, quiet and still. His entire being seemed to be enslaved by the heavy burden he was carrying. His DuPont lineage was his family legacy, but it was also his way of providing a life for Christine that he believed she deserved—even if it meant his own life. His eyes were filled with desperation and fear of losing her.

I spoke determinedly, refusing to be intimidated by him. "It's not about the money for her," I firmly declared.

He scoffed, his lips curled in a sneer, "You think I don't know that?" He slumped in the chair and closed his eyes, perhaps trying to escape the harsh reality of his words. "Christine has never been moved by material possessions, but the fact still rattles me. If I am not a DuPont, what can I give her? What could she possibly want from me?"

Augustus slumped into the creaky chair and ran his fingers through his locks, shaking his head in shame.

"Hell, I'm not even a king anymore," he muttered. "I'm just a bastard with nothing."

The weight of Augustus's words felt like a boulder on my chest. I sighed heavily through my nose, adding to the oppressive silence of the room.

"And I'm just a royal guard with not even two thousand dollars to his name," I whispered, pushing back the tears that were threatening to spill down my cheeks.

The air seemed to thicken around us with despair as we stared into the void of our own broken dreams.

Christine stormed into the kitchen like a whirlwind, her blonde hair wet from her shower. We all held our breaths as her eyes narrowed on Augustus. In a second, she grabbed the collar of his shirt and lifted him toward her like a rag doll, her grip strong and her body thrumming with rage.

"Do you think I care if you're a fucking king?!" she hissed, bringing her nose to his. He gulped thickly, and she snarled in response.

"No," he squeaked out.

"I do not," she said, pushing him back an inch before letting him go with a rough shove. Her silver gaze smoldered with intensity. "I've loved you for years. *You.* Not your fucking title, asshole." Her stare instantly shifted to Atticus. With each heavy step, she pounded the floor, her anger accelerating with every movement. Her heaving chest, red-hot and ready to burst, was enough for anyone to feel fear. But still, Atticus remained still as a statue.

Without breaking eye contact, she spat out her words with a venomous intensity. "Your money means nothing here. Your name has no power over me. I love you because you see my heart, my soul. You have no idea how much it hurts that you don't trust me enough to believe that."

The air in the room shifted, crackling with a new kind of energy. It was both menacing and intoxicating, and soon it seemed as though all the oxygen was sucked from the room.

Rage boiled within her as she spun around and advanced on me, her breathing labored and eyes aflame. Her voice trembled as she spoke, her passionate words cutting through the air.

"I love you." She paused, jerking her head of wet hair from side to side, droplets landing on her flushed cheeks. "I love you for coming for me at my darkest hour, for holding me close and mending my broken pieces."

She continued while glaring at all of us. "We're going to take down Lord Nathan and Theodore DuPont because they're a threat to our family—to me." Her voice grew stronger. "This kingdom deserves a monarch that gives a damn. And you know what else? We're going to do this together." Her gaze pierced me, challenging me. "I swear, if one of you tries to leave, I'll drag you back here kicking and screaming."

Her words were like a puncturing fist that had landed cleanly in my gut. It was rare to see her so vulnerable, so exposed. Though she was the one that looked like she was going to break, her strength and conviction to fight alongside us was perhaps the greatest weapon I had seen. It was like a piece of a fearsome warrior had finally been revealed.

An unfamiliar energy vibrated through the room, as if there was something beginning to stir. It was small, but it was there—a promise that this was only the beginning. My chest swelled with new purpose.

She stared at all of us for a moment. "Figure your shit out and find me when you're ready to work together," she spat. With that, she turned around and left the room. We stared at the floor, momentarily speechless.

Augustus trailed behind her like a lost puppy. "I'm going to talk to her."

I nodded and watched as he disappeared around the corner.

In the now quiet kitchen, Atticus and I stared at each other, our eyes communicating all the words we couldn't say. I didn't know what to make of this whole mess, and I was sickened at the thought of Christine hurting.

We had to make this work.

"If I untie you, will you leave?" I asked.

He looked at me. "If I leave, do you think she'll forgive me?"

"No."

He let out a grunt. "Then I guess I'm staying."

My fingers quivered as I unsheathed the pocket knife from my waistband. I crept toward him, my feet shuffling softly across the floorboards. I positioned the blade of the knife against the rope binding his wrists, its cold steel grazing his skin. A line of warmth rose up his chest as I pressed it further against him.

"Swear to me you won't leave," I said slowly, my breath wafting across his neck.

He stayed quiet. His eyes met mine, begging in silent desperation. But I held firm, the knife pushing further into his flesh.

"I promise," he finally rasped, his voice shaking with reluctance.

My heart fluttered and I relented, lifting the weapon away from his body. "Okay then."

I savagely sawed through the rope, freeing him from his restraints. His towering frame shadowed me, radiating with a power and strength I could only dream of having. My breath quickened as his smoldering eyes traipsed down my body, and he grinned mischievously.

"I hope you enjoyed having me at your mercy, Leo," he purred seductively. "It's the only time you will ever have power over me."

I licked my lips, trying my best to hide my trembling

nerves. "I have power over you every time Christine steps into the room. Don't forget that," I warned him defiantly, my voice wavering slightly. He flashed me another lascivious smile as I stepped back, still unable to break away from his gaze.

Chapter Thirteen

CHRISTINE

My eyelids felt heavy and my heart was still pounding in my chest. I spent the whole day in my room, afraid to move or think, terrified that if I did, I might just go insane. I was embarrassed. Ashamed. Hurt. I slept alone and woke the next morning still feeling exhausted. I'd asked the guys for space, and they reluctantly gave it to me. We were all on edge and I needed time to think.

I hated that my love for all three of them was being questioned, and I hated that it also felt like something I should be ashamed of. If Vivian knew that I was forcing her son to share me, she would probably faint. My mind was racing with the possibilities, my hands clenching together in my lap.

I took a deep breath and gathered up a few strands of courage, then went downstairs. Vivian was in the kitchen, humming something as she went about the morning routine, setting out plates on the table and fetching cups from the sideboard. The smell of freshly baked bread and breakfast casserole wafted up from the oven.

When she saw me standing in the doorway, her face lit up with excitement. "Ah, Christine! Good morning!" she exclaimed. "Come sit down."

I slid into a seat at the table across from her while she poured milk into two glasses and placed them in front of us. "Are you feeling better?" she asked.

I nodded. "I'm sorry about yesterday."

"Don't be silly," she said warmly, reaching across to squeeze my hand between hers. "Of all the crazy things that have happened the last few days, that's the least concerning."

I let out a choked laugh. "I suppose you're right."

"Well, I'm happy to see you." Vivian smiled and offered me a cup of tea. "It's been so long. Leo missed you dearly, and I was so happy when you returned. I hated having him banished to the damn countryside. Only saw him once or twice a year."

Seeing Vivian now made the guilt eat at me, festering in my body like an infection slowly poisoning me from the inside. "I'm—I'm sorry about that."

She shook her head. "It's not your fault."

But it was. He was sent away because of me. Leo was away from his mother and sister for three years because I was sent away. He was a casualty because he rescued me that night. "Now, why don't you tell me what's really bothering you?"

I looked at her contemplatively, chewing on my bottom lip nervously. Vivian and I had always gotten along. She was kinder and more motherly than Isabelle was and reminded me of my mother.

I swallowed hard. "I don't know where to begin," I admitted.

"How about you tell me about you and Leo?" She smiled. "You're together, I assume?"

I nearly choked on my drink. "We are," I said, clearing my throat. "I mean, we weren't, but—"

She waved her hand as if to say it was alright. "I understand." She leaned in over the table, eyes bright. "Leo can be very convincing." I could still hear the warmth of his voice in my ear.

"I suppose he can," I agreed.

"Well, whatever you're worried about, you can tell

me. I'm here for you." She patted my hand and gave me a soft smile.

"Thank you, Vivian." I leaned against her shoulder. "You have no idea how much that means to me."

"I think I do," she said wistfully.

I winced, thinking about how to say what I wanted to say. "I love Leo," I blurted out. "He's everything to me, and I know I've only been back a short amount of time, but I can't imagine living my life without him."

Vivian smiled warmly. "And I'm sure he feels the same way."

"But he's not the only one…" My stomach roiled with nerves and guilt. How could I tell this woman that I was dating her son and two other men?

She seemed to sense my apprehension, and her smile faded, her face growing solemn. "What is it?"

"I'm…I'm, I'm in love with all three of them," I blurted out, my words tripping over themselves.

"Pardon me?"

"I mean, I was. I guess I still am, but it's just so complicated."

She frowned lightly, raising an eyebrow in suspicion. "Are you sure this is love and not lust?"

"I'm sure," I said staunchly. "This has been a whirlwind and it's been difficult, but we've had to learn to trust each other—to open up and let our guards down.

It has taken a lot of time and patience, but somehow, we've made it work. Mostly. We've connected on a level I never thought possible." My hands started to tremble as I spoke of them, and the words tumbled out in a jumble. "They love me the way I am—the real me—and they accept me for all my flaws and weaknesses. They are so different from one another, but when it comes down to it, they have each other's backs, and nothing can rattle them. They make me smile and laugh and want to be better."

Vivian's eyes sparkled as she finally spoke. "I had my suspicions last night. Leo was like a shadow of his former self when you left, like he'd been possessed. When you came back, it was like he was my old Leo again. And I knew Augustus has always had feelings for you. Atticus is…protective. I was curious who you'd choose."

I cringed. "I'm so sorry. I'm sure this is uncomfortable to talk about. I'm in love with your son, and now I'm telling you that he has to share me."

"Don't be silly." She waved her hand, shooing away my concern. "That's the way it works."

"I love all three of them, just in different ways," I said, shrugging. "Leo is…he's strong and powerful, but at the same time, he's caring and protective. He knows just when to listen and when to intervene. He has a commanding presence that makes you feel safe and protected."

"And the others?" she asked with a smile.

I paused, collecting my thoughts.

The morning sun cascaded through the windows and filled the room with dancing light. "August is like an unpredictable thunderstorm," I declared. "He's fierce and aggressive and egotistical, but at the same time, tender and kind. He is loyal and endearingly sweet."

"And Atticus?"

"He's my peace," I said, nearly breathless. "He makes everything okay again. He's my anchor and I don't know what I would do without him. He's my haven. He comforts me and shows me that I'm capable of more than I ever thought I was. That I'm perfect just the way I am." My voice quivered slightly. There was a lump in my throat that wouldn't be swallowed back down. "He sees the real me, the good and the bad, and he loves me anyway." I let out a sigh. "I just worry about the logistics of it all."

"But, Christine, it's not so strange. I wouldn't worry yourself so much."

I blinked at her. "What do you mean?"

"If you're worried how I'll feel, don't," she sighed. "Leo is more than capable of making his own decisions.

I want my son to be happy. That's all any mother wants for their child."

I shifted in my seat. "But what if…what if I can't make him happy? What if I'm forcing him into an impossible situation? If I go back as queen, we'll never have a normal marriage. A normal life. What about children? What if he never gets the future he wants?"

"What if?" she echoed me. "What if you take the crown and it's a disaster? You will regret not taking the chance to be happy."

"But what if that chance is with three men?" I asked. "What if he truly loves me and can't stand the thought of me with another man? What if it's too much? What if I can't give him everything he needs?"

"Oh, sweetheart," Vivian sighed, her eyes softening. "That's life. That's being in a relationship. The only way to know is to try."

"If I try and fail…"

"Then you have a life worse than the one you had before. And if you're lucky, you'll learn from that."

I smiled. "That's an awful lot of pressure to put on a relationship."

"If you can't handle the pressure, then maybe you shouldn't be in the relationship in the first place."

I looked up at her, a million thoughts running through my mind. She was right. If I didn't try and the stakes were this high, I'd always wonder what would have happened. And if it was good, I'd never forgive myself for not being brave enough to see it through.

"I just don't know how to make it work."

"You just need to love each other and forgive each other when you make mistakes. You need to be loyal and committed, and you need to work together as a unit. You need to love one another so much that you're willing to change to make the relationship work. So much that you're willing to make that sacrifice. Yes, it's hard sometimes, but you have to make time for each other, and that means being with each other, no matter the consequences."

"The consequences, so far, have been death and war," I said, a sad smile on my face.

"That is the consequence of being a queen. Leo, Atticus, and Augustus need you to be the best that you can be. I hope you can rise to the challenge."

"I hope so, too," I said. "I'm terrified," I admitted, playing with the hem of my shirt.

"Of what?"

"Of disappointing all of them. Of royally screwing this up. Of losing the people I love."

"Love is a powerful thing, Christine. It can make fools of us all. It can make us do things we would never have imagined ourselves doing. It can make us believe in things that we otherwise wouldn't believe. But it can also make us stronger than we ever thought possible."

"I've known Leo long enough to know that he'll go to the ends of the world for me," I said.

"I hope you never have to test that."

I nodded. "I hope I don't, too."

"You're fortunate, you know."

"I am?"

"To have so many men willing to challenge the world for you. I've never seen Leo so brave and so determined before," she said.

I sighed. "And I don't really know what to do about that."

"You love him," she said. "And that's all you need to know. I can tell you're both in love, and if you love him, don't throw that away. Don't deny him the chance at happiness with you."

I smiled, but it was a sad smile. "That's easier said than done."

"It's never easy," she said. "But it's always worth it."

"How do you know?" I asked. "How can you be so sure?"

"Because I've been there. Because I've seen what love can do. And I've seen what it can't. I've seen what it can turn a man into and what it can take away."

I cleared my throat. "Leo told me about his father."

A shadow of pain crossed her expression. "Yes, I'm sure he did. There's still a lot of hurt from that, and I wish I could forget it. But he was a good man."

I nodded, keeping my mouth shut.

"It's been a long time," she said, and it seemed like she was talking to herself more than to me. "I've thought about it enough to last a lifetime. He left us alone for a younger, prettier thing. It made Leo scared to open his heart up.

"I don't hate him for leaving me," she continued. "But I hate him for what he did to my son. I hate him for turning Leo into someone afraid of his own heart. I hate him for making him believe love is a poison and that it's best to keep your distance from it. But most of all, I hate him for making Leo so terribly lonely."

I reached out and covered her hand with my own. "I promise not to make him feel lonely," I whispered.

"There you are," Leo said while walking into the kitchen. "What are you two ladies conspiring over?"

"Nothing," I said with a smile, standing up. I walked over to him and wrapped my arms around his waist. He seemed stiff at first, nervous for his mother to see us like this and worried about the questions she likely had. But slowly, he put his arms around me and pulled me close. He nuzzled his face against my neck and kissed gently.

"Hi, I missed you," I whispered.

"I missed you, too," he said.

"You know," Vivian said, "I don't care."

Leo's eyes widened in surprise. "You don't?"

"No," she said. "I don't. I've been sitting here, watching you two, and I can see how much Christine adores you. I think I know you fairly well," she said, looking at Leo. "And you'll figure this out, my darling boy. Just next time, don't attack Atticus in the sand, Christine. You got these kitchen floors so dirty."

I let out a laugh as Leo stared at his mother. "She knows?" he asked me, his voice a whisper.

I nodded. "I told her my intentions with you, Leo Winthrop," I goaded.

"Oh, did you?" he asked and smirked. "And what were those intentions?"

"That I intend to be with you," I said, looking right into his eyes. "And that I intend to be good to you, no matter what."

He raised one eyebrow, looking amused. "]And she gave her blessing?"

"More or less."

Leo shook his head. "More or less."

Chapter Fourteen

CHRISTINE

"Are you still mad at me, love?" August said while slipping into my bedroom. I was lying in bed, thumbing through a book Daphne lent me.

I looked up at him and then looked down at the pages once more.

I was mad. Furious, actually. I understood that his insecurities ran deep, and I never wanted to be a source of pain for him. But hearing all of them talk about me made my skin crawl.

Talking to Vivian helped, but I was still navigating the pain of it.

I didn't love August because he was a king. He was

so much more. I loved him because he looked at me like I was the only person in the world. I loved him because his words made me feel like I mattered. I loved him because he was a goofy teenager who couldn't keep his hands off me. I loved *August*.

A feverish heat coursed through my veins as I watched him, his tawny eyes as warm as the sun, standing there. I could feel my heart choking out my words, and I burned with the desire to be close to him.

"I have no idea," I uttered in a faint whisper. "It seems like we don't have a place or even an idea of what to do next, and it's scaring me."

He stepped even closer, his intense gaze never wavering from mine. He slowly sat on the edge of the bed and asked me in a hushed voice, "If you could make a home anywhere, where would it be?"

With a racing heart, I pushed my book aside and stood up to meet him. Our skin seemed to melt into one as our bodies were entwined, sending an electric current through me. His lips, soft and gentle, seemed to erase all the turmoil that had taken root in my heart. We were completely absorbed in each other—an endless exchange of passion that surrounded us in a realm of bliss.

When we finally parted, he planted a kiss on my forehead as if it was not enough for him either. That gave me the courage to tell him, "I would go with you wherever you wanted me to—even if it was on the moon—not caring about our whereabouts as long as Atticus and Leo were with us and we were together."

He caressed my neck with his rough, calloused hands. I quivered in response. His warm breath tickled my face as his forehead met mine. I was vulnerable, bare and exposed. It felt like I was begging him to look into my soul and recognize the hidden depths of my love for him.

He took a deep breath. "I never wanted the throne. I've been spoiled and pampered since I was born," he said, then he paused. "But I wish to protect you and to put you on that throne because you have a pure heart and you care for our people."

I shuddered as realization struck me. "The people deserve a murderer?" I asked, my voice barely audible.

He pressed his lips together in a knowing grin. "No," he murmured, his breath tickling my skin. "The people deserve someone strong enough to take charge. Someone patient enough to put up with my crap, ruthless enough to survive anything, and loving enough to capture the hearts of three men."

My heart raced as I studied him, wide-eyed and speechless. He thought I was someone capable of ruling a kingdom? I wanted to believe his words, but it was never something I planned for myself. Lord Nathan and Theodore DuPont had forced me into the role—marrying August meant he would assume the title of king, something he was born to do.

A shudder went through me as our gazes locked and held for a few moments too long. A pool of desire formed deep within me, and I wanted nothing more than for him to take me in his arms and make me forget the world beyond these four walls.

How was I supposed to lead?

I searched his gaze, savoring the way the intensity poured from his eyes and wrapped around my body. How was I supposed to lead?

"You don't have to be ruthless," he added quickly, his deep baritone sending ripples of pleasure up my spine. "But you must have the courage and strength to stand up for what is right. That's what a good ruler does. And it's why I was never cut out for the job. I'm too selfish, love."

I bit my lip and looked up at him, basking in his warmth like a sunflower in the summertime. "You're not as selfish as you think," I whispered, my voice barely audible.

He leaned in and kissed my jawline, sending a shiver down my spine with each brush of his lips. His intoxicating scent filled me, competing with the musky smell of the room. "You make me a better man," he breathed against my cheek, sending goose bumps along my skin as he pulled away.

I nodded, my throat tight with emotion. His gaze seemed so sure that it gave me the confidence to believe in myself—and him. But then, reality hit me like a ton of bricks—was it really possible for someone like me to rule?

"When they see you on that throne," he said softly, his fingers tracing circles on my arm and sending sparks through my veins with every touch, "they will know without question that they are looking at a powerful leader who has been through hell and back—and won."

I wanted what he promised—to make a better life for us—but first I had to acquire the skills necessary to lead. With determination, I vowed that no matter what awaited us, whether danger or love, I would fight until we reached our goal together as one unit: Atticus, Leo, August, and myself.

I nibbled my bottom lip, tasting the salt of my tears. "We can't go back to the castle, August. Lord Nathan has built an army. I know I talked a big game in the kitchen, but I was worked up."

I felt drawn to him like a magnet. He seemed to sense it too, because he stepped closer to me. "I actually have an idea on how to handle that," he said softly as his intense gaze locked on mine.

"How to handle what?" Leo said, disrupting the moment as he suddenly appeared in my bedroom.

"August said he had an idea on how to handle Lord Nathan," I answered, forcing myself away from August's captivating presence and wiping the tears from my eyes.

"And here I was hoping we'd just hide here forever," Leo replied. His low voice was a contrast from August's but still sent a shiver up my spine. "I'll get Atticus." My heart sank at the thought of losing the serenity of being alone with August so soon.

We meandered our way to the living room, where Daphne and Vivian were already waiting for us. Atticus stood there, his arms crossed over his chest, and he asked with a matter-of-factness, "So, what's your grand plan, August?"

August shifted uncomfortably in his seat, tugging at his collar. He started to say something just as I interjected with a hushed voice, "August. Tell us."

He slowly exhaled and Leo brushed against my hand—a subtle gesture of support. Then August began, "Redview. It all started there. Three years ago, a rebellion broke out, right? Lord Geralt helped my father contain it. The archives said over three hundred people were killed."

"Eva mentioned that when we were tracking down Lord Nathan," Atticus reminded us.

I furrowed my brow in confusion. "Who is Eva?"

August rolled his gaze to mine with a deep intensity. "The most annoying teenager I've ever met in my life."

I uttered a mumbled, "Oh."

"So, what should be done about it?" Leo asked, his frown deepening.

August grimly replied as his fists clenched, "They've tried to pin the blame on another lord, but Lord Nathan has been cultivating his army on deceit. People living in Aldrich are suffering from oppressive taxes and the effects of their crumbling infrastructure. Lord Nathan saw an opportunity to use that to his advantage. Little do they know, his family is not only responsible for the massacre that occurred in Redview, they benefited from those circumstances, and they continue to reap the rewards financially. Unaware citizens have been taken in by Lord Nathan's machinations, and he's made himself out to be a savior."

Atticus scowled, adding, "But if they had the slightest clue that it's his own family that caused all this bloodshed…" His voice trailed off as the mood in the room filled with a sense of rage mixed with anxiousness.

"And if we made promises for real change…" I gritted out, my fingernails digging into my palms.

"Then we could turn Lord Nathan's army against him and have more of a chance to take him out."

Atticus steeled himself. "He still has DuPont men."

August narrowed his eyes. "We both know they're more loyal to you. If Lord Nathan loses his army, they'll still be outnumbered. Once they realize Theodore DuPont has lost his upper hand, they'll switch sides. DuPonts don't have the numbers."

I scoffed in disbelief. "What makes you so sure?"

Atticus exhaled heavily. "Criminals are only loyal to survival. Besides, my father let me out of that cell because he *knows* some of our contacts are still loyal to me. People will go where the money flows." He refused to make eye contact with me, body tense in the chair. We still hadn't made up from our fight. "It's a good plan, August."

August was paralyzed, his gaze wide with disbelief. "Really? I had a good plan?"

Atticus's eyes softened as he tried to keep a light mood, but the fear and powerlessness within him was apparent. "It's a good plan. But how exactly do you plan to spread the news? We're hiding, remember?"

"Redview," I murmured, feeling my throat tighten with anxiety. "We go to Redview."

The room was dense with trepidation, and I glanced around, unsure if they had heard what I said.

Atticus's forehead creased in worry. "Are you aware of the risk we'd be taking if we go there? We are not exactly welcome anywhere now that we have a bounty on our heads."

August's voice rang steady and confident. "Most of Nathan's soldiers are at the castle now. We can meet with the wives; they'll help us."

I nodded in agreement, my voice growing stronger. "We can't keep running forever; the DuPonts will come for us no matter where we go. We need to stand up and fight against Nathan's army. We have each other's backs; none of us will have to do this alone."

Atticus held my gaze, and his voice was unswerving when he spoke back to me. "That's right. No one will be left behind to face danger alone."

August shot me an apprehensive glance before I shifted my focus to Leo's mother and sister. I opened my mouth, my words caught in my throat for a brief second. "You... Stay here," I said finally, my voice wavering. "It's not safe for you to accompany us."

Daphne rose from her chair, but Vivian stepped in

before she could respond. "Yes," she affirmed. "Don't worry about us."

Atticus nodded, his lips twitching into a tight smile. "I'll call Hudson and get him to stay here as well. He'll keep watch over the two of you," he said with a gruff voice.

I could feel Leo tense beside me, his body rigid in surprise. After a beat, he croaked out a soft thank-you to Atticus, who merely shrugged and replied with a murmured, "We're all family now."

Vivian's face lit up at the sentiment, her eyes glowing with admiration as she looked up at him. With a satisfied nod, she clapped her hands together and declared that she would go pack some meals for us; the trip was going to be long and arduous. She grabbed Daphne's wrist and pulled her along as she headed for the door. My heart was beating rapidly as I watched them leave, my mind reeling with worry.

I inhaled the heavy air of anticipation that surrounded us.

I stole a glance at the three brave men I loved. We needed to clear the air if we were going to survive this. "Okay, gentlemen," I said. "We each have to hold ourselves accountable not to do anything heroic."

The intensity of Atticus's gaze told me he was brimming with disagreement, but he kept his mouth shut.

With that kind of self-control, I could feel the sexual tension sparking between us.

"And you," Leo added, pointing at me. "No heroic bullshit either, Christine."

I bit my lip and glanced at Atticus. His clenched jaw let on how much he was struggling to contain himself.

Leo squeezed my hand.

My throat felt suddenly dry and my pulse quickened as I looked into Atticus's eyes. His face might have been hard and uninviting, but beneath his stern facade, I could make out his loving expression and admiration—the same emotion he'd had since the day we first laid eyes on each other. Did he feel it too? "Are we…good?" I asked hesitantly.

Atticus swallowed hard, and I could see he was fighting something inside himself—a fierce battle of emotions that he didn't want me to see. Finally, his lips set into a thin line and he nodded. "I'm fine."

My gaze skewered Atticus, my lips a thin line, too. "That's a pretty uninspired speech, Atticus. If you have something to say, now's the time."

Atticus stiffened, his jaw clenching. His anger was palpable in the room, like an electric current that ran through us all. His voice was tight when he said, "What I said in the kitchen…"

August laughed. "When you were tied up? I really wish I'd taken a picture."

Undeterred, Atticus continued. "My words still stand, but I want to make something crystal clear."

I crossed my arms over my chest and scowled. "Well then, out with it."

He cleared his throat, his eyes burning into mine as he said, "I'm sorry. Every goal I ever set—every plan I ever made—all of it was with you in mind. I devoted my entire life to protecting and providing for you. You'd love me no matter what, but if I can't even give you the world, then how can I respect myself? How am I supposed to win if giving up is all that's left?"

"You can't keep shouldering this alone," I argued as I watched him. He seemed so entrenched in his own thoughts that he didn't even notice me getting up from the chair and making my way to him. I straddled him, pressing my body close to his. "I love you, Atticus. Not only for who you are, but for who you want to be. Not for your last name. Not for your empire. Not for your goals, but just for *you*."

Atticus froze, not sure how to react, but I felt his arms wrap around me as if they acted of their own voli- tion. His face was so close that I could feel his breath. His eyes were searching mine, and his grip on my body tightened, as if he were trying to commit my curves to memory.

After a moment of intense longing, I leaned in and kissed his temple and said the words that had been gnawing at me. "Please don't do this to yourself again. Please stop trying to do everything on your own. You tried when you locked me up. It doesn't work with me."

He let out a heavy breath into the crook of my neck before he spoke, and when he did, his voice was filled with promise, reassuring me of better days ahead. "I won't," he breathed. "I promise you."

My heart fluttered at his words, warming me from the inside out. I pulled away from him slightly and looked into his eyes while I wrapped my arms around his neck and said the words that I had been too afraid to say out loud until now: "I forgive you."

"I love you," he replied as if there was no other answer he could give me.

My lips widened into a smile so big it almost hurt my face to contain it all. "And I love you," I said back and sealed it with a kiss.

Chapter Fifteen

CHRISTINE

August's voice quivered, a deep longing reverberating with each syllable as he spoke. "The last time I was here, I thought you were dead, love." He stared longingly out the window, his gaze unfocused and blank.

We had spent all day driving to Redview, filled with anticipation and apprehension of what was to come. Too exhausted to speak, we each grappled with our own demons as we approached the edge of the kingdom.

The hotel we chose to stay at was run down and sullen. The windows were a dreary gray, and the curtains hung soiled with cobwebs. The furniture was caked in dirt and years of neglect, and the bedding was worn and stiff. The lampshade had been torn off from one corner, leaving the lightbulb exposed and flickering softly in the night air.

I drew a deep breath, daring to speak up despite the somber mood. "We never really talked about that." August spun around to face me, and I saw a spark of some emotion behind his eyes, even in the dark.

Atticus was seated on the edge of the bed, meticulously cleaning his gun while Leo stood silently against the doorframe. I could feel tension in the air as I waited for August to respond.

Finally, he spoke. His voice cracked with emotion, and it sounded like he was trying to contain an unbearable pain. "It was terrible," he said almost inaudibly. "I never want to exist in a world where you're dead… never. Being here…reminds me of that."

Leo cleared his throat. "You ready, Atticus?"

We'd decided that the two of them would secretly scout the town for someone to talk to—someone with influence. I stood out too much, and my picture was plastered on every screen across the kingdom.

Missing Queen, million dollar reward…

Atticus stood up, his gun now clean and ready for action. "Yes," he replied. He glanced at Leo in understanding and nodded before turning to August with a look of compassion.

"We'll be back soon," he said quietly, placing a hand on August's shoulder.

Leo jumped out of the room, eager to get started on whatever mission they had been assigned, while Atticus lingered behind for a moment longer. He looked into August's eyes and shook his head slowly, a gesture of sympathy and understanding that was not lost on him.

August's jaw clenched as he listened to the men's words, and then he gave a curt nod of agreement. As their footsteps faded away and the door clicked shut, he stood motionless, his body quaking in an effort to contain the turmoil of emotions that had been raging within him since our arrival. I watched as beads of sweat formed on his forehead and his breathing became labored, betraying all of the inner conflict that was spilling out from deep within.

A single tear trickled down his cheek. He lifted his tear-streaked gaze toward the window one last time before turning around and slowly walking toward me.

He took my hands in his with a desperate strength and pulled me tight against his chest. He clung to me like he was a shipwrecked man, frantically grasping onto a broken piece of wood. His face was buried in my hair, and I could feel his hot tears falling onto me.

I could tell that he had a long road of healing

ahead, but at least now I knew he was ready to start that journey.

"Are you okay?" I heard him ask, his voice thick with emotion. "Are you nervous?"

I shook my head, trying to sound as confident as I could. "No, I'm good," I said softly, a slight quiver in my voice. "This should be easy, right?"

His grip on me loosened, and I felt his shoulders droop in resignation. "I'm scared," he choked out, his voice barely above a whisper, tears now streaming down his face. "I don't want to lose you," he sobbed, his voice breaking with anguish. "I can't. I can't lose you again."

Tears cascaded down my face, mirroring August's agony. I embraced him tightly in my arms, my head resting on his chest.

"You won't," I murmured comfortingly into his ear. "I'm never leaving you August, never."

I drank in his heartbreaking gaze as he scanned my face for hope. We stood there in an exquisite embrace, our souls aching for a blissful union that would never be but yearned to exist.

My hands tenderly pushed him onto the bed while I straddled him. I looked deeply into his eyes before pausing to kiss him on the lips.

"I'm not going anywhere," I whispered with conviction as my lips caressed his forehead.

"Love," he uttered despondently as I nestled myself in his embrace. His voice of despair was so strong that it brought out the worst in me—the ache of a broken heart and an unfulfilled wish for a beautiful love story.

He kissed me with such desperation, like he was trying to burn the memory of me into his soul. His touch became more intense as his hands roamed my body hungrily. He yanked off my shirt and I gasped as he flipped us over and slammed me against the mattress. His mouth moved to my neck, sending shivers down my spine as he bit and sucked. His hands moved progressively lower, gripping my hips and pulling me against him. His heart raced, as the intensity of the moment took over. He kept grabbing me harder, as his lips moved down my body, every brush of his lips sending a shiver down my spine. His hands explored my body, pushing and pulling at the same time. He tasted every inch of my body, and I felt his emotions coming through each touch—desperation, yearning, hunger— until I could feel it radiating through us both.

My fingers tangled in his thick hair as he crashed his lips onto mine, my body shuddering at the warmth of his breath. His weight smothered me as he intensified his kisses, and I could feel the desperation in him, his mouth aching for me.

"I dug through so much wreckage," he murmured,

propping himself up to look in my eyes. "Clawed through stone and wood. And I wanted to just—to give up. To sleep and forget the pain. To find someone to blame and murder them." I ran my knuckles down his cheek, trying to soothe him. "I never understood how someone could kill without remorse. Especially my father… But not until after you were gone from me." His eyes welled up with tears, and he blinked hard, struggling to keep himself composed. "I wanted—God, I wanted to fucking kill them all."

He pressed his face hard against my skin, his lips almost biting my neck. His tears were icy against my nerve endings, sending shivers throughout my body. I tried to keep myself together, but the overwhelming emotion in the air broke me, and tears spilled down my cheeks.

"It was so damn scary how ruined I was. How absolutely mad. I'd never been so…" His broken words were muffled into my skin, his hot breath engulfing me like a blanket of warmth.

I clutched his shoulders firmly, trying desperately to give him some comfort. My heart ached for him and I wanted so badly to make the pain go away, but there was nothing I could do. This was his breaking point, and anything I did would be futile.

"I felt so powerless," he murmured softly, his voice

trembling with the hurt in his soul. He pulled away from me, his eyes meeting mine with desperation and need. "But you know what, love?"

"What?" I whispered through my teary voice.

"This experience has forced me to mature. I need to end this charade of entitlement and take my rightful place by your side, Christine. For too long, I have been the epitome of selfishness and neglect toward you, and I'm so sorry." His lips smashed hard into mine, claiming my mouth with an intimacy both foreign and familiar. "You've changed me, love. I didn't know I could feel this way. I want this, but I know it will be difficult and I will make mistakes, probably more than you can imagine." He softly brushed the loose strands of hair away from my face, allowing his fingertips to linger longer than necessary against my skin as he waited for my acceptance or denial.

Still looking deeply into his eyes, which were heavy with a mixture of despair, pain and a burning desire for something more, I spoke in a voice barely audible. "I know you, August…better than you know yourself. I believe in you and all the amazing things you can accomplish if only you try."

He ran his fingers along my cheekbone as I gasped with anticipation. His lips trailed across my own, sending a flood of heat throughout my body and making me quiver.

"I love you, Christine," he murmured against my skin.

I didn't respond, but instead grabbed the back of his neck and pulled him close, inhaling his scent. His lips were hot and demanding, pressing into mine with a kind of fervent passion that set my heart on fire. I wrapped my arms around him tightly and felt his body shudder with pleasure as our tongues intertwined in a wild frenzy.

He pulled back slightly as he said it again, "I love you."

Without hesitation, I kissed him again and tried, through my touch, to express the deep emotions I was feeling. I clung to him fiercely and he responded in kind, his fingers teasing me with an insatiable hunger that couldn't be contained. His lips tasted like honey, and his touch ignited me, threatening to rip me apart with pleasure.

"I love you too," I whispered between kisses, completely overcome by the intensity of our embrace.

We slammed into each other, and we kissed with increasing fervor, our tongues feverishly exploring each other's mouths. August pulled away and grabbed my neck as his mouth moved downward. His calloused fingers brushed against my skin, and I could feel them shaking with need. I quickly tried to undress him, both of us frantically trying to get his clothes off faster.

I heard a low rumble of laughter as I struggled to remove the belt around his waist. His hands tried to stop me, but I wanted to have him naked, I wanted to feel the heat of his body against mine again. There was a silent understanding between us that needed no words as we removed each other's garments.

August brought me closer, and our eyes met. I was captivated by the intensity of emotion in his gaze, and I could not look away. Each touch became more passionate and urgent than the last, until he pulled me hard against him. When his lips were at my ear, his breathing was labored, but he whispered something that made me shudder.

"Christine, I love how your pulse races. How your skin feels warm beneath my touch. I love the little ways you gasp when I kiss you. Every sigh is a symphony. Every moan makes me want to sink my teeth into your bottom lip. I love the way you live, beautiful. So vibrant. So *mine*."

He was perfect, wild and untamed.

"Love, let's feel alive for a little while. Take what pleasure life has to offer us," I murmured, feeling an irresistible desire course through me. He roughly tilted my head back and captured my lips with his, our tongues colliding as his fingers curled tightly around my neck. Passionately and yet tenderly, I felt his hold on me, and the sigh that escaped my lips was driven by passion.

As I melted into him, the heat between us intensified, and I felt my body ache for him as I reveled in this moment of pleasure. August's eyes filled with hunger and adoration as he watched me, awaiting my consent. The craving that consumed me took command, and I reached out to pull him closer, biting my lip as I beheld him hovering above me.

He tenderly kissed my neck and shoulders before his lips moved sensuously to my breasts. He lingered there, brushing feather-like kisses against my skin as I ran my fingers through his hair. When he at me again, I could sense his uncertainty and apprehension.

"Fuck me, August," I urged in a whisper, feeling a wildness surge through me. "Make me feel everything."

He growled in pleasure and anguish, his contorted face a mask of unbearable torment. Before I could do anything, before I could convey my emotions through words, he was inside me. He moved urgently, impatiently and clumsily, each thrust more frenzied than the one before. I could sense his battle as he fought to restrain himself, his eyes begging me to understand his struggle to make love to me the way I deserved.

The sharp pricks of pain from his savage actions made me flinch, but I embraced it. The burning heat between us was all I could feel. All I could taste was him, my vision filled with the naked desire in his eyes.

He groaned raggedly, his breath coming in deep, shuddering gulps of pleasure and pain. I clawed at his back as he pounded me relentlessly, our bodies blurring together in a desperate dance.

"Oh, God," he cried out, his voice rippling through me. His lips found my throat and neck as he drove into me with all the intensity of a wild storm. I felt like I was on fire, my whole body trembling with aching desire. His thrusts were hard, rough, and so deep I could barely tell where one of us ended and the other began.

I felt him sink deeper inside me, as the sound of our bodies slapping together in the quiet room filled my ears. I had never been this hungry for someone before, this hungry for *August*. It was a primal need that went beyond sex, beyond the physical desire for human contact. It was a need for intimacy, for love. It was a need for August.

He stood up and reached for my hands, pulling me up to him. I wrapped my arms around his neck, my thighs around his waist, and held on as he thrust into me again and again. I watched as his eyes glazed over with lust. "I love you, Christine. Can you feel it? Can you fucking feel me?" he grunted.

"I feel you, August," I said. "I love you."

After pounding into me for what felt like an eternity, he laid me back down on the mattress. My body tensed and the world around me vanished. I was in my own little universe, a place of pleasure and sensation. I looked up at August, mesmerized by the way he looked at me. The way he dragged his hungry eyes over my skin made me feel invincible, as if nothing could take me away from him. Nothing could take us away from each other.

August's lips pressed into mine, desperate and insatiable. The hard, rough sex made me pant for breath, yet I wanted more. I took his hand and clasped it on my neck, taking in his warmth as he drove deeper into me. His tongue explored my mouth as if it were a secret chamber, and with each thrust, I could feel him struggling to contain himself.

"Don't hold back," I whispered into his lips, my body awash with pleasure.

He looked into my eyes with a sad, patient smile on his lips. Leaning closer, our lips connected and his tongue rolled over mine as he fucked me harder. Then he broke the kiss to whisper, "I want to give you every-thing I am, everything I can be."

I closed my eyes and let out a shuddering breath as our lips connected once more. His movements were becoming more insistent as his grip tightened, and I could feel him losing all control. His sweat-drenched body became frantic, his hips thrusting with an animal-istic intensity.

"I know," I whispered, my words muffled against his mouth. I ran my hands down his back and felt his slick skin, the sweat between his shoulder blades. Finally, I kissed him again, tasting him as he pounded into me, and I felt myself on the edge of ecstasy. "I know you do," I uttered.

August and I slammed into one another with a ferocity we both had been eagerly craving. His hands were like iron, pulling me against him as we devoured one another in an uncontrollable, lustful rage. Our bodies moved in a frenzy, and I felt his muscles tense as he reached the peak of pleasure. His chest heaved and my own body shook as our climax surged together.

I gasped, feeling completely and utterly undone from our frantic session. He kissed me again and nuzzled my neck, whispering the words I knew he truly meant, "You are amazing, Christine." My tears mingled with sweat as I blushed and bit my lip, remembering a time when these words were said daily and with such adoration.

August pulled me tight, his heart pounding against mine, our breaths heavy as our lips touched in a slow, tender kiss. He laid his forehead on mine, his eyes still filled with fire and longing. He slowly pulled out of me and ran his hand over my naked flesh.

"Christine, I want you to know that I…" August's voice trailed off and he gazed at me, his eyes soft, loving, and full of determination. I felt tears prickle in my eyes, and I reached up for a quick, tender kiss against his lips. He pulled me close and I pulled the blanket around, snuggling into his chest. "I will be a good man—for you. Always for you, love."

He kissed the top of my head, and I sensed the shame in his voice. He thought he was nothing without me. I knew he was wrong, but I didn't have the heart to tell him. I had to be strong for August and let him know that our family, our home, was worth fighting for.

August held me close, his head buried in my hair. I moved my hand over his skin, feeling the light, standing hair on his arm. I pressed a kiss over the pulse beating in his neck and closed my eyes. I could picture my life with him, the way it was before our lives changed forever. I wanted it back—the innocence. But at the same time, I wanted it to be *better* than before. I listened to his breathing, the soft beating of a strong and healthy heart.

"I love you, Christine," he murmured against my skin. I held him as close as I could and pictured our life together.

"I love you, too."

Chapter Sixteen

LEO

"Let's hurry up," I barked, my anxiety gnawing at me. I stole a glance at Atticus and rolled my eyes when I saw his smug grin. "Eager to get back to our queen?"

I deftly dodged a passerby, jogging to keep pace with Atticus as he made his way down a shadowy alley. In truth, I was well aware of Augustus and Christine's plans for the evening. Though I had accepted our peculiar arrangement, that didn't make it any easier to stomach the thought of Christine being taken by him in that hotel—hard, with passion, and relentlessly.

"Let's just finish this," I snarled.

Atticus paused and turned to face me. "You have improved a lot since you joined us. I feared that I would have to strip Christine of you completely, but your ability to adjust has been surprisingly impressive."

I openly scoffed. "I can only adjust because I have no other choice."

A tinge of tenderness illuminated his features for a second. "Because the alternative…"

My gaze dropped to the pavement before locking back on him. "Losing her isn't an option—so I'm willing to take whatever piece of her that I can get."

"Good," Atticus hissed as he stiffened his back. He glanced toward the door, then settled his gaze upon me. "My sources have informed me that one of the rebellion leaders is from this very district. We must find his mother. She is our best chance to——"

A sharp, snarky voice cut him off. "Hello, boys."

We both whipped around to face the mysterious intruder. I vaguely recognized her outline in the faint moonlight.

"Eva," Atticus snarled. "What the hell are you still doing here?"

The small figure slowly walked toward us, and I could make out her features as she stepped closer into the light. She was a young woman, dark hair cut short and features that were too soft for a warrior, yet here she was. Spritely and determined, she kept her chin held high as she addressed us.

I recalled seeing her in Redview when I came here to tell Atticus that Christine had disappeared, but I never got the chance to ask who she was before chaos ensued.

She gestured toward the buildings surrounding us and looked back at Atticus with a sly smile on her lips. "Your father wanted me to stay and keep an eye on things here," she explained matter-of-factly. Her arms were crossed in defiance over her chest, daring him to challenge her words.

Atticus's jaw tightened as he ran a finger along his chin. "I had a feeling they sent you to spy on Augustus and me when we came here to see Lord Nathan," he said scathingly.

She bowed mockingly, her gaze hard. "I'm a good little soldier, am I not? My father sends a command and I do it—no questions asked."

I felt the air suddenly grow oppressive and heavy. Anger poured through her words. Atticus spat, "I suppose you intend to run to my father and tell him we're here." His eyes were blazing with distrust and fury.

She sneered at us, her lip curling in contempt. "So, what are you two up to?"

"Going to see someone," Atticus replied coldly.

"Who?"

"That's none of your business," I growled, clenching my jaw.

She chuckled darkly, her eyes glinting with malice. "Oh, but I think it is. If you don't want me to make a phone call to Theodore DuPont, then you'd better start talking."

Atticus and I exchanged a wary glance before the former sighed heavily. "What is it that you want? If you're gonna betray us, then just do it. I'm not going to kill a kid."

Eva's lips twisted in a mocking smile. "Oh, so kind." Her gaze flickered between us. "I've been stuck in this godforsaken town for weeks, and this is the only remotely interesting thing happening, but you won't even give me the satisfaction of a fight?"

Atticus let out a harsh laugh that bordered on a sob. "Guess I'll have to disappoint you."

"Where's the queen?" she asked, her eyes darting suspiciously around.

"Gone," I hissed through gritted teeth. I glared at Eva, my hands shaking with rage.

"I bet she's close. You probably can't crawl two

feet without her hovering." She scrunched her face and looked me up and down, a smirk playing on her lips.

Atticus spoke to her like she was an annoying little sister. "Eva. I don't want to hurt you, but I *will* tie you up if you threaten Christine's safety."

"Go ahead and try it," she threatened.

Atticus took a step closer, and Eva burst into laughter as if this entire standoff was utterly preposterous. What had this kid been through? What kind of darkness did she know?

Once her gales of laughter ceased, her voice lowered to a whisper. "What if I wanted to switch sides?"

Atticus's response was sharp and authoritative. "No."

"Why not?" she asked cautiously.

"Because I don't trust you," he answered, eyes narrowing with suspicion.

"I don't trust you either," she retorted with a sly smile, "but that doesn't mean there's nothing we can do for each other."

My stomach clenched in apprehension. "What's your price?"

She beamed with determination. "Respect. Freedom."

Atticus furrowed his brow in confusion. "What do you mean?"

Her expression twisted into a scowl. "My father is only ever using me as a pawn to get favor with Theodore DuPont, but when the job is done, he locks me away again. I'm tired of working for both of them."

I cautiously scrutinized Eva with a hint of suspicion. She appeared to be an asset, but I wanted to be sure. I shifted my gaze toward Atticus. He seemed to like her, but I still had my doubts. I slowly turned back to Eva. "And…you'd work for us?" I asked hesitantly, keeping my guard up.

She nodded her head, her features set in a hardened determination. "Yes—for now at least." She paused, her expression defiant as she squared her shoulders and looked me directly in the eye. "But eventually I want to go to high school and university. A place where I can learn and become my own person, away from my oppressive father and Theodore DuPont." She then looked at Atticus. "On top of that, I want to manage one of your income streams—preferably the weapons deals." She clenched her fists angrily. "I have some good ideas on how to expand that area of your business, but every time I mention them, my dad takes credit for it. I'm done with him stealing my work."

Atticus's throat tightened as he locked eyes with

Eva. Her demand for participation in his mission was not to be taken lightly. He spoke with care. "Eva, I understand your eagerness, but what you're asking for is not that easy. We are in the midst of something dangerous, and I'm not sure if my team is willing to—"

"Then I'll tell my father," she interjected. Atticus heard an icy threat in her voice. Her finger rose before he could speak again. "If you don't let me help, then I'll tell Lord Nathan and Theodore DuPont about you. But if you need me, I'll stay away from your mess and help if you ask." Eva's gaze didn't waiver as she spoke, determination radiating from her being. She held up her hands. "I can't live like this anymore. My whole life has been surrounded by death and destruction. I just want...I just want to enjoy myself for once."

Atticus glared at me as if he expected me to talk some sense into Eva, but I felt my own resolve falter when I saw the same look in her eye that my sister had when I'd tried to reason with her in the past. I slowly turned my gaze toward the red door.

"Do you know who lives here?" I asked.

Eva snorted with laughter. "Mindy Little. Mother of Ryan Little, who declared himself an officer in Lord Nathan's rebellion army." She sneered and shook her head, her lips curling in disgust as she spat out her next words like venom. "She's a lying, backstabbing moron that wants to sleep with Theodore DuPont."

Atticus and I jumped back, like the words had struck us like lightning. We spun away from the door and raced down the alleyway toward the main road, trying to put as much distance between us and that house as possible. "Shit," I muttered. "That could have been a disaster."

"You're welcome," Eva said, her bouncy stride filled with an underlying deviousness. "If you really want to talk to a woman in charge, I suggest Yasmin Lee. She lost two sons in the massacre three years ago and runs a local soup kitchen. Everyone here loves her and she's got pull. I could introduce you, if you'd like, but she'd probably prefer to chat with your queen."

"I'll manage," I murmured, my voice heavy with distrust.

"And I hope you'll manage to keep me updated," Eva said, trailing after us.

"If you want us to trust you, then you'll have to prove yourself," Atticus declared firmly, his tone laced with determination. "We will investigate your suggestion with caution and make sure Christine isn't walking into a potential trap."

I could feel her eyes burning into my back. "Fine. If you need me, I'm staying at the same hotel as you. Next door, actually. If you could tell your queen to keep it down, that would be great."

We stopped walking to stare at her. She grinned. "If I wanted to hurt you, I would have called my father the second I saw you rolling into town. Think about my offer, DuPont."

* * *

"So you're Christine?" Eva said while looking her up and down. I wished we had called ahead to let her know we were bringing her, because Christine's hair looked like Augustus spent the last hour holding onto it while he fucked her from behind, and there was a large hickey on her neck.

"I am," she said while sitting up on the bed a little taller. "And you're Eva?"

Eva pulled a knife out of her pocket, and Atticus rolled his eyes. "I hear you trained with Hudson."

"Sometimes *I* trained him," Christine said with a playful wink.

Eva nodded. "Okay, I like her. Let's kill some motherfuckers."

"Language!" I snapped. Eva was definitely raised with a bunch of criminals, because she was only seventeen but definitely talked like a hardened sailor and acted like a jaded middle-aged divorcée.

"So Yasmin Lee. Tell us more about her," I said.

Eva walked over to a small table in the corner of the room and swiped up a bag of chips. After opening it, she crunched on one of them before speaking with her mouth full. "She's kind but fierce. You can tell she's been through a lot. She started a soup kitchen a few years ago to help out people in the area that lost jobs or homes in the massacre. Now she's one of the most popular people around here. Everyone loves her. She's not on your side, but she's not on Theodore's side either. She's neutral. Just wants to help people."

Eva wolfed down another chip. "She's been trying to get Lord Nathan to help her get more social services to the community, but he keeps blowing her off."

"So we offer to help her," I said.

Eva popped another chip in her mouth. "She doesn't look like a fighter, but she's stronger than you'd think. Caught me stealing from her storage room and grabbed me by the ear. Made me work kitchens for a week."

Atticus laughed. "I like her already. When can you get us a meeting?"

Eva checked her watch. "Soup kitchen is open tonight. I can take you there."

I nodded. "Sounds good to me. What about you, Christine?"

"Oh, I'm in, for sure." She flashed a seductive smile. "The sooner we get this over with, the sooner we can leave Redview. I'm anxious about your mom and Daphne."

Eva walked over to the bed and sat down on the edge beside Christine. "Christine, there's something you should know before we go any further."

"What?" Christine asked with a look of concern.

Eva hesitated. "I found out a lot about Lord Nathan and his family while I was gathering intel. When you were in the castle, my father called me to let me know what was happening there. My father likes to brag when he gets gossip. Most of it was predictable evil villain bullshit, but there was some-thing that stood out to me. Are you...pregnant?" She scowled while asking the question, as if it bothered her.

"What?" Christine replied. "Pregnant?"

My heart galloped like a thoroughbred, my breaths labored and restless. I saw Atticus taking a step closer to Eva, her face a mask of pure resignation. Augustus's lip curled with an expression of repulsion. "I heard them mention the doctor," she said, barely above a whisper. "They...tested your blood?" Her voice trailed off as I glanced around the room. The walls felt as though they were closing in on us.

Christine vigorously shook her head, her blonde hair cascading down her back. "No, I'm on the shot. Or I guess I was back home. But…I had my period." Augustus clenched his jaw as she paused and trailed off into thought, desperately trying to do a mental calculation. "I had my period seven weeks ago…" Augustus was barely breathing as horror crept into his veins. Atticus's icy voice cut through the air like a razor blade. "Go get a pregnancy test. Now." Augustus looked like the earth beneath him had been ripped away as he hesitantly met Christine's gaze, her eyes reflecting his own dread.

Christine's voice wavered as she clutched her stomach, her brow furrowed with disbelief. "I don't feel different." Her eyes darted around the room to meet Atticus's gaze. She looked terrified as Atticus snapped his fingers and called out to Augustus in desperation. "Get me a fucking test!"

Augustus flew off the bed and scrambled away. I dropped beside Christine and gaped at her. She was fighting for her life just a few days ago and dragging Atticus into the freaking house. Was she hurt? Was the baby okay?

"Look, I just wanted to tell you that they were planning to *get rid of it*," Eva said. "Apparently, Lord Nathan was really fucked in the head about you having a bastard child. Wanted it done before you got married. I guess they didn't tell you?"

Christine's head shook violently, her eyes widening in despair. She couldn't believe what she was hearing. "No. Surely they wouldn't do something like this. I would never have—"

Suddenly, Atticus grabbed Christine's trembling hand, holding it firmly and reassuringly as he looked into her eyes. His deep, resonant voice effortlessly filled the air. "It's okay," he said, his gaze unwavering. "We'll figure out something. We'll get through this."

A sorrowful sigh emanated from Eva's lips as she looked Christine in the eye. "I'm truly sorry to be the one to tell you this. I just…when I heard it, I didn't feel right about it."

Christine stood there, her mouth agape, not a single word coming out. She simply nodded in understanding. The air was thick with tension, the sound of Augustus's hurried footsteps echoing in the hallway like a ghostly whisper.

Eva's voice broke through the silence, gentle and understanding. "Maybe you guys should talk. Come get me when you're ready to see Yasmin."

Eva left with a quick nod, and the moment she was

gone, Atticus enveloped Christine in his strong arms and held her tight against his chest.

"I'm so sorry," he said, his voice cracking. "We'll get through this. You're gonna be okay."

Christine sat there, a stoic statue, as tears slowly dripped from her downturned eyes. "I need to know," she said, her voice faltering.

"It's going to be okay," he murmured into her ear.

"How is this going to be okay?" she replied weakly, her face buried against his chest. "I'm scared, Atticus. What if the baby gets hurt? This is a terrible world to bring a baby into right now."

The sound of his breathing quickened, and he squirmed uncomfortably beneath the weight of her words. "I'm sure the child is—" I started to say.

"I don't even know if it's true. Could just be another mind fuck from Lord Nathan," she replied, cutting me off.

Before anyone had time to fully digest what was said, the bedroom door flew open with a loud bang and Augustus rushed in, a box of tests thrust into Christine's hands. "Got these from the pharmacy across the street. Please hurry," he pleaded with her.

With her head shaking slowly in disbelief, Christine made her way into the bathroom, and Atticus turned toward Augustus, his usually vibrant face now drained of all color, a look of sheer anguish across it.

"What do we do if it is positive?" he asked softly, not wanting Christine to hear him from the other room.

Augustus sighed heavily, his brow furrowed in worry. "Well, whatever happens, we will have to support her," he said firmly, looking between me and Atticus for agreement. I didn't know how I felt about this. We both nodded before turning our attention back to the bathroom door expectantly, waiting for Christine to emerge with news of our fate.

The room was silent as we all waited for Christine. I felt a heavy weight on my chest, knowing whatever the results were, our lives would be drastically different. It didn't take long before Christine opened the door and thrust a thin-looking stick into Atticus's hands.

He read it quickly and then locked eyes with Christine, both of them filled with an emotion that none of us could fathom. He took a deep breath before finally speaking. "You're pregnant," he said quietly.

This announcement sent shockwaves through the room. I had suspected that this was what was happening, but hearing it confirmed knocked the wind out of me. Christine gasped and Augustus swore loudly as reality sank in.

Christine stared at Atticus, her face pale and her

eyes wide with fear and uncertainty. She let out a shaky breath before breaking down into tears, her entire body shaking from the magnitude of what she just learned. Atticus wrapped his arms around her and held her close as she sobbed uncontrollably against his chest.

We all stood there in silence, not knowing what to say or do next. Finally Augustus spoke up, his voice gentle but firm. "No matter what," he said, looking between Atticus and Christine for emphasis, "we are all here to support you." Silence stretched for a lingering moment until he spoke again. "Is it…is it mine?"

"I don't know," Christine answered. "Maybe? Probably? Possibly?"

Augustus stood up and rolled his shoulders back, like a man preparing for war. "Whatever the answer is, we will do everything in our power to keep you safe and raise this child. Together."

I felt like I was watching a train wreck. This couldn't be happening. It was all too much to take in. I had to get out. I walked out of the bedroom and across the hallway to my room, closing the door behind me. I collapsed against the door, my whole body shaking with fear and frustration. I dropped down to the floor, my head in my hands. I felt my throat tighten, and my eyes burned from being squeezed shut so tightly. How could this be happening? How could everything that was so good and happy just be ripped away from me so quickly?

A baby changed *everything*. Christine would have to choose Augustus. They'd have a *happy little family* and forget all about me. All about us.

An ache welled up inside my chest, and I tried to ignore it. I held my breath, like that would somehow stop the inevitable conversation. I rolled to the side and leaned against the wall while thinking about everything.

My door creaked open and a pair of footsteps fell across the carpet. My hands covered my face, doing nothing to hide my tears. I felt a hand gently touch my shoulder, and I looked up to see Christine kneeling down beside me. Her eyes were red and puffy, and her face was blotchy. But when she saw me looking at her, she smiled softly and reached out to give me a hug.

"Everything is going to be okay," she said. "We'll figure this out, together."

I didn't believe it for a second, but I hugged her back. "I'm sorry," I whispered, my voice hoarse with emotion. "I should be taking care of you, not crying in this damn room."

My eyes burned with unshed tears as I felt her soft hand rub my back. "You need time to process," Christine said. "I've been through so much in the past few days. But right now, I need my best friend to tell me everything is going to be okay."

I barely heard her words as my thoughts raced through my head. I felt like I was watching my life slowly slip away from me, like a life preserver being pulled from my grip by a cruel and merciless God. I felt my heart sink lower and lower, unable to find the strength to keep fighting.

"I love you," I whispered as we held each other. "I love you so much. How do you feel? Do you need anything?"

"I need a second opinion," she joked. "I've always wanted kids, but this is sudden. And not exactly the best time to get pregnant. Now it's not my life I have to take care of." She looked down at her stomach.

I looked up at her and smiled. "It's going to be okay," I said. I felt a small sliver of hope well up inside me. "You can do this. I know it's hard, but you're strong. You have always been strong."

I could always tell when she was using her "strong" face. Her eyes squeezed shut and her lips pursed together. She turned her head and looked away. She breathed in deep before turning back to me. "We will do this together, right?" she asked, her voice shaking. "Whatever is happening, we'll stay together, right?"

"I'll stay with you as long as you'll have me," I said,

my face crumpling up as I tried to fight against the tears. I'd chosen my words carefully. Christine would leave once this baby was born.

I wanted to believe that everything would be alright, that I still mattered once the baby came and we both would be able to move on. But deep down, I knew the truth. The moment this baby arrived, she'd forget about me and build a life with the father of her child. That was something I couldn't ignore, no matter how much I wanted to.

Chapter Seventeen

CHRISTINE

I stomped down the street, my hood pulled close as I held my middle. Ever since I saw those two pink lines, I felt this overwhelming awareness of my stomach, as if it weighed me down. I was sure I was going to be sick, but I kept walking, trying to keep myself from thinking of the surreal situation I was in.

August was beside me, his boots scuffing against the pavement. "Are you sure you're okay to do this?" he asked, his voice gentle yet strained with worry.

I swallowed hard and nodded, though I wasn't entirely sure. I was still reeling with the fact that Theodore DuPont and Lord Nathan knew about my pregnancy before I even did.

I took a deep breath and looked up at August. "Let's just get it over with," I said, my voice trembling.

August hesitated, then grabbed my hand and squeezed it. I could feel the warmth of his touch, and a feeling of comfort flowed through me. He nodded in agreement, and together, we made our way toward the soup kitchen.

My stomach fluttered with nerves. I didn't know what I was doing. I didn't feel pregnant. I was sore, sure. But I'd also fought my way out of a castle and gone on the run. If a regular person had tried to fight off the guards like that—not that anyone else could have—they'd have been killed immediately. Fuck, it was so reckless. It was dangerous, but it got the job done. What if I'd gotten hurt? What if the baby had been hurt? I didn't know what to think about that—it was too bizarre, too terrifying to really take in. "Christine?" August asked again.

"She's fine," Eva said tersely. "Stop hovering."

I didn't know her well, but I liked the girl. She reminded me a lot of myself—the way she joked and the way she thought about things. Something about her energy made me feel connected to her.

"Have you had any water today?" Atticus asked. I ignored him. I hadn't been taking very good care of myself. Hadn't been careful. A surge of guilt swept over me like a deluge.

"I think so," I spat.

"Here." He opened a bottle of water and helped me drink it.

"Thanks."

"How are you feeling?" Atticus asked while helping me up a curb.

"I'm fine."

"No. You're not fine," he snapped.

"Christine, maybe we should just take the night off?" August suggested.

"She's fine," Leo grunted angrily from ahead.

"Oh, for fuck's sake. Let's all just go back to the hotel room. We need to sort ourselves out before we meet with Yasmin," Atticus shot back.

I appreciated their concern, but I didn't need it. It made me feel weak, like a child that needed to be coddled, and I didn't have the energy to fight. "We need to do this," I said. "I want to get out of here as quickly as possible."

"I agree with Christine." Eva crossed her arms, and her brow wrinkled in concern.

"Are you sure?" Atticus asked.

"Look, I said I'm fine," I snapped. "If I have to say it one more time, I'm going to lose my shit."

Leo marched ahead of us, his face a mask of anguish. He kept his emotions tightly reined, so I had no idea what storm was raging inside of him. He had taken the news worse than the rest, and I worried he was replaying the moments we had shared and wondering why I hadn't chosen him again. His voice was pure gravel as he spoke through gritted teeth, "Let's get this done so Christine can rest. She's been pushing herself too hard."

"Fucking hell," August cursed before following him inside.

Eva nudged me. "I don't know how you put up with them. We should be a two woman team and just kill Theodore on our own."

I laughed and shook my head. "I like you."

"I'm likable," she replied.

Atticus strode in front of us, leading us into the soup kitchen. My heart raced like an engine as I took in the dull-hued walls and shiny industrial kitchen. The long windows made the room feel airy, but there was still a lingering smell of fried food.

We stepped further into the main room. Every single face stared right at us, some with curiosity, others with suspicion. A hushed murmur spread as we passed by each table; they knew our faces and they were determined to find out what we were doing here—right in their place of solace.

I could feel their eyes pressing onto my back, like a heavy weight that prevented me from moving. I quickly glanced away, trying to ignore the judgmental stares of people who were just trying to survive.

Eva urged me forward and I stepped into the realm of the unknown. My three men were at my heels, poised for attack. Eva knocked on the door that led to the offices, and a female voice called out, "Come in."

Eva pushed the door open. In the room, multiple women were situated at their computers, and an older woman was seated in the corner.

"Eva!" a warm voice sang in delight. "I had been wondering where you were!"

"Hey, Yasmin," Eva spoke hesitantly, glancing at me as she stepped aside.

Yasmin's pupils dilated as they fell upon me, and her face contorted into tense concentration. Her hand crept under her desk, as if feeling for a hidden weapon.

"Are you…in trouble?" she asked calmly, her voice thick.

"Nope. They just want to hear about your plans for Redview and see if they can offer any assistance," Eva chimed in, her voice clear and sure.

Yasmin slowly rose from her chair, eyes unyielding as she studied each of us. She was a stunning woman—so elegant, with gentle features, intense eyes, and a warm smile. Her long dark hair was drawn back into a neat ponytail. She wore a simple plaid shirt and sweatpants—an outfit that the other workers in the kitchen had donned.

My heart raced as anxiety surged through my veins. Oh, God. I needed to stay calm.

"Everyone out, please. I'd like to speak with Eva's friends," she commanded in a brittle tone, far removed from the warmth of her earlier greeting with Eva.

The three women practically ran for their lives, pushing us aside as they scurried away. Eva quickly threw herself into the nearest chair, physical and emotional exhaustion taking its toll.

My three burly men remained firmly at my side. "If I had known the queen was coming, I would have at least tried to make this a more hospitable atmosphere. However, I can never bring myself to bow before someone who hasn't earned it," Yasmin declared with a bitter edge. Her voice shook as if she fought back betrayal.

I grinned maniacally while removing my hood. "It looks like we already have something in common."

Yasmin's lips curved into an icy smile, but her gaze

was blank. "I've heard you and your companions are in some trouble."

I narrowed my eyes suspiciously. "Yes."

"You're on the run, aren't you?"

"We are," I replied, my voice quivering.

She then glanced pointedly at August. "Please forgive me, but I have no desire to converse with King Frederick's son in my presence. That man single-handedly ruined this entire kingdom." Her voice was shrill with anguish, her body quivering as she spoke. I could see the pain in her eyes and knew there was no turning back for us now.

August took a deep and steadying breath before striding forward. His voice carried into the room, unwavering. "He's not my father, ma'am. And I'm relieved that I share no blood with that abhorrent man."

Yasmin let out a rattling sigh. "So the rumors were true then. I thought for sure Lord Nathan was speaking out of his ass."

I inhaled sharply, my voice cutting through the silence like a hot knife. "He's certainly lied about several things," I retorted, standing my ground. "I came here to discuss them with you."

Yasmin shot me a quizzical glance, her expression darkening. "Why? I'm just a woman who runs a soup kitchen."

Eva slammed her hand down on the table, her voice rising steadily. "Come off it, Yas! You practically run this town!"

I swallowed hard, my gaze firm. "Lord Nathan has been lying to you all this time—and he needs to be held accountable."

Yasmin scoffed, folding her arms with a haughty air. "All men in power lie. At least Nathan inspires change."

My blood boiled at her words. How could she be so naive? "He may bring change, but at what cost? I hear he makes a lot of promises he can't keep—or refuses to keep. Redview needs help, and he's just another man trying to capitalize on your anger."

Yasmin's frown deepened. "What are you asking me to do?"

"Reform your town," I replied. "I need your help, but I also need your leadership. You're the most respected woman in this city, and if you say something, men listen."

"Sadly, that only goes so far."

"Let's turn the tables," I declared as I slammed my fist onto the table, showcasing my determination. "Let's make sure Lord Nathan doesn't remain the most influential person in Redview, and you can take the steering wheel of this town."

Yasmin's face contorted with elation and excitement

as her eyes burned with the fire of a thousand suns. "How?" she inquired.

I breathed out a sigh and straightened my back. "It was Lord Nathan's brother who committed the heinous massacre in Redview three years ago. I heard it from King Frederick himself. Lord Nathan is using this to bolster his military power. The only reason he got an alliance with Theodore DuPont is because of *your* rebellion. You gave him an army and Theodore saw an opportunity."

Yasmin leaned back in her chair, a faraway look in her eyes. "I need proof."

My voice oozed with conviction as I took another small step toward her. "You know it's true," I said, my gaze fixed.

A heavy silence filled the room as she squared her shoulders in defiance. "I need proof," she repeated firmly, her eyes locked on mine in a battle of wills.

August swooped in from the shadows with a rough voice, "I have proof. I found it in the archives." Then he added with a sly smirk, "I can have it sent to you by tomorrow morning. My trusted advisor, Adonis, has scans of the reports." His words hung in the air like a challenge as we both stared at him skeptically.

I narrowed my gaze at Yasmin, my face stern and determined. "I need you to make sure everyone knows what he did. His family shouldn't be allowed to profit off of murdering innocent men, women, and children," I demanded. "King Frederick gave his family assets as payment for destroying your town. Land, precious stones, oil. All of it is going to him instead of Redview. And now you all work for him. It's wrong."

Yasmin's face reddened with rage. "No one will listen to me," she spat out, her voice filled with venom and spite. With a wild look in her eyes, she set her jaw and held my gaze, signaling a fierce challenge I had no choice but to accept.

"Then make them listen, Yasmin. Don't let anyone stop you from doing what you know is right. This is your town and you have the power to change it. Lord Nathan will bleed these soldiers dry. All we need is a spark of distrust."

Yasmin scrutinized me, her eyes boring into my own. For what felt like an eternity, we were entrapped in this moment of tension. I could feel her searching for any weakness or doubt in me. Finally, she broke the silence with a single question.

"Why are you doing this?" she asked.

My eyes narrowed and I stood firmly before her.

"I'm not the same fragile girl who ran away three years ago," I stated with conviction, my voice growing in volume as I gathered confidence. I knelt down before her, meeting her gaze fiercely. "This place is my home, too, and I'm not going to let these selfish men ruin it for their own agenda. I never wanted to be a queen, but sometimes destiny hands you something unbearable and you just have to make the most of it." My words felt heavier with the truth swirling in my stomach. I was going to be a mother. I had to make this world better for my child. Our child—whoever the father may be.

Yasmin seemed to ponder my words for a moment. She nodded her head slowly and I watched as her walls of defiance began to soften. Her face softened too and her expression shifted to one of understanding.

"You're right," she said finally. "Sometimes destiny hands you something so unbearable that you must take action." Yasmin sat up, rolling her shoulders back. "You have the courage to stand before me, ask for my help in stopping the brother of the man who destroyed this town three years ago. You have the courage to ask a grieving woman to take the lead in her own township and fight for her people. So far, it seems you're better than half the men in that castle."

I bit my lip and gave her a nod. "Thank you."

"I can't guarantee the men will fight for you," she said.

"I just need them not to fight for Lord Nathan. I'm capable of taking care of everything else."

"And what happens after you take the throne? How will you help Redview?" she asked.

"I will do everything in my power to pay you back for your help and friendship," I replied. "But more importantly, I'll give power to those who have their people's best interest at heart. How would you like to be a Lady of the Court, Yasmin?"

Yasmin's eyes widened. "Me?" she asked.

"Yes. You're the best one for the job. You just need to get Lord Nathan out of power for good."

She sighed. "Alright. I'll do it."

I smiled. "Welcome to the revolution, Yasmin," I said.

She grinned, and with her eyes locked on mine, she slowly bowed.

Chapter Eighteen

CHRISTINE

"Get off your feet, love. You should rest," August said while tucking me into bed.

"I'm pregnant, August, not dying," I snapped, making him cringe.

He tucked me under the covers while Atticus stared out the window. Leo was sitting at the foot of the bed, staring at his hands like he was trying to memorize his lifelines. "I'm just going to say what we're all thinking," August said, his voice scratchy. "The baby is totally mine."

Atticus turned his head to us, a scowl on his face. "And what would make you think that?"

August stood taller, a proud grin on his face.

"According to my research, if she had her period seven weeks ago, then that means she ovulated about four or five weeks ago, and I vividly remember fucking her brains out then." He paused to look at me. "Respectfully, love."

I sat up and stared at him. "You looked up ovulation?"

He stroked my cheek. "I needed to know."

Crossing my arms over my chest, I glared at each of them. "Would it make any difference if it was Atticus's or Leo's baby?"

"Well, no," August stammered. "But I mean…this baby is *mine*. That's different."

Atticus cleared his throat. "We don't know for sure. Some women ovulate at different times. Plus, Christine has been under a tremendous amount of stress. It could be mine."

"It's definitely not mine," Leo snapped, the hurt in his voice making me sigh. "The royal guard makes all their men get vasectomies."

I sat up and scooted to the edge of the bed. "You know that this baby is all of yours, right?" I whispered as I reached out to hold Leo's hand. "I know things are complicated, but when I said I want you all, I meant it. Which means we're *all* having a baby."

Leo looked at me like I had stabbed him. "That

sounds really idealistic, Christine. But let's try and think about this objectively. You want all four of us to raise this baby?"

"Well, yes, why not?" I asked all of them.

"Christine, your child will be a royal," August explained.

Atticus cleared his throat. "My child would be a DuPont."

Leo looked bitterly at the ground. "And if it were my child, it would be nothing more than a bastard. You're planning on marrying August still, right?"

"Yes."

Leo stood up. "So if it's his baby, the child will be a royal. He's the one you intend to marry, yes? Regardless of his father, August *will* be king." He paused to wave a hand at Atticus. "And if later on down the line, you have Atticus's child, he or she will still be a bastard, but no one will think twice about it. They'll be protected and provided for by the DuPont name. But if it were my child—not that it could be..." He swallowed. "It would be a no-name bastard with no title, no recognition. I'm...struggling with a lot of things. I want to believe you when you say that we're all in this together, but what if everything changes when that child comes along? What if you decide it's too much work—it's too twisted—to love us, too. Then what? Atticus and I will be forced to just give you up?"

Atticus laughed. "I'm not giving her up. I don't care about marriage. I already own Christine's fucking soul. I've got a death grip on her heart that no ceremony or piece of paper can get rid of."

August held his hand up like a stop sign. "For the record, I'm not giving up, either. I'm not where I thought I would be in my life right now, but I would go through hell and back to prove to Christine that I'm a good father and husband." He pulled my hand up to his mouth to kiss my knuckles. "Atticus might not want a ceremony or piece of paper, but I'm excited to do that with you."

Leo raised his head to look at both August and me. "If Christine chooses you over us, or if you both decide you're just better off without us, then I don't want anything to do with the baby. It would hurt too much. It's your choice, but I won't be involved."

"Leo, it's not like that," I said, hurt in my voice.

"I'm not saying it is. But I don't think I could handle watching you two love each other, building a happy little family without me. I could never be okay with that."

Atticus sighed. "I'll love the child like they are my own."

"I'm not going to give you up, Leo," I croaked.

"The only person pushing you away is yourself. I'm telling you that I want all of us to find a way to make this work. It's still new and we have a lot to process but—"

"But when you're done processing, will you decide staying with August and only August is the best course of action?" Leo asked.

Atticus scoffed. "Doesn't matter what she decides. I'm telling you, that's not going to happen. I'm not going anywhere, whether she wants me or not. So the only person ending this is you, Leo. Let's give you two some time to talk."

The room fell silent. Atticus stood up and motioned for August to follow him. After a moment of hesitation, they both left the room, closing the door behind them. I looked at Leo, hoping he would say something to make this better, but he just covered his eyes with his hand.

"I don't know what I'm supposed to say," I said softly as I stood up. I took his hand and pulled it away from his face. "I realize that I can't control you, I can't force you to try. I want us to find a way to make this work," I spoke as I lightly stroked his face. "I know that once we figure it out, we're going to be stronger than ever."

I reached my arms up to wrap around his neck. "I'm not choosing August or Atticus. If we move forward, it will be *all* of us. How can I convince you that I want this? I want *you*? If you can't believe me, then we're never going to work, Leo. All I have is my faith in us, and all you have is…"

"What?" he choked out.

"You have this crippling sense of doubt that I couldn't possibly love you, and it destroys me." He kissed my cheek as tears streamed down my face. "I'm desperate for you, Leo. Please believe in us."

"I don't know if I can."

My heart sank to my stomach, and I stepped back from his grip. "You're killing me."

"It's killing me, too. What do you want from me? Maybe I just don't love you enough to share. Maybe it's just not enough."

"You don't love me?" I asked, my throat closing. I knew this was a possibility when I went on this journey, but it still cut me deep. "What more can I do? You have to have faith that you are important to me—that I *love* you."

"How can it be special if you give the same damn thing to two other men, Christine?" he roared. "Love doesn't work like that!"

His outburst made me deflate. There was so much lingering between us, but I felt like there was never going to be a happy ending for us. "I'm sorry I asked so much of you, so much that you couldn't give. I'm sorry I fell in love with you." I fell to my knees and sobbed. "I know it's not enough and that it's not enough for you, but it's still there."

"We were doomed from the beginning, Christine. It doesn't make sense. You're having a fucking baby with someone else."

"It could also be your baby, too! We could all raise this child together!" I screamed. "I can't do this anymore, Leo. You're not willing to fight for us, so I'm done."

"I can't do this anymore either, so I guess we're both letting each other go," he said quietly. I stood up and ripped my clothes off, one article of clothing after another, the anger boiling inside of me with each passing second.

"Christine, sex isn't going to fix this," Leo sighed.

I glared at him, fury radiating from me. "I'm not naive enough to think that it will, Leo. But if you're going to give up on us and throw away all the moments we shared…then I at least deserve a good goodbye."

"Christine—" He cut me off before I could finish, but I wouldn't let it stop me.

"You're telling me that you don't love me anymore and that I can't force you to feel something," I spat out each word, my voice thick and angry. "So if this is really it, there's nothing else left to do but make this last moment count."

I stepped toward him as August and Atticus slunk into the room to see what was going on. Atticus ran his voracious gaze over my body, while August seemed to find amusement in the situation.

"Do you want us to leave?" Atticus crooned.

August looked hungrily at me. "I would love to find out what thoughts are passing through that mind of yours."

My voice was dripping with vitriol as I spoke. "Come in."

Rage coursing through my veins as I glared at Leo. "Come on," I snarled, nostrils flaring. "Since you can't decide whether you love me or not, why don't you show me goodbye the only way you know how? Fuck me with no regard for my feelings, take what you want and then leave. Just like that."

"Christine," Leo growled.

My vitriol spilled out in a rush of venomous words. "Is this the part where you leave me for the last time?" I growled. "Tonight you can take everything from me." I savagely unfastened my bra with trembling fingers, and it slipped to the ground.

August and Atticus stalked in, their eyes captivated by my rage. I was incensed. I was livid. But before Leo would go, they would all get a taste of my wrath. I wanted him to feel my pain and indignation. I wanted him to be crippled by having ever considered leaving me.

August and Atticus stopped at the edge of the bed, and they both watched me with hunger in their eyes. I walked over to them and shoved my hand in Atticus's pants, making him gasp. "Yes, Little Monster. Show him what he's missing."

My movements were feral, my skin burning with rage as they both touched me, exploring my body with anxious hands. My lips bit into August's, punishing him as he kissed me back, eager to feel the extent of my ire. Every thrust of my tongue brought a new surge of fury until I screamed.

August kissed my shoulder, his hands slipping over my breasts to tease my nipples. I moaned as Atticus pulled his cock out of his pants so I had easier access.

"Do you want to go, Leo?" I spat, my voice seething with hatred.

Leo let out a wild growl. "What the actual fuck, Christine. Is this really what you're after?"

I shot him a deadly look. "Say goodbye, Leo," I snapped.

No one said a word; instead, I slowly sank onto my knees and engulfed Atticus's hardening cock in my mouth. I savored the salty taste and ran my tongue around the tip as August and Atticus both groaned in unison. I grabbed both of my breasts firmly and circled my nipples with my thumbs. When I looked up, I saw August rubbing himself through his trousers. If looks could kill, Leo would have been dead.

I pulled Atticus deeper, my nails digging into his flesh, as a malicious glee filled me at the thought of Leo watching. Leo let out a pained groan, his hand curling around his own erection with a ferocious grip.

"Christine," he growled in warning.

I paused and pulled away from Atticus, glaring at Leo with hatred burning in my eyes.

"Do you want to leave?" I asked, my voice dripping with malice. "Do you want to fuck me and then run away from me like usual? Will that make it easier for you?"

Leo stepped forward, his eyes blazing with an icy rage. "Christine." His voice was a mere whisper, yet it was filled with more hostility than any scream ever could be.

I lunged at Atticus and pinned him down on the floor. His breaths were staggered as I shifted my hips to straddle him. I growled before I pounded my body down against Atticus's erect shaft, eliciting a stifled moan from his throat. "Fuck me, Atticus. Hard. I want you to show him how you'd act if I told you I didn't love you. Show me how you'd act if I was about to walk out that door. I want you to fuck me with all the hate that you can offer, Atticus. Show me how you'd act if I broke your heart," I commanded, my eyes boring into his own, begging him to understand.

With a primal grunt, Atticus thrust up, pushing himself deep into me in one powerful surge. I braced my palms to his chest to keep my balance as he lifted his hips from below and drove himself deeper and deeper into me, with each passing thrust more urgent than the last. Our eye contact never broke, and I could feel Leo's sorrowful gaze burning into us from where he stood.

I cried out as Atticus jolted his hips up and speared his cock into me in one more powerful thrust. "If you were leaving me, Little Monster, I can assure you, you wouldn't be on top," he said before gently picking me off of his lap and standing us both up. He walked me over to the bed, gently laid me down, and slowly stripped out of his pants.

"If you said you didn't love me, I'd drown in your cum until you realized how fucking wrong you were," he said before prying my thighs apart and licking up my slit.

Beside me, August fell onto the bed with a thud. He ripped off his pants, tossing them carelessly in the corner before he joined us on the mattress. His hands held my breasts tightly as he groaned, his eyes never leaving Atticus's lips as they moved against my slick pussy.

Leo stood there silently, his expression one of searing pain and desire.

Atticus's lips curled into a menacing sneer. "I'd make you suffer until you begged me to take you back. Then I'd fuck you so hard you wouldn't be able to take it anymore." His voice boomed through the air, and my heart pounded in my chest. I felt hot tears streaming down my face as I succumbed to his demands, his words like razor blades cutting through me. His rough hands pulled my hips closer, and he rammed into me. He moved like a man possessed. His thrusts were hard, fast and unrelenting. My lips opened in a guttural cry as I felt myself coming undone, until finally he pulled away and looked up at me with a cruel stare. "I'd fuck you until you begged me to stop."

The promise he uttered hung in the air as I tasted them with my parched lips. I could almost feel August's amusement radiating from his smirk.

"Fuck that pretty mouth, August," Atticus sneered, his grip on my skin tightening as he leaned closer to me. "Show her what we would do to queens who want to leave us."

I could feel my body quiver as I turned my head in his direction, my eyes now level with August's hard cock. Atticus's dick pressed against me as his hands moved up and down my body, his grip becoming more intense with every movement. He drew me closer, his intention clear, and with one hard thrust, he was inside me.

August surged inside of my mouth, and they both started to fuck me in tandem.

I cried out as Atticus slammed into me.

I stilled my body, forcing Atticus to guide all of our movements. I was holding my breath, and I was going to make them both show Leo that they wouldn't let me leave without a fight.

I felt the mattress dip, and in an instant, Leo's hands slid up to my breasts, and August came to life, forcing more of his cock down my throat.

"Now you want her?" August spat at Leo. "Now you want to touch her? Feel her? Wait your fucking turn."

My pussy started to clench around Atticus's cock. The pleasure made my pussy ache for more. I cried out and Atticus pushed harder.

August pulled out of my mouth. "Are you going to sit there with your dick in your hands, or are you going to give Christine what she wants, Leo?" he asked roughly before thrusting past my lips once more. August held my face with both hands. Atticus's cock was deep into my pussy. Leo roamed my skin while watching us. Atticus started to fuck me harder and faster. "Fuck her face, August," he growled.

Atticus's words made August come hard down my throat. I sucked every drop of it down, swallowing and drooling over his cock until there was nothing left.

I loved how August and Atticus worked together. I loved how they loved me and how they worshiped me. My body's desire for them increased. I wanted them to fuck me harder and faster, but I also knew that I needed to show Leo that he wasn't going to leave without a fight.

I took a deep breath, held it and then exhaled hard.

I was trying to show Leo that I didn't need him to breathe, and I didn't need him to be there. I wanted him to see that I would be fine without him.

Even if we all knew it was a lie.

I felt my pussy tighten around Atticus's cock, milking him until he couldn't hold on any longer. He groaned and then started to come inside of me.

I could feel myself shaking and my body quivering with pleasure as Atticus quickly pulled out of me and stood up.

"See, Leo?" I said, my voice shaky. "That's what a

man does when he refuses to lose the woman he loves. Seems you're always the one watching. One of these days, you need to step up without someone forcing you, because from here on out, none of us are going to make you do this. You're either in or you're out. Now get the fuck out of my sight."

Leo opened and closed his mouth, seemingly stuck in indecision. And then, rage crossed his features, this unbridled explosion of emotion that twisted his expression up into something feral.

"I didn't get my goodbye, Christine," he snapped before unbuckling his belt.

I spoke as he tossed his pants across the room and stripped out of his shirt. "I'm not sure I want a goodbye anymore. As you can see, I'm more than taken care of here."

"Frankly, baby, I don't fucking care," he sneered before grabbing my hips and pulling me toward the edge of the bed.

"No," I said firmly, pushing against his chest. "No goodbye. No more. You missed your chance."

"Did I, now?" he asked, his eyes narrowing as he stared at me.

"You said you weren't sure if you loved me, Leo. I can't handle that," I said before rolling over and trying to get away, but he wasn't having any of that. I yelped as he yanked my hips back, moving like lightning. He gripped my thighs and pulled me close. I looked over my shoulder at him before trying to crawl away again.

His eyes burned into mine, and his lips curled into a snarl. "Give me my goodbye," he demanded as he pushed my shoulders down and forced my ass up in the air.

My eyes widened. "No."

Atticus and August sat back on the bed beside us, each one watching with a heavy, hungry gaze as Leo dragged his hands up and down my body, squeezing and pulling me closer to his cock.

"Are you going to stop this?" I asked Atticus.

"We both know you're capable of stopping him, Little Monster," Atticus replied. He then bit his lip and sat back. August seemed unsure but followed his lead.

I felt Leo's cock brush against my ass, and I shuddered. I could feel the weight of his stare, the same as Atticus, who sat right next to me at his side. I blushed and squirmed with every touch, every squeeze, as Leo's thigh pushed mine apart.

"You wanted a fight, Christine? You fucking got one." He slid his hands down my thighs and over my ass, pulling me back to his groin. He gripped my hips and stared down at me as he settled himself at my entrance. I moaned, arching my spine, as he brushed his tip against my slick opening still dripping with Atticus's cum. My pussy throbbed and ached for him. I wanted him to fuck me, but I didn't want to give him that satisfaction.

"You don't get to fuck me, Leo. You get to watch the man who does." I closed my eyes, trying to control my breaths as he pushed the tip of his cock against my opening.

"You forgot something, baby," Leo said. "You'll be with them, but you'll think about me."

He sunk his cock into me, making me gasp as he filled me up. He started to fuck me, and his strokes were hard, fast and deep. I felt his cock rub against my pussy walls. I gasped and writhed, my hands gripping the sheets. I was going to come hard, but I wasn't going to beg him for it. He sped up his movements and I closed my eyes, trying to fight the urge. I knew I was fighting a losing battle, but what did it matter, anyway? What did anything matter?

"Your pussy will always love me, Christine. Even when you don't."

I sobbed, biting my lip as he rocked against me. His skin slapped against my ass. I could feel my orgasm building up deep and low in my stomach, a blinding white-hot light that burned my skin from within.

"I'm going to ruin your cunt, baby. My cock is going

to be the only way to feel, Christine. You'll need it to make sense of the world. I'm going to ruin you."

I felt the sting of pleasure, and I knew he was right. He already ruined me when he gave up on us. I was going to give myself over to him and keep fighting him until he finally gave me what I wanted.

Everything.

All of them.

He fucked me harder until he was slamming into me. He groaned as he thrust into me, and I moaned, aching for his cock, desperate for his touch.

He leaned over me and grabbed my hair in his hand. He removed a hand from my hip and slowly trailed it around the front of my body, over my clit and up to my breasts. I was throbbing. I held my breath, waiting for him to move his hand back to my hip and fuck me harder. Instead, he took his hand away, leaving my pussy pulsing in need. I mewled in protest. I couldn't last much longer. I could feel the pressure increasing, my orgasm building up inside of me. I was moaning and crying out. All I wanted was for him to fuck me harder and faster, to pound into me and to dig his nails into my skin.

But then. He just stopped.

"Feel that, Christine? That's what a fucking goodbye

feels like. And we both know neither of them will finish what I started."

"So close," I cried, my voice shaking.

"You still need more, don't you?" I could hear the amused tone in his voice. I wanted to kill him for doing this to me, for leaving me hanging. But I was so close, so close to an orgasm that my entire body was electric.

"Please," I pleaded, my body shaking, my arms and legs trembling.

"What are you begging for, baby?" he asked, his voice deep and throaty.

"Don't stop," I begged. "Please."

He growled and leaned over me, gripping my thighs. I was begging, pleading for him to fuck me. I was so close.

And then, I felt him put distance between us. I collapsed on the bed, the pleasure fleeing my body. I heard him put on his pants. I listened as he walked toward the door. I sobbed when he left without a word.

Leo said goodbye. And it was far worse than anything I could have ever imagined.

Chapter Nineteen

CHRISTINE

I let out a sigh while looking back at the car. We spent the day resting in silence, deciding it was safer to travel at night. I was ready to get out of this town and take time to process everything.

"I got this, boss," Eva said as she thrust out her hand for a shake.

"You sure you don't wanna join us at the beach house?" I asked in a hopeful tone while turning back to look at her.

"Ugh, no offense, but unless you're planning on kicking those guys out, I'm gonna pass. The awkward tension is thick, girl. No way am I going to be near whatever you've got going on." She twisted her face into an exaggerated grimace. "Plus, if my dad thinks I'm being good here, he just might let me in on his secrets. And Yasmin's cool."

"If you need anything, call us—me specifically—okay? Don't forget."

Eva rolled her eyes and smiled wryly. "Look, I've been handling myself since I was twelve, so no worries here. But sometimes everyone needs a lil help, right?"

I shoved her shoulder and we both shared a laugh. "That's all I'm saying."

"So, as your friend, let me give you a piece of advice." Eva winked at me. I followed her gaze to the car, where Atticus, August, and Leo were waiting for me. What a dumpster fire. After everything that had gone down, I was not looking forward to a road trip with all of them. We all still had to stick together.

"Hit me with it." I shrugged as Eva cocked an eyebrow at me.

"Dump them!" she laughed.

I rolled my eyes and groaned. "It's too late for that now!" I held my stomach as I chuckled nervously. "But we can figure this out somehow." I didn't necessarily believe my own words, but I didn't want to drag Eva into all of my problems. She'd been forced to grow up at a young age, but that didn't mean I was going to contribute to that. I let out a puff of air. "It's crazy, right? Everything?"

"Not really," Eva said with a shrug. "What's crazy is the fact that you didn't remember to take your birth control while boning three dudes."

"Nice," I replied flatly. "Be safe. I'll text you."

She waved her fingers and walked through the parking lot, away from us. The moment she was out of view, it felt like a weight settled on my shoulders. The weight of my long night and the exhaustion I felt hit me full force. I was nursing a broken heart and still reeling from the fact that I was pregnant.

The car seats were like two worlds apart: August and Leo in the front, and me with Atticus in the back. Even though I was sitting right behind Leo, I felt distant. I wanted to reach out and touch his long golden hair with the tips of my fingers, but was afraid the gesture would be rebuffed. Leo glanced at me through the rearview mirror, almost as if he could read my mind. He said nothing, but his eyes asked, *are you okay?* Every muscle in my body tightened as I felt a rush of emotion crash over me. I had never been so torn, and I wasn't sure what to say.

"How are you, Little Monster?" Atticus asked.

"I'm alright," I replied faintly, not wanting to give

away my inner turmoil. Leo started the car, and drove us out of the parking lot.

Maybe, when we got to the beach house, we could escape this emotional crisis. I had no idea what kind of relationship we'd have after all this was done. We could take down Lord Nathan and Theodore DuPont, but then what? Would Leo quit his job? Would he leave us behind? Or would he stay and force both of us to linger in this unfulfilled state indefinitely?

The air between us screamed of heartbreak as Atticus spoke louder than necessary for Leo to hear. "You were up all night crying. Maybe you should rest some more." We all looked exhausted, like we hadn't slept in days—but I knew it was the weight of the last few weeks weighing us down. So much had happened and it was tough to process. Leo didn't say a word. He just stared ahead into the night, lost in his own thoughts.

"I rested all day. I just want to get to the safe house," I replied.

"I need the royal therapist. He'd know what to do," August sighed, watching the scenery pass by. But, his hope was quickly quashed by Leo's sharp retort.

"I don't need a therapist."

"What you need is a kick to the dick," Atticus sneered, pulling me close and caressing my hair.

I wanted to tell them all to shut up, all my men clinging to their unresolved dramas and unspoken pain, but Leo beat me to the punch.

"Why don't we try going on a silent six-hour drive?" he proposed, and I felt a twinge of sadness. His knuckles had turned white gripping the steering wheel, his noble attempt at regaining control of the situation.

August scoffed in disbelief, "A silent drive? That sounds terrible."

Surprisingly, Leo's voice was gentle and kind when he offered, "You could always sleep." His words reminded me of when August was younger and Leo tried his best to keep him in line. It sent a wave of nostalgia throughout my body.

August pouted, a glassy sheen of desperation coating his eyes. "I'm not tired. Remember when you used to bore me with stories from your days at the military academy to get me to sleep?"

Leo grunted, momentarily unable to respond, and the awkwardness of the silence settled.

August nodded excitedly, a glimmer of hope beneath his words. "Okay. Let's do that."

I swallowed a bitter laugh, immediately regretting having allowed myself such an indulgence. August never ceased to amaze me with his ability to disarm stress and tension with empty words and nonchalance.

Though his lack of genuine emotion was sometimes disconcerting, it was also something he was admittedly good at, avoiding feasible confrontations and allowing him to pretend everything was alright.

"I guess I'm supposed to tell you a story," Leo said with a glum expression, his voice trailing off into an empty silence.

August leaned forward in anticipation, a coy grin tugging at the corner of his lips. "Oh, this should be good."

"Fine," Leo spat out in a resigned tone. He cleared his throat, gathering his thoughts before beginning. "As you know, I went off to the military academy at eighteen. The first few months were hell; I was young and stupid and had no clue what I was doing. The others were mostly a year older than me, and they loved having someone they could pick on. But I was determined to prove myself, so I kept pushing forward."

He took a moment to chuckle darkly at the memory before continuing. I tightened my hold around Atticus's arm, feeling the weight of Leo's story pressing down on me. He slowly recounted his experience of being mistreated, always striving for acceptance, but never quite grasping it. His words painted an image of a confused young man battling with his demons, desperately seeking an escape while trying to find himself.

Leo's voice was barely a whisper in the confined space of the car. "Like a fool, I decided to enlist. Everyone said it was a mistake. But there was one guy, another guard trainee named Darren, who took me under his wing. He was one year older than me. He warned me about the perils of war and told me to keep my mouth shut if I wanted to survive. I didn't, but I listened to him anyway. He was a real good guy. The kind you don't find so often nowadays."

The darkness inside the car seemed to deepen as Leo fumbled for the words he knew would come next. "He was killed in action not long after that." Leo paused for a brief moment to collect himself. His voice grew husky, barely a whisper in the confines of the car. "I was pretty messed up because of it…so when an assignment came up for the castle, I applied without thinking twice. I didn't think I'd get in, but this pain in the ass, spoiled rotten playboy—"

"That's me," August interjected with a wry smile.

"—Augustus," Leo continued with a hollow chuckle, "was a handful, and no one else wanted the job. So I thought, 'What the heck? It's better than going off to die in some overseas conflict.'" His laughter died out. "Wasn't quite sure what I'd gotten myself into… but here we are. I thought for sure I wouldn't last a day," Leo added. "But I guess I learned how to be a good guard. Protect him while giving him his space. I wanted to quit a million times—"

Atticus made an uncomfortable sound in the back of his throat. "But you decided it was worth it, putting up with August, when you met Christine."

Leo's gaze flicked to the rearview mirror, meeting my eyes. "It wasn't exactly love at first sight," he admitted sheepishly. "She was young. I was protective of her innocence, her gentle demeanor. She reminded me of a broken toy, and I wanted to put her back together. It was painful to see a gentle creature like that in a cruel castle, and I felt compelled to help her."

His voice softened almost to a whisper. "The first time I saw her…it was like seeing a fairy princess in the castle gardens. She seemed almost unaware of the world around her. I was mesmerized by her beauty and vulnerability. But I never wanted to be with her in that way. I just wanted to keep her safe." His Adam's apple bobbed as he swallowed hard and looked away.

August's gaze was drawn to the window, like a moth to the flame. As the cityscape zoomed past, August appeared deep in thought. He turned to Leo and spoke in a soft voice, a gentle plea, like a cry in the night. "I know you wanted to protect me and take care of me, too, Leo. Can't you just admit it? One positive thing? My heart can't take another rejection from you."

Atticus laughed. August rolled his eyes and sighed.

Leo looked thunderstruck and uttered barely anything but a sullen, "I guess."

August snorted and crossed his arms. "It's called communication, dude. I'm hoping for compliments, and you're coming up with zilch."

"Jesus Christ," Leo said, letting out a pained sigh and pressing his palm to his forehead. "Can I just get on with the story?"

"Only if you include more bits about how much you love me, too," August replied teasingly.

Leo gritted his teeth, white knuckling the steering wheel. "I gave August the space he asked for, working in the shadows. And I kept Christine safe, too. She wasn't necessarily my job, but I made her my responsibility. But then something happened to the fairy princess who was blossoming into a beautiful young woman, and I...I couldn't protect her. I failed her." The last words were carried away in a whisper of his pain and regret.

Atticus shifted in his seat, tension radiating off of him.

"I got really good at pretending nothing happened," Leo continued quietly. "My job was taken away from me, and I slowly disappeared inside myself. I felt like I didn't deserve anything, or anyone... Hiding away seemed easier than facing the shame of what my failure had cost me."

I croaked his name. It was a struggle to stay quiet; I had been pushing my emotions down, keeping them in check until now.

August shifted uncomfortably. "I guess it was hard to transition back to the castle and all its memories, huh?"

Leo's laugh was harsh and self-mocking. "Hard? Try impossible. I wanted Christine to go away; it just felt right. But I also wanted her to stay, even if every time I looked at her, I saw myself for the loser I am. Every glance like a knife to the heart, until…"

"Until what?" I asked, unable to control myself.

"I realized what was hurting me was love. Love that I couldn't do anything about."

August frowned. "I mean. You did plenty about it. I heard you loved her good and hard all night long just a few days ago. Maybe you need to stop blaming yourself. Maybe that's why you don't feel like you're enough."

Leo's eyes burned with anger and pain. "It's not just my fault," he spat. His words were laced with exhaustion and a sour sting of self-loathing. "The fault lies in the hands of Lord Geralt, Lord Nathan, King Frederick, you"—he glared at August—"and Atticus."

August sighed as if Leo was being overdramatic.

"Sounds like you have a lot of feelings to work through," he exhaled.

Leo shook his head and chuckled bitterly at August's lack of understanding. "I'm not processing my trauma," he said through gritted teeth, "I'm admitting the truth. If you had been there, you would have let her down too."

August gave a grave, heavy sigh. His dark eyes lingered on my face, filled with regret and heartache.

"I did fail her," he murmured. "But I learned my lesson. That's the thing about life. You can only do your best. You've got to release all the crap that doesn't make you feel good, but not let those truly special people go."

I could barely speak, so I just nodded as his words settled around us like a heavy blanket of snow. My mind raced, swirling in a whirlpool of what-ifs and fear of potential heartbreak. I didn't want to get attached only to lose it all again—the old wound still ached like a sore reminder of what could happen if I reached out too far. Yet despite everything, I craved having Leo wrap his arms around me and tell me that everything would be alright.

"My royal therapist would be so proud of me," August said with a playful clap of his hands.

"I don't want to talk about it anymore," Leo said.

I clenched my hands into fists, feeling my rage

bubble over. I wanted to scream, wanted to throw something. Words flew at Leo like a torrent of fury, desperate hope, and longing.

"Of course you want to run away the second the conversation gets too hard. You pretend. That's all you ever do. Pretend that I'm not in love with you, that the things I said were empty words, that I don't want more from you than to be my shadow. Pretend that you'll survive if we're not together," I spat.

My anger evaporated as soon as Leo whispered his reply; the sorrow in his voice was like a dagger to my heart. "And I guess I'll pretend that you're not pregnant with another man's baby."

Atticus pulled me close and gave me a comforting squeeze. "Christine," he said tenderly, "there's nothing wrong with celebrating this pregnancy. I'm excited for this baby."

"Are you excited, August?" I asked.

August twisted in his seat to face me, and his expression was a mask of trepidation. "It all happened so fast we haven't had the time to take it in," he said in a dazed voice. "I mean, I like the idea of having a kid—I think. But that doesn't stop me from being scared shitless of actually having one. What if I drop her? Or what if I... Oh, God." He trailed off, his forehead wrinkling in concern.

I reached out, placing a hand on his arm. "You think it's gonna be a girl?"

He shrugged, an uncertain glint in his eye. "I hope it is," he said finally. "A beautiful little princess who looks like her mama? I'd just pamper her rotten."

A soft smile tugged at the corner of his lips before quickly falling away with an almost painful tilt of his head.

Atticus huffed an uncertain laugh. "I'm hoping for a boy, but if I have a daughter…I'd have to string up any suitor who glanced her way. I've already envisioned a thousand scenarios in my head."

I snickered. "Judging by your tendencies, I'd say your son would be a real charmer. I guess I'll be on the lookout for any little girls coming to win his heart," I said with a chuckle.

August's face twisted in agony. "God, if they have even an ounce of my DNA, they'll be troublemakers. What if they end up wild and partying too hard? Or maybe pop pills and screw some girl named Candy and have to take some strong ass antibiotics for a few weeks for a totally normal and treatable disease that I no longer have?"

A hysterical laugh erupted from me, reverberating through the car. "August, you need to take a step back and relax. Our kid is going to be one of a kind."

Atticus chuckled, but his voice was icy as he asked the dreaded question, "What about you, Leo? Boy or girl?"

The car swerved as Leo stepped on the gas. He scrunched his face, exhaling slowly. "Girl," he at last said, his voice heavy with defeat. "I used to take care of my sister when we were younger, and I think I'm better with girls than boys. I bought her first pack of pads when she got her period."

My mouth dropped open before I could stop myself, and I blurted out, "No way! That's so sweet." Once the words escaped me, I remembered we had been arguing just minutes before. My heart sank as my amusement evaporated away.

Leo managed an awkward smirk and returned my gaze for a split second before returning his attention to the road. His lip curved into a half-hearted smile as he spoke. "I think I may have gone a little overboard at the store; Mom was working double shifts, and I guess I felt like I had to step up and take care of this for us," he sighed.

August's eyes widened with panic. "I forgot about periods. What will we do?!" he exclaimed, his voice ringing throughout the car.

Atticus's chuckle sent ripples through the tense atmosphere. "Then we'll buy her pads and chocolate and a heating pad," he said, eyes twinkling with amusement.

"A heating pad is the best present ever," I muttered, a faint smile touching my lips despite the abject fear that lingered in the air.

August's brows knitted together as he blurted out, "Oh God, I'm not ready for any of this. What if she has some health condition or someone hurts her or…or…" His expression plummeted at the thought of it all.

Atticus smiled sympathetically. "Before we come up with all the worst case scenarios, we should celebrate. We're having a baby!" he declared joyfully, punctuating his words with a short laugh.

August reiterated his sentiments quietly. "We're having a baby," he said, his voice somewhere between melancholy and excitement.

Leo smiled softly, his eyes brimming with tears. "A baby."

I placed my hand on my stomach, gently rubbing circles and feeling the life growing within me while I whispered, "We're having a baby."

Chapter Twenty

LEO

"We're almost there," I said as we drove across the bridge leading to the beach house. The bumps in the road caused Christine to stir in the back seat, and I heard Atticus softly cooing over her.

"Christine is still asleep," he said adoringly as his fingers gently ran through her hair, a contented smile on his lips. "Her body needs rest now more than ever." His voice was tender, and both Augustus and I could feel the emotion radiating from him.

"I'm just glad she'll be able to relax for a few days," Augustus said with a sigh of relief. "I can't wait to get her into a warm bath, get some food in her belly. She hasn't complained of nausea, has she?"

Atticus smiled, though there was a bit of sadness in his eyes. "Not yet. But she probably will soon. Glad at least one of you is as obsessed with her as I am," he said wistfully.

My heart hammered against my ribcage when I glanced at Christine's fragile figure sleeping in the rearview mirror. I had put her health at risk with my selfishness. "Do you think she's too stressed? Stress isn't good for a baby."

Augustus sneered, his piercing eyes burning into me. "So now you care about stress? You didn't seem to care last night."

My jaw was tightening as I tried to stay in control of my rage. "Yeah, I fucked up," I muttered. "But I care about her."

Atticus's voice was low and menacing. "Once she's tucked up safe in bed, you and I are gonna have words. Don't forget that I warned you what would happen if you ever insulted Christine about our relationship again. I told you to sort out your own demons, Leo. But you didn't listen. And now it's not just her that's at risk. It's our baby too. So if you do anything to jeopardize my child, I'll kill you."

I could hardly breathe as I muttered my response. "I'm gonna apologize to her."

Augustus's eyes bore into me with disdain as he leaned back in his seat. "Might be too late, Leo."

I snarled, "I know it's too late," aware that my voice wavered as a result of my fury.

I pulled into the beach house driveway, and the crunching of the tires echoed in the stillness. I stared at Christine.

Atticus was possessive and protective, his rough hand sliding under her shirt to caress her skin as he leaned in close. He kissed her softly, then glanced at me, seething with anger and panic. His dark eyes were smoldering with a mix of worry and testosterone. "What now, Leo?" he growled.

My fists tightened into a white-knuckled hold as I stifled the tears that threatened to brim over my cheeks. "I don't know, alright? All I know is that I love her, and I'll be damned if I let anything happen to her," I bit out, letting my gaze pierce his.

"She's my everything," he growled possessively, his voice low and intense. "I was very clear about my expectations of you."

I nodded, swallowing the lump in my throat.

"I heard that," Christine whispered breathlessly.

Her icy blue eyes slowly opened and locked onto mine in the mirror.

Atticus tugged her out of her seat, gathering her in his strong arms. He smiled down at her, his voice low and sultry. "You ready to sleep in a comfortable bed, Little Monster?"

"Let me talk to Leo, first," she said drowsily, her voice raw from lingering sleep.

Augustus's eager voice cut through the tension in the car. "Dibs on snuggling Christine tonight!" He jumped out of the vehicle before Atticus could respond.

"I'll be just outside," Atticus said before glaring at me and following after Augustus.

I flinched at his threat. "I'm really sorry for everything that happened, Christine. I'm just trying to figure it all out."

Christine closed her eyes and let out a long sigh, not responding in the slightest. The silence was deafening as I repeated my apology.

She opened her eyes to meet my gaze in the mirror. "Leo, I want us to work more than anything, but you're going to have to prove it to me," she said resolutely. "I need you to fight for me—or walk away."

She opened the car door and stepped out.

My nostrils flared as I tried to breathe. I watched her, unable to move. I knew she was right. The idea of walking away from her, of losing her forever, was too much. I didn't know if I could fight for her; I wasn't prepared for that.

She glanced back at me as she walked toward the house.

I sat there for a few moments before slowly following after her.

The beach house was consumed by darkness as we approached the entrance. Atticus and Christine were walking ahead, her holding his arm tightly and him tracing circles on her skin with his fingers. It made me sick to my stomach, this stupid longing for something I knew would never happen. Augustus was whispering something to the two of them, a secret I wasn't in on.

Just as they were about to walk up the steps, a deafening shot cracked in the night, and Atticus's body fell violently to the soil. Christine screamed out in horror as Atticus stared at his hands in shock. She rushed to him, tears streaming down her pale cheeks. His shirt was drenched with a deep red, and my heart stopped as I saw the gaping wound in his chest. The sharp corrosive smell of blood filled the air, and I felt my body go numb.

The clamor of chaos erupted around us, and time seemed to stand still. Christine fell to the ground in a heap, her contorted face mirroring the fear that had taken hold of us all. Augustus rushed toward her, but an unseen force seemed to be holding him back. I drew in a shaky breath and sprinted up the steps leading to the front door, feeling like I was running through quicksand. Suddenly, a sharp pain burned through my side as a bullet ripped through the air, followed by another and then another. Blood trickled down my arm as I pushed forward with every ounce of energy I had left. Christine's screams swarmed around us, and I prayed we would make it out alive.

My head thundered with adrenaline, and my vision tunneled down to a single point. Everything was moving so slowly, like I was stuck in a dream. Augustus's voice roared around me, but I couldn't understand what he was saying. I saw Atticus glance up at Christine, and it felt like my entire world cracked in half when he groaned a single word.

"Run!"

I lunged for Christine, throwing myself between her and the approaching men, shielding her with my body. I scooped her up in my arms, barely feeling the weight of her as I stumbled backwards. She was screaming and fighting me every step of the way, desperate to get back to Atticus.

Augustus's voice echoed around us as he yelled for us to get in the car, but it seemed like every shadow was spilling out of the house and rushing toward us. The men in black had their guns raised, ready to fire any second. Fear surged through me as I sprinted toward the car, dragging Christine behind me.

My heart was pounding, fear coursing through my veins as one of them launched toward us, Christine standing frozen in a moment of terror. He barreled toward her with a predatory savagery, his body looming like a massive mountain above us. His face was a twisted mask of fury, and his shaved head glinted in the moonlight.

I had no time to think; I acted on instinct. I dove at him, my limbs carrying me faster than I knew my body could go. My fists flew forward with fervor, barely dodging the click of his gun. I kept punching his face, his blood spilling onto the pavement beneath us as he screamed in agony. He flailed at me with his thick hands, but I felt nothing. All I heard was Christine's sobs and Augustus's screams; all I could feel was the fierce determination to protect her no matter the cost. Atticus had told her to run, and by God, I would make sure she did.

I unleashed a barrage of punches, kicks, and slashes, aiming for the man's face with each strike. I felt my knuckles bruise under the force of my blows, but I didn't care.

"Get the queen!" one of them shouted. "Kill the others!"

I felt a sickening crunch as I snapped the man's neck and spun around just in time to see Christine grabbed by two men, her screams filling the air. She fought them briefly but then stopped, turning to me with a face filled with terror and rage.

I scanned the area, trying to spot Augustus and Atticus, but there was no sign of either of them. I was powerless; I couldn't protect my family.

Christine remained still, watching as two more men threw me to the ground beside her. I was desperate; I wanted her to live. Tears streamed down my cheeks as I begged for her life. "Please, don't hurt her."

"I won't fight," Christine said firmly to the men holding her. "I won't fight." I knew she was thinking of her child; she couldn't risk getting hurt. Even though her face was contorted in rage, she didn't move.

The two men pinned me against the unforgiving ground. Somewhere, Augustus's desperate roar bled through the air.

They viciously carried her away, shoving her into their darkened car and locking it. To my right, I finally saw Augustus. He was hovering beside a lifeless Atticus as he started throwing futile punches at the men that had him pinned down.

"Leo, get up," he screamed as he hopelessly tried to break free and rescue her.

I furiously thrashed against my own captors and unleashed a flurry of punches so powerful they felt like thunder, until I managed to free myself from their grip. With the taste of metallic blood still lingering in my mouth, I quickly clawed my way toward the car. They were pulling away, headed back down the bridge.

Augustus escaped the two men fighting him and leapt forward with all his might, his fist pounding against the hood of the vehicle and his foot viciously kicking the metal. His voice cracked with fear and rage as he hurled obscenities. "Bastard!" he screamed. "Bastard!" His cries echoed throughout the night air, like an omen of what was to come.

I sprinted, trying desperately to race after them, but the car vanished in a blink of an eye, leaving us in its wake.

"What the hell is happening?" I shouted in terror, panic rising in my gut.

"I don't know!" Augustus cried out.

Suddenly, another bullet whizzed inches from us, and my heart plummeted. Augustus scrambled toward the closest assailant and engaged him in a fierce battle. He jabbed his fists mercilessly into his attacker's face, causing a stream of blood to trickle down. I watched, frozen in fear as he wrestled the gun away from the assailant's grasp and pointed it straight at him.

I didn't have time to see Augustus shoot the man, because another attacker pounded the gravel toward me, and I sucked in a deep breath before fighting him. Adrenaline coursing through me, I threw punches and kicks with a ferocity I didn't even know I had, a desperation fueled by the sight of Atticus motionless on the concrete and Christine captured in their grip.

Out of the corner of my eye, I saw Augustus shoot and another man went down, but three more swarmed him. We were outnumbered, and my body and spirit ached from the barrage of attacks, my stitches barely hanging on. Gunshots were ringing through the air, and then, a low scream like a lion's roar filled the space.

I pushed into the attacker with all my might, sending him reeling with a blow to his face. I stepped forward, ready to fight again—for Christine—when Augustus shouted for me to move. Two shots blasted in quick succession, and two more bodies hit the ground.

I heard a yelp of terror from the assailant standing closest to me. Stiffening, I looked past him and saw a nightmarish sight: a figure dressed in glistening crimson, standing in the entrance to the porch. It was hard to tell if it was man or beast, but two menacing pistols were clenched in its grasp and pointed without wavering at the assembled assailants. Its voice rasped in a half-choked, almost insane rasp. "Run, you bastards!" it bellowed before unleashing a torrent of thunder-blasts toward us. Bullets ricocheted off the trees, sparks flying, as we scrambled for safety. In mere moments, the assailant's bullets had carved a swath of destruction around us, leaving only pools of blood and slumped over corpses in their wake.

Augustus and I dove to the ground, our bodies shaking with fear. We could hear him taking out each person one by one, and each time the sound of a gunshot boomed through the air, our hearts dropped. When everything had gone silent, I cautiously looked up and saw Augustus motionless on his back. His eyes were bloodshot and wide with terror. He was alive but had taken a lot of damage from the fight. His clothes were drenched in sweat and splattered with blood. I couldn't help but feel like this was the end for us both.

I sprung up, my heart hammering against my chest, and locked eyes with the rugged man standing on the front porch. I felt like I'd seen him before, but I couldn't place him.

Augustus was the first to realize who he was. "Hudson!" he exclaimed.

The pieces started to fit together in my brain. He was Atticus's right-hand man, sent to protect my family as soon as he heard about the impending danger. How could I have been so stupid? I had been so wrapped up in saving myself that I hadn't thought about them.

With a burst of energy, I rushed over to him, desperation gripping my heart in an icy embrace. "Where is my mother and Daphne?" I shouted, barely able to keep myself upright. Blood coated my clothes, and the metallic tang hung heavy in the air.

"They're hiding in the pantry," Hudson gritted.

I breathed a sigh of relief. "Fuck," I choked out. "Thank you."

Augustus's sobs echoed around us, and I whipped around to see him throwing himself toward Atticus. I had to make sure he was still alive. I desperately dropped back down, finally heaving a sigh of relief when I felt his pulse beating beneath my fingertips. He was alive. And then his eyes opened, and he looked up at me with a tender and eerily calm look.

"Christine?" he breathed out, his voice barely audible.

"They have her," Augustus replied, shaking his head in disbelief as tears streamed down his face. "They have Christine." The fear on both of their faces was apparent, yet the last shred of hope that lingered in their eyes was undeniable. In the midst of danger and death, we had to find a way. "We need to get you to a hospital," Augustus added desperately.

Without hesitating, I wrapped Atticus's arm around my shoulder and pulled his body up from the cold ground. His breathing was labored, each breath ragged and uneven. His face was stained with blood from a deep gash in his chest, and I could feel the pain radiating from him with each step we took forward.

"Where are we going?" Hudson asked.

"We're taking him to a hospital," I said. "Grab my mother and Daphne."

"They could come back," Hudson argued. "They'll be expecting you to go to the hospital."

I growled. "I don't care, and we can't stay here."

The realization that I was putting my entire family in danger by bringing Atticus to the hospital hit me hard, but I had no choice.

Hudson ran off to do my bidding, and Augustus took the opportunity to wrap Atticus's other arm around his shoulder, each of us gritting our teeth against the pain and helping each other navigate through the area. The pain Atticus felt was evident, the hollow look in his eyes only adding to the fear that hung over us all. I had never seen him scared before, and it shook me to the very core.

We painfully lowered his body onto the back seat of the car, and he groaned in agony.

"How bad is it?" I cried out in terror.

"It's okay," Augustus tried to reassure us through gritted teeth and clenched jaw.

"No, it isn't," Atticus whispered painfully. "She's gone." Atticus grabbed my arm and pulled me urgently toward him, his grip tight and unyielding. "You need to go after Christine." His blood was soaking everything in sight, the metallic smell drifting in the air. His face was so pale and ghostly, like a white sheet of paper. We had no time to spare.

"I will," I swore as I felt his grasp loosen slowly, and my heart clenched in panic.

Augustus bellowed out a scream of frustration and fear as Atticus's eyes slowly fluttered closed and his body went limp.

And in true DuPont fashion, Atticus's last words were a demand.

Chapter Twenty-One

CHRISTINE

Rage shrouded me like an unrelenting cloak of despair as I was tossed into the car, barely noticing the cold leather seat as it welcomed my numb body. The driver peeled out of there, and I sank helplessly. I couldn't fight them. Not without risking the baby.

The red blotches that stained my clothing seemed to mock me with the last vestiges of Atticus, as though they were a cruel reminder of how death had claimed him. No words could offer any comfort, no amount of reassurance or explanation could take away the ache in my broken heart. I looked out at the world through eyes blurred with tears, not knowing which direction I was heading. All I wanted was to escape, to find a place hidden away from the chaotic sorrow that had consumed my life.

The men who captured me didn't speak. They were on edge, worried about what would await them when we arrived at the castle.

"You weren't supposed to kill DuPont," one of them murmured softly.

"We'll blame someone else," the other said back.

He was dead.

Atticus was dead.

I didn't even know about Leo and August, but I feared the worst.

It was a long drive. Exhaustion and fatigue finally hit me, and I fell asleep somewhere between the safe house in the castle, but was woken up by a gruff voice when the car stopped.

I opened my eyes in confusion, momentarily forgetting my dire circumstances as I took in my surroundings. The castle walls were tall and imposing, with no hint of warmth or welcome emanating from inside.

My captors dragged me out of the car, pushing me forward toward the entrance. Fear and grief rose up within me like a tsunami of emotion, threatening to sweep me away in its powerful tides. But I held fast, determined not to break down here in front of them.

We stepped into the coldness of the castle's hallways, and every dark corner seemed to taunt me with its eerie presence. My captors quickly deposited me in an empty room and shut the door behind them. The frigid atmosphere penetrated my clothing and settled into my bones like a heavy blanket of misery. Tears surged up in my eyes as grief overwhelmed me with a crushing force. Everything within me screamed out in agony—the confusion, sadness and despair had taken on a living form, consuming me in its depths.

The ache for Atticus clawed at my heart, silencing any protests from my lips as the tides of sorrow rolled over me until all that remained were muffled cries into the emptiness surrounding me. My raw emotion echoed off the walls until eventually it faded away, leaving only stillness behind.

I stayed on that cold floor for what felt like eternity, alone with my thoughts, exposed and vulnerable until finally exhaustion hit me once more, beckoning for sleep's embrace.

And so I lay there on the hard ground, allowing myself to drift away in numbed peace, knowing that however uncertain tomorrow may be, today belonged only to grief.

"It's all your fault!" a maniacal voice shrieked, breaking through my sleep. I jolted up and saw Theodore DuPont leering at me, his blade glinting in the moonlight. "I knew you'd be the death of him." His clothes were disheveled and covered in blood. His icy eyes had turned to a deep malevolence as his face contorted with a crazed intensity.

I desperately scrambled to my feet as my eyes frantically searched for an escape route.

"Did you hear me?" he roared. "My son is dead because of you! You killed Atticus!"

The words felt like a vise crushing my heart as guilt and rage burned inside me.

I tried to contain my fear, using it instead to bolster my courage. "You murdered him," I said grimly, my voice shaking as I warily glanced around the room. "You wanted to punish us for some twisted plan of yours."

He stepped back, adjusting his collar as he was clearly taken aback by my words. "He never would have been there if it weren't for you."

"You killed him," I said with more force, as bile rose in my throat and my pulse raced with terror. "You let your ambition consume you, and it cost Atticus his life."

He shook his head, his movements jerky and frantic. "No. No. This is your fault."

I sobbed. "I loved him!" I wrapped my arms around myself. "I loved him."

"You didn't love him. Women like you are incapable of love. It's why Isabelle didn't choose me. It's why you wouldn't choose him."

I felt my chest cave in as I looked at him in wonderment. "Is that what you tell yourself?" I shrieked. "You had Lord Nathan kill Isabelle. Do you blame him for her death, too?" I took a step closer to him and tipped my chin up. "You killed them both. And for what? You're a married man with a beautiful, selfless wife. You had everything and you threw it away. Not me."

I was shaking with fury as I held his gaze, and I saw a flicker of doubt cross his face. I knew he couldn't bear to admit that I was right, but it didn't matter.

"Are you going to spend your life blaming everyone for your failures?" I asked with an icy calm.

"Shut up! Shut up! Shut up!" he screamed while holding his ears.

"The woman you fell in love with was strong and vibrant. She didn't want you because you're weak, Theodore. Atticus was twice the man you'll ever be. Isabelle didn't love you. She couldn't. Because you were a coward. Because you wanted to tame her."

He stared at me in disbelief. "You're wrong."

I let out a bitter laugh. "Do you know why I love

your son?" I narrowed my eyes. "I love that he helps me blossom, where you pluck petals. He loved me for who I was. He—" I paused, realizing I was already speaking in the past tense.

A tortured sob left my lips, and I shook my head, my vision blurring as tears escaped down my cheeks. "You're a coward," I said dispassionately, my eyes averting his gaze in shame. "You love to control people. You tried to control Atticus with all your threats. But he defied you."

"I'm a DuPont," he said between clenched teeth. "I demand you show me respect!"

"Sure. I'll show *you* some motherfucking respect!" I screamed, my stomach heaving with a crazed emotion I was desperately trying to control. "You're a coward!" I repeated with manic conviction. "Your son defied you, so you ripped the life away from him. You're the real demon. You're nothing."

I held my stomach protectively and he eyed the move, his expression saturated with calculative intent. My chest was heaving with terror as the silence built. "You're pregnant," he hissed in a harsh whisper.

I didn't answer him. I refused to admit it out loud in his presence.

He took a step closer to me, the air between us alive

with terror. "You're having a DuPont," he growled threateningly.

I shook my head vigorously, barely able to breathe or speak in the face of his overwhelming horror. "No—"

He took intimidating steps closer to me, and he towered over me, his searing glare reducing me to a shaking wreck. His voice was low and full of menace. "At first, I was going to take away your privilege of birthing a DuPont, but now this is my last chance."

My voice caught in my throat as icy fear twisted my insides. "W-what do you mean?"

He curled his fingers tightly around my wrist. A sinister glint flickered within them, and I felt the full weight of his evilness. With a low growl, he spoke with a rabid intensity. "The second this baby is born, he's mine. I'm going to fix this. I'm going to fix everything."

A wave of terror swept over me, sinking into the depths of my being like an anchor. Desperate to free myself from his grasp, I croaked, "W-what did you say?"

"You won't be able to control me anymore," he growled with a twisted grin. "You'll be insignificant. Useless."

His hand then groped my abdomen, and I watched in horror as he pressed harder and harder.

"You're hurting me!" I shoved at his chest, sending him back a step.

He chuckled darkly. "I'm trying to, Christine." He brushed his lips across my ear. "I need to make sure that you never defy me. A firm hand makes a strong child. And this baby will be indestructible."

I cringed as his face moved lower, and his hot breath, laced with alcohol, blasted my bare neck.

"No—"

And then he kissed me.

He suddenly lunged forward, pressing his hard body against mine, smothering me with his weight and might. I tried to push him away, but his force was too strong. I clawed at his armor-like chest, desperate to break free and escape my fate. My shrieks of anguish were muffled against his lips. In that moment, I felt trapped and help-less, just like the girl Lord Geralt had once tried to conquer, enslave, and take away all those years ago.

He finally broke away from me, and I crumpled to the ground in a heap of despair. I never wanted to go back to that moment of terror and despair again, but alas, here I was. The fear coursed through my veins as I shook uncontrollably in the aftermath of my emotional breakdown.

"My son is dead," he screeched, thundering his fists onto the buttery oak wall, splinters flying into the air.

His eyes were hollow and sinister, like empty pits of a man possessed by evil. "You're not a DuPont. And I will take what is mine!" he rasped through his teeth.

The room felt colder. I shivered as I took a step backward, fear and sweat seeping from my skin like droplets of honey. "You will serve many purposes in this castle," he hissed, his voice like a whip cracking in the air. "You will become queen. You will marry Lord Nathan! And you will birth me a new heir."

I shook my head frantically. "You can't have my baby!" I screamed, shaking with terror.

He tilted his head, his face blank. My blood ran cold as I heard those next words that seemed to pierce the heavy silence of the room. "I thought you would've learned by now," he snarled. "I will do as I please. No one will stop me."

My lungs emptied as I looked upon him with terror. "What is wrong with you?" I sobbed harder. "Why? Why are you doing this?"

He moved forward, a menacing glimmer in his eye. "Because you should've been mine, Isabelle. Because you *will* be mine." He stepped closer and closer, his breath reeking of madness. "I've tried to control you. But you're too strong for that."

"I'm not Isabelle!" I yelled desperately.

"No?" he asked mockingly, his lips curling into a

sinister smile.

I frantically shook my head.

"Ah, Isabelle. Together, we shall rule the world." He reached for me and I screamed in fear.

"No! No! No!" I yelled, shaking violently. "Stop it! Stop it!"

He grabbed my dress and I thrashed in his grip. "A DuPont is to rule over his subjects."

I struggled to break free as his grip tightened. "You're wrong! I don't care about power! I don't want it! I don't want it! I don't want it!"

"You will learn to crave it."

He brought his face closer to me, and I squirmed, kicking and wiggling with all my might. "You will learn to consume it."

I felt his hand brush my bare side. "Or I will consume you first," he whispered.

I was breathing hard, my nostrils flaring, as I stopped fighting him.

He dragged me across the room, kicking and screaming at the same time.

"Please, stop!"

I knew I was capable of fighting him back, but I just *couldn't*. I couldn't force myself to be strong. I couldn't bring myself to fight. Not with the grief terrorizing my system. Not with the memories assaulting my brain.

He grabbed me by the delicate skin of my arm, digging his fingers into my flesh. I yelped in pain, my eyes watering from the sharp sting. "I'll take your power and I'll take your strength," he said in a low, hissing tone. "I'll take your baby and I'll take your life." He stared at my stomach. "I will destroy you, Isabelle. You'll finally be mine."

"I'm not Isabelle," I sobbed. "I'm Christine."

I felt my body go numb as his words from before seemed to echo in the air between us. He stared at me with a twisted sense of glee in his eyes. His grip on my arm tightened, cutting off my circulation and causing pain to course through me.

My heart hammered against my chest as I tried to break free from his grasp, but it was no use. He was too strong for me. I whimpered in terror, feeling all the energy being sucked out of me.

He continued to look at me crazily as he spoke again, "I can tame you. I can fix everything." His voice was low and menacing, and I knew that whatever he said, he meant it.

In a desperate attempt to escape, I thrashed around, but he simply tightened it once more. Tears streamed down my cheeks as I looked up into his face in horror. "No," I whimpered softly.

He gave a low growl before continuing, "Careful,

Isabelle. We don't want to hurt the baby." He paused before looking down at my stomach with an eerie gleam in his eye. "Elizabeth will be thrilled. We can start over," he said with a sneer on his lips. "This was the way it was always meant to be."

A chill ran through me as I shook my head frantically. "NO! I'm not Isabelle!" My voice had been reduced to a whisper, but the desperation behind it was evident.

"Yes, you are," he replied calmly, his voice filled with malice that made my skin crawl. He took a step back to look at me from head to toe before continuing, "You have always been Isabelle."

His words left me stunned and horrified beyond belief as they slowly sank into my mind like burning hot embers into flesh. How could this be happening? How could this be real? Nothing mattered anymore except for the sheer terror.

"Get some rest," he spat before releasing me. "We have a coronation and a wedding tomorrow."

"Both?" I choked out.

"I'm tired of waiting. You will submit, Isabelle!"

I held my hands up in surrender. "Okay," I choked out. "Okay."

He stood up and straightened his clothes, eyeing me with that dark gaze that made me sick to my stomach.

Chapter Twenty-Two

CHRISTINE

I stared into the mirror, my eyes wide with horror as I saw the tightly-fitted, lacy monstrosity enveloping my slender body, barely hiding the bruises that were scattered like a wildflower garden. A horde of people had been swarming around me for hours, slathering my skin in makeup that resembled war paint. I felt numb, both physically and emotionally. I was completely overwhelmed by grief and misery. My men were gone, just like my freedom and my inner strength that had disintegrated with Atticus, so the only thing I had left was myself.

The air around me was thick with tension, nobody ever daring to say a word about what had happened last night or about my tears streaming down my face or lips. Everyone was just as scared as I was.

I knew what I had to do—succumb to Theodore DuPont's demands and marry Lord Nathan or risk my unborn child's life and keep fighting until the end. But what did I have left? Nothing. Not anymore.

Just my baby, and Theodore DuPont was even threatening to take that, too.

My body twitched as a maid approached me, her gloved hands gripping a small black box. "Lady Christine," she said softly, her voice cutting through the loudest silence I had ever heard. I timidly glanced at the box she was offering me, my breath freezing in my lungs as I spotted a simple black ribbon wrapped around it.

My heart thudded painfully against my chest as I realized what it was—my wedding band from Lord Nathan. A reminder of defeat, a punishment for loving someone else. My gaze shifted toward the ring that August had picked out for me, my beloved Augustus, who I would never see again. Tears pooled in my eyes, and my throat tightened, struggling to contain the cries that threatened to escape me.

"He requests you wear it instead of..." Her voice trailed off as I stared helplessly at the two rings—symbols of what could have been and what would never be. I wanted to run away and never look back, to take back my freedom and reclaim my life, but there was nowhere to go. I was trapped between two unfulfilled desires, and there was no way out.

With trembling fingers, I took the box from the maid's hands, not knowing if this action would cause me more pain or bring me some kind of peace. All I knew was that I had no other choice.

"Lord Nathan insists on seeing you before the ceremony, Your Majesty," the maid announced.

I scoffed, a dread knotting in my stomach. "I thought it was bad luck for the bride and groom to meet before the wedding?"

The maid nodded and exchanged a glance with her friends. She lowered her voice. "If I may speak, my lady."

My heart thudded as I tried to keep my breathing normal. "What is it?"

"It's not just your life on the line," she said, tears streaming down her face. "We've all lost friends and family. I implore you to—"

"I won't do anything that'll irritate Lord Nathan," I said, cutting her off. I was aware of his power over us all in this manor, and no one was safe if I made him angry.

"Gratefully, Lady Christine," she muttered before hastily exiting the room. My heart sank, pumping a rush of adrenaline through my system as I heard the door clatter closed behind her. I reluctantly squared my shoulders in preparation for Lord Nathan's entrance. I shouldn't succumb to him, I had to be brave—I was the heir to the throne, and he was nothing but a conniving pawn.

When he slunk through the door, I forced down my fear and steadied my voice. "Lord Nathan," I snarled, my ire boiling over in my chest. He wore a pristine black suit with a deep blue vest and a rage red tie, his hair slick and his skin like porcelain. His deep blue eyes were clear yet seething with egotism. I wanted to scream in his face, but instead I buried my warring emotions deep inside and faced him with a stoic mask of composure.

"My, what a stunning bride you are. I can almost see why my brother was so smitten with you," he said.

I kept my mouth shut, too broken to speak. To think. I didn't have the strength to fight him.

"You caused quite a mess when you ran away," he continued, his voice brimming with glee. "The maids were scrubbing blood off the floor for days. But we finally got you back." I tried to contain my rage as I closed my eyes and opened them again, releasing a deep sigh.

"Was there anything you wanted, Lord Nathan?" I asked, my voice quivering with inner conflict.

"So submissive." He sneered. "I knew killing your men was the best way to break you. Theodore was anguished, but it was for the best, don't you think?"

My insides were boiling with terror, and my heart pounded a thousand miles per hour. I could feel my muscles tighten and my teeth grind together, each taking a tremendous amount of effort to stay composed.

"I believe I have something to propose," Lord Nathan said, his eyes ablaze with an insane fervor as he glanced at the ring box in my grasp. Fearfully, I opened it. Inside was an exquisite silver ring—its band broad and encrusted with a massive blue stone, artfully adorned with a silver filigree design. "I thought this would be perfect for you," he murmured softly, his eyes glistening with crazed pleasure.

"Why?" I queried, fear coursing through my blood. My conflicting emotions—rage and grief—throbbed inside me in an endless battle for control.

"It's my mother's ring. My brother had been holding onto it until the day he died. I assume he intended it for you. It's a symbol of our power. Now a symbol of our union. We'll be wed soon, wife."

"Christine," I said, trying to steady my shaking voice. "My name is Christine."

He snarled, with a malicious glint in his eyes that sent an icy chill up my spine. The way he savored the moment, it was clear he was enthralled with the idea of tormenting me. "If I'm being honest, I have no desire to wed you, *wife*. My desires are far from what you'd expect from a gentle-hearted man. But there is something dark about marrying you. Something that brings me a wicked pleasure. Something that sends a rush of heat through my veins and almost makes me queasy with anticipation."

I found myself aghast in a state of fearful paralysis, feeling the looming terror as my racing mind fought against my inner turmoil. I could barely croak out, "And what would that be?"

His lips twisted into a satisfied smirk as he clapped his hands together and spoke, "I think it's such a glorious thing to break such an intrepid woman—the woman who killed my brother. Don't get me wrong, I'm grateful that the bastard is gone. But it's still just so…wonderful."

My body tensed as I squirmed, trying to reclaim the self-control I had lost. With a deep breath, I found the courage to re-establish my dignity and spat out, "I assume you want revenge?" He simply chuckled, further raising the hair on my neck.

He grinned. "Anger is better spent on more ambitious ventures, don't you think? You're nothing. Just a girl with the right blood flowing through her body. A pretty face. I don't need revenge. If my brother let you best him, then I say he deserved it."

He took one step closer. And then another. DuPont guards came into view, both of them clutching guns as Lord Nathan approached, prepared to shoot me if I tried anything. "Why are you doing this to me if you don't want me?" I asked through clenched teeth.

He nonchalantly continued, as if we weren't discussing the most horrifying experience of my life. "I have always been envious of my brother. He was blessed with the lion's share of my parents' love and attention, while I was left in the shadows. Yet here I am, in possession of something he could never have. How amazingly delicious!"

I felt my knuckles tighten around the box, and my eyes flooded with rage. "I will end your life. Just like I ended his."

He took a single step forward, taunting me with his audacity. Our faces were so close I could hear the slow rasp of his breath over the pounding of my heart, and I knew that one swift move would be enough to break him down once and for all. His death was imminent.

"You won't kill me, Christine," he said with a smile. "You'll want to keep DuPont's baby safe. You'll be my wife." He bent down to pick up the ring box. "You'll wear this ring every day, reminding you of our union."

I could feel my pulse racing. Anger was boiling inside me, and I had to remind myself what was at stake.

My baby.

I had to keep my head in the game. It was the only way I'd survive. "You're definitely braver than your brother was," I said.

As expected, he grinned. I knew Lord Nathan's weak spot. He was like every other pathetic lord in this kingdom. He wanted to prove himself.

"Oh?"

I gave him a grin full of malice. "He screamed when I killed him. Was so terrified. I wonder, will you beg for mercy when I kill you, Lord Nathan?"

"I never beg, darling. You'll learn that soon enough. Get ready. The ceremony starts in an hour."

A small noise escaped me. A crack in my numbness. I felt the fight return. "I'll kill you, you motherfucker."

"My. The more you talk, the more I look forward to fucking you."

I gritted my teeth, clenching them until my jaw ached. "You're a psycho."

"I'm a survivor, that's all." He took one last step forward, and the guards raised their weapons. "And, it's time for you to take your place as my wife. Do something with your face. I expect my bride to be flawless." He turned and headed for the door.

I flexed with rage, every muscle in my body tense. Nathan's cologne was heavy and cloying. I wanted to lean back and gag. The smell lingered long after I heard his footsteps travel down the hall. Someone shut the door, locking me in with his suffocating stench and the remnants of his threats.

I let out a weak breath, feeling alive for the first time since returning to this castle. A fight grew within me. I didn't want Lord Nathan to win. I didn't want Theodore DuPont to steal my baby. I had to fight.

I turned to look at the mirror once more, steadying my breathing as I tried to come up with a solution. I could still fight. I had to be careful but—

"Is it true?" a soft voice full of agony asked.

I spun around and gaped at Elizabeth DuPont as she slipped into the room. She wore all black, her eyes rimmed red as she stared hopelessly at me.

"Elizabeth," I croaked.

She took another step toward me. "Is. It. True? Is my Atticus…" Her expression crumpled.

I opened and closed my mouth, not sure what to say to this woman or whose side she was on. "Atticus is…" I didn't want to say the word.

"Tell me, Christine. I have to know. We don't have much time. Just…is he dead?"

I swallowed the thick ball of emotion and slowly nodded my head. There was no way Atticus survived that gunshot to the chest. I had to accept it. I had to say goodbye.

Tears fell down her face, and she looked away.

"Oh, God," she groaned, gripping her temple. "I have a headache," she muttered. "I need to go lie down, but I can't." She shook her head and looked back at me. "I keep thinking it's all a bad dream. I'm just going to wake up and be with him, but it's not going to happen. He's dead. Atticus is dead." She leaned against the wall, sliding to the ground in a heap.

I rushed to the other side of the room and knelt beside her, patting her back awkwardly, and she silently sobbed into my shoulder. "I'm sorry," I whispered, feeling the sting of hot tears on my cheeks.

More tears fell from my eyes, and I felt myself break again. Atticus was gone. He was truly gone. I mourned all the time we didn't have. All the experiences we never got. Time. I just wanted more time.

"And you're pregnant? Is it his?"

I shrugged. "I don't know. Your husband says he's going to take my baby, Elizabeth. We have to stop him."

She shook her head. "We can't. I'm not strong enough."

I looked her in the eye. "Yes. You are. You can help me, Elizabeth. We can—"

She cut me off. "I'm not strong. For years I've endured Theodore. He liked to hurt me… At first, I thought he hated who I was…" She paused to stroke my cheek. "Then I realized he hated me because of who I *wasn't*."

I swallowed. She knew about Isabelle.

"Elizabeth. You have to help me. For Atticus. For…" I paused to grab her hand and press it to my stomach. "You have to help me for your grandchild."

She stared at where our hands touched and shook her head. "I have to go," she murmured before pulling back. I felt my stomach drop as she pulled herself off the ground and dusted herself off.

"Elizabeth, please," I begged.

"I'll see you at the coronation and wedding," she replied, her tone vacant.

I punched the wall when she disappeared through the door.

Chapter Twenty-Three

CHRISTINE

"I solemnly promise and swear to govern the people of Aldrich. I will, to my power, cause law and justice, in mercy, to be executed in all my judgments. I will, to the utmost of my power, maintain the laws of humanity and the true profession of right and wrong. The things which I have here before promised, I will perform and keep. So help me God."

I uttered the sacred vow, my voice reverberating off the walls of the cathedral. A shiver inched up my spine as I felt the priest's eyes on me, like a hawk sizing up its prey. He slowly lifted the golden crown, which glittered brightly under the light of the chandeliers. I closed my eyes as he lowered it upon my head, its weight an eternal reminder of my responsibility and burden.

"Let it be known to all gathered," he proclaimed, "that I have bestowed upon this woman the honor and rights of the queen of Aldrich."

The cathedral was eerily silent, only a few sniffles reverberating in the distance. I opened my eyes and surveyed the scene before me. The lords were captive in their pews, the guards' spears shimmering in defiance, while I stood amongst them, crowned and unafraid—the queen of Aldrich.

I slowly spun around, surveying the solemn crowd, my face contorted in rage. Lord Nathan had made good on his promise and taken away my kingdom, leaving me with nothing more than a broken spirit. My eyes roved over each of my loyal lords and ladies, maids and peasants alike. Despite our imminent downfall, the support of my people was unflinching.

A single clink of a drinking glass reverberated through the room, and I blinked back tears of frustration. Never before had I felt so utterly alone in a room full of people. The sound of a lively melody suddenly filled the void, but no one was brave enough to take the floor. This was no celebration. There was no song and dance in honor of my defeat.

I closed my eyes, trying to remember what it felt like

to be free. But it was gone—I was missing in action. When Atticus died, so did his Little Monster.

My vision tunneled as the reality of what I was about to do overwhelmed me. I stumbled to catch my breath, the anticipation sucking the air out of the grand chamber like a vacuum.

The room hung silent in a state of suspended animation. Every eye was upon me, though I could barely make out their faces in my bleariness. Anxiety pooled inside me like lead, anchoring me to the spot.

Then, a symphony of rustling and whispers. I snapped my head up in time to see Lord Nathan emerge from the shadows with a malicious look on his face. He had been at the forefront of it all—this union of marriage and coronation that had rocked the kingdom to its core.

The crowd stayed silent as I stood there, waiting for the fate my life had become.

"You look stunning, my queen," he crooned, his voice oily and smooth. He sneered before leaning in and whispering for all to hear, "I can't wait to fuck you while you wear the crown."

I snapped, my teeth gritted in rage. His arm looped through mine, and I could feel his grip tightening. My eyes flickered over the crowd before finally settling on Elizabeth and Theodore DuPont. Elizabeth simply stared ahead of her, vacant in her gaze. Theodore's eyes bored into me, a hint of madness dancing within them as he saw me crowned—as if my being here only further solidified his demented belief that I was Isabelle to him.

Lord Nathan grabbed my hip, his grip possessive and cruel. The orchestra continued to play their dulcet tunes, but all I heard was the thundering of my heart. He slid closer to me, his words a damning promise for all to hear: "I'm going to soak your bastard baby with my cum."

Elizabeth gasped, and in that moment, I felt all my muscles tense and a feeling of indignation surge through me. I wished to have a weapon of my own so that I could break free from this place. But as I started to turn, I saw Elizabeth reach into the depths of her dress and pull out a glinting dagger. With a confidence that shocked me, she locked eyes with her husband. At the same moment, the band stopped playing. Elizabeth screamed with rage as her voice echoed through the court, "This is for Atticus, you son of a bitch!"

The crowd gasped in horror as Elizabeth plunged the sharpened blade into Theodore's neck. Scarlet liquid gushed forth and sprayed all over those nearby and soaked her own skin in its warmth. Lord Nathan lunged forward while Theodore crumbled to the ground, choking on his own blood in his last desperate attempts at life.

Elizabeth let the knife slip from her hands, and Theodore took one last breath before he died.

The lords ran out of the chamber in a frenzy, leaving Elizabeth standing still in the center of the room. Her gaze was transfixed on her deceased husband, but no emotion stirred upon her stoic face. Then Lord Nathan stepped toward her with a chilling glare, and I was about to rush to her defense when two guards clamped Elizabeth's arms together and pinned her to the ground. "No! No!" Nathan shouted, his voice trembling with rage. He strode closer, thrusting his finger at me. "This is all your doing! I know it! You will pay for this!"

Cries of agony reverberated off the walls, echoing into the chapel. Suddenly, the main doors were ripped open with a booming crash. In their wake, a powerful gust of air brought with it an absurdly enormous group of men. Clad in mismatched armor, they looked as if they had only recently emerged from a long and grueling battle. Leo, August, and Hudson strode in at the head of the army, followed closely by Eva. Before any of them had a chance to draw their weapons, the DuPont guards raised their guns menacingly. The tension in the room became tangible, and I didn't know what to expect next.

A raging scream tore through the air as Lord Nathan clamped down on me. His fingers dug into my skin, his strength stronger than I'd anticipated. He yanked a jagged blade from its sheath hooked to his waist, the sharp edge pressed against my throat. Fear seized me in its chilling grip.

My men roared and surged forward, but it was too late—I was already at his mercy. I glimpsed Leo running toward us, the fire in his eyes igniting a spark of hope inside me, Eva right behind him. August took down a DuPont man with a flying tackle and slammed the head of his hammer into the man's skull, and for a brief moment, he made eye contact with me—and I knew what had to be done.

Hudson killed the DuPont guards holding Elizabeth and pulled her into his chest, stroking her hair as he stared at me. "Fight," he mouthed.

I stomped on Lord Nathan's foot, making him groan in pain. I squeezed my eyes shut and braced for the feel of the blade sliding through my skin.

But it never came.

Nathan's grip slackened and I jolted from his grasp, my breathing heavy. Pools of red liquid cascaded from his throat, staining the marble floors beneath us. I glanced up at Eva, who stood imperiously with a blade pressed to Nathan's throat. Her lips twisted into a sadistic smirk as she pushed the weapon deeper into his flesh.

"Surrender," she commanded coldly.

"You will never win this fight," Nathan croaked, undeterred.

Leo snorted in derision and surveyed the room with scornful eyes. Nathan trembled and held Leo's gaze as I felt a fire ignite in my chest. I moved to stand amongst my men.

"You tried to take my wife," August growled, veins popping from his neck.

"You tried to take my baby," Leo bellowed, his body shaking with fury.

My heart thumped wildly, a sense of empowerment taking hold. I held Eva's gaze for a moment before turning to Lord Nathan.

"Bow to me, Lord Nathan," I commanded, my tone now laced with hatred. Taking the shining sword from Eva's grip, I pointed the blade toward Nathan's chest. He locked eyes with me, his face a mask of rage. He didn't move, so I stepped closer and pressed the sharpened steel into his chest. "Now!" I screeched, the venom making me tremble.

He dropped to his knees in surrender—eyes wild,

breath ragged. His hands shook as he begged for mercy. Bile rose in my throat as he pleaded, but I hardened my heart.

"You murdered Atticus," I spat, my voice razor-sharp. "You deserve a fate much worse than death. And I'm going to kill you."

With a sinister notion of amusement, Lord Nathan sneered and said, "Kill me, and my guards will kill you."

I fixed my gaze upon his face and bellowed in defiance, "Your men work for me. They know of your lies, Lord Nathan!"

Panic brimmed in his eyes as he spluttered, "You don't have the nerve to take my life. You're too cowardly."

A feral rage erupted within me, and as a live wire of fury, I charged forward and struck his face with all my strength, my fist slamming against his jaw. The crack echoed off the walls of the cathedral. He staggered back with a howl of pain and looked up to see me poised like a hawk over its prey. With a voice of thunder and fire, I declared, "You know what, Lord Nathan? I'm the Bloody Queen. And as my first decree, I sentence you to death!"

With one last swipe of my blade, I severed Lord Nathan's head from his body. A collective gasp echoed through the cathedral. His head spun through the air and tumbled to the floor in a sickening thud. Blood spurted from his neck in a gory fountain, coating the marble ground with thick drops of red.

The room was silent except for my heavy breathing.

My sword clattered to the ground, and I felt Leo's strong arms encircling me, pulling me into him. I shuddered in his embrace, my heart pounding in my chest. It was finally over.

My arms felt heavy as I lifted them and pulled away. Leo wrapped his hands around my wrists, a calloused grip cutting through the violence that filled my veins. His lips landed softly on mine, uttering a promise of love in the midst of this carnage. I whispered it back as a dozen men knelt before me, their voices a chorus of loyalty.

Leo released me, and August surged forward to wrap me up in a warm embrace. He murmured against my skin, his words a promise to keep me safe. His kisses were sweet emblems of love and affection in this place of death and destruction. I held him tightly, desperate to capture the moment and carry it with me forever.

In a wild frenzy, Leo began barking orders at the shell-shocked soldiers. August tugged on my arm, urging me to flee. But I couldn't. I was determined.

"We're not leaving," I declared. "We're getting

married right here. Right now." My voice echoed in the smoldering ruins, the ashes of our fallen enemies still dripping off our bodies. "The world needs to see that we are an unstoppable force." Leo grabbed my hand and August's and pulled us together, joining us in an iron-clad embrace as the surviving Redview army and lords cheered in victory.

Astonishment pierced my core as my dearest friend Leo uttered the words, "I think Atticus might be sad to miss your wedding."

Stunned, I could only squeak out my disbelief. "He's alive?" I gasped. Perplexed, I stared into Leo's eyes, searching for the answer I desperately needed. He gave a small nod, and a faint smile brushed across his face.

"He might not be well enough to walk you down the aisle, but he's okay." My heart was bursting with joy and relief; the tsunami of emotions felt like an ocean wave crashing into me.

A million questions flooded my mind in a single moment, but I had to start somewhere. "What happened?" I asked.

Leo looked around. "He was hurt pretty badly. Needed emergency surgery. But he survived."

Elizabeth's voice cracked with hope as she cried, "Atticus?" and ran toward us, Hudson scurrying to keep up. Leo glanced between me and her, and I gave the slightest nod. She had saved us.

"He is," Leo confirmed.

Elizabeth gasped and Hudson held her up as she clutched her chest.

"Where is he?" I demanded.

August grinned, a cruel glint in his eyes. "I had to knock him out before he followed us into that damned castle, otherwise he'd be dead by now," he said with perverse satisfaction. "He's in a secure place, no doubt cursing us all."

"Take me to him," Elizabeth and I said in unison.

August smirked and laced our fingers together. "I was so looking forward to a bloody wedding, love," he said mockingly.

I chewed my lip and smiled softly at him. "We'll still have time for our wedding tonight," I said, warmth flooding my veins at the thought, "but first, I have to see my Monster."

Chapter Twenty-Four

ATTICUS

Heavy and sluggish, I blinked a few times, peeling my eyelids apart like I was opening them for the first time. It felt like pushing two brick blocks apart to look around. Every muscle in my body tensed, and my chest felt heavy, like it was filled with concrete. It hurt so fucking bad. My heart pounded in my ears, and just when I thought it would burst from trying to push out of my chest, the pain dissipated.

The bullet almost lodged itself in my heart. The doctors said I was *lucky*.

Good thing I didn't have a heart anymore. The

fuckin' thing was a nuisance, so I handed it to Christine for safekeeping. She needed what little love I possessed more than I ever did.

"Atticus?" Christine said hesitantly. The sound of her soft voice made me smile for a moment.

My chapped lips burned as I smiled and croaked, "Little Monster."

Her hair was plastered to her head and neck, dripping a trail of water onto the floor. A T-shirt that could not contain her beautiful curves was too big for her frame. The tight pants clung to her long legs. Her eyes had dark circles under them, and tears leaked from them when she saw me. "You saved her," I choked out when I saw Leo and August standing in the corner of the hospital room.

For so long, I thought I had to rely on myself to keep my Little Monster safe. I didn't trust anyone else to do what was necessary. But when I was fighting for my life, they were fighting to save hers. Maybe it wasn't so bad to have them loving her too. They stepped up when I couldn't, and I'd always be in their debt for that.

"I thought you were..." Christine cried before stroking my cheek. She cried silently, a few tears dripping down her cheeks as she looked at me.

I pawed at her hand, my fingers so fucking slow like I was trying to move through molasses. Even that simple movement was enough to make me feel like I was going to pass out. "I'm here," I gasped, since I was out of breath. "I'll always be here, Little Monster." I was open]and vulnerable in a way that I had never been before.

"I love you," she whispered, kissing my fingers.

That one sentence was more than I could ever dream of. "I love you more." My heart beat faster. Were there tears in my eyes? "Are you okay? Is the baby…"

"Leo and August wouldn't let me see you until I got checked out," she said while side-eyeing them. "Baby is…good." I breathed out a sigh, releasing some of the tension in my chest. "I got to hear a little heartbeat." Before I could fully start breathing again, she continued, "I'm a little weak and they made me get some fluids, though."

My chest constricted. "You heard the heartbeat?" I asked. I wanted to be there for that moment. I wanted to be there for every moment.

"It was beautiful," Leo said, his voice a daze from his spot in the corner.

August approached the side of the bed with a smile. "Sorry I knocked you out, brother. Couldn't risk you getting hurt again."

"You fucker," I groaned, making him laugh like the asshole he was.

Well, August wasn't a complete waste of talent

anymore. Damn, who would've thought the ex-royal would actually have a heroic bone in his body? No matter what had happened in the past, I was proud of him. He'd stepped up for Christine, and that was all that mattered.

"Hey, August?" I said while trying to keep my tone as sincere and humble as possible. Compliments were never my strong suit, but I owed him this one.

"Yeah?" he replied without taking his eyes off the horizon.

"You stepped up for Christine when she needed you most. You proved yourself more than I ever could've imagined. Being your brother is an honor that I don't take for granted." I clapped him on the back. "You're a good man, August. A really good man."

August's mouth was left gaping open in shock. I could see the awe and pride in his eyes, swiftly followed by disbelief and embarrassment. He choked out a timid, "Um, yeah," his voice thick with love. "Thank you, bro. Don't get soft on me now. Just because you almost died doesn't mean we have to get all sentimental." He chuckled and lightly tapped my hand with appreciation.

"Of course not," I replied with a smirk, my chest stinging as I forced out a laugh. I glanced over at Leo, who was still standing in the corner, distant but still in our presence. "Get over here, Leo," I commanded with a gesture of my head. We had come too far for any of us to not be part of this moment.

The deep-set circles around his eyes were evidence of the sleepless nights he had spent agonizing over all of us. He kept his distance, attempting to protect us from being hurt again, like Christine had been.

My voice was unwavering and powerful as I spoke, "That's an order."

He hesitated for a few moments, but eventually he obliged and made his way to Christine's side. She was perched on the bed, nestled beside me. He stood there, feeling the weight of our love and admiration for him, and a sense of closure settled over us while he opened his arms to embrace her.

"I'm glad you're okay," he growled, his muscles tightening as he attempted to suppress the rage that lingered beneath. We were all still wrecked about what had happened to us. Christine went to him, wrapping her arms around his neck and pulling him into an embrace. He held her for a moment before reluctantly releasing her.

"Thank you both for protecting Atticus," she whispered, squeezing him close.

Leo glanced at me, conveying a silent message. "We're family, Christine. We all have a stake in this."

"We've all made it here," she said, her voice shaky with emotion. Tears sparkled in her eyes, and Leo tenderly wiped them away with his thumb. "I never thought I'd have this again."

He stroked her hair and nodded understandingly. "I'm glad you're here. I'm glad you're safe. I made a mistake thinking I could do this alone. It'll take all three of us to protect you and our baby."

"Our baby," she murmured, her hand caressing the bump on her stomach as she laid her head against his shoulder. "Damn it, I can't believe this is my reality." Christine tightened her embrace and stared up into Leo's eyes. "You're stuck with us now."

"I wouldn't have it any other way," he said.

A voice from the doorway broke up the tender moment, and I turned to look at my mother walking through the door, followed closely by Hudson. "Can I come in?" she asked.

My mother had always been such a gentle creature, controlled by a husband who treated her like a pet. But she had a fierceness in her gaze that felt unnatural. "Mom," I said.

Christine and Leo stepped back with reverence as

she slowly approached the bed. Her eyes were filled with tears, but Hudson's gentle touch on her shoulder seemed to be the guiding light. "I'm so glad you're okay," she stammered, her voice broken with emotion. "I…I couldn't bear the thought. I'm sorry, Atticus."

She tenderly grabbed my hand and I felt some semblance of strength return to my body. "Mom, it's okay," I whispered.

"No. It's not." She leaned closer, her face mere inches away from mine. "He will never hurt us again, Atticus," she spoke in a shaky voice, laced with determination. "Never again."

I looked up at Hudson and saw a firm expression on his face, as if he was conveying a deep-rooted resolve to keep us safe without words.

"Of course not, Mom," I assured her with a warmth in my voice. "You're safe now."

Mom's gaze shifted between Christine and me, her lips trembling as she spoke. "She showed me how to defend myself, Atticus. She's…" Her voice trailed off as she wiped a single tear from her eye. "She's a special one."

I turned to face Christine, who was now weeping silently. "You did it, Elizabeth," she said. "I'm so proud of you."

I couldn't understand what I was hearing. "Mom, what happened?"

My mother inhaled deeply and stood up, her petite frame radiating strength. "I killed him, Atticus," she declared through clenched teeth. "I killed your father." She bent down to press a gentle kiss onto my forehead. "And I'd do it a hundred times over if it meant protecting you and your family from any harm. I used to think you got all that fearlessness and bravery from him." My mother lovingly caressed my dark hair. "But now I realize that you inherited some of it from me too."

I reached up and grabbed her hand, pressing it against my forehead. "How are you feeling?"

"Been better," she said with a quiet laugh. "But I'll get through this. I'll get through it knowing that you're safe. That your love and unborn child are safe, too." I could feel her hot tears land on my skin. "And I get to see all of you together." She pulled her hand away, and I saw the look of fierce determination in her eyes as she announced, "I'll never stop protecting you and yours. You'll always be my son."

"Mom," I whispered, my voice cracking with emotion. I reached for her hand again and held it against my chest. "You made the right decision. You did."

"I wish I had done it earlier," she said, her voice pleading with me. "That way, you wouldn't have suffered."

Electricity surged inside of me, my throat closing up at the overwhelming weight of guilt and sadness that had been lifted from her shoulders. "Mom—" I felt bad that she had to do this. I should have saved her sooner. I should have realized how twisted my father had become.

"No, Atticus. Don't speak," she pleaded, her voice filled with conviction. "There's no reason to feel guilty. You're safe. You're all safe." She then turned to face Christine, who was still fighting off tears, and grabbed her hand. "I'm so sorry, Christine, for what you had to go through. I should've protected you and Atticus better, but now I'm here to do so. I'm sorry."

Christine furrowed her brow and shook her head. "No, it's okay, Elizabeth. You saved me in the end." She tentatively stepped forward and seized a hold of my mother's hand. "I'm happy you're here."

Elizabeth smiled. "I should let you all discuss tonight. Leo, I saw your mother and sister in the waiting room. I'll be with them if you need anything."

"What plans?" I asked, but to my frustration, they ignored my question.

Leo gave her a smile. "Thank you, Elizabeth."

Once she and Hudson were at the door, Hudson paused to look back at Christine. "You did good today, Christine. I'm proud of you."

Christine smiled at him. "Thank you, Hudson."

Once they were gone, I sat up a bit in my bed. "What plans?"

August grinned wildly. "Today, I'm taking my girl to the altar."

"She wanted to get married standing in Lord Nathan's blood—that would have been something," Leo joked, but his eyes echoed a deep-seated hurt. I glowered, wishing I could dig into his mind and get rid of his doubts. Christine was mine—ours.

"I still have an idea," Christine interjected, her voice gentle yet purposeful. "I thought a bonfire behind us while we said 'I do' would be nice."

"Little Monster," I murmured, admiration practically dripping from my mouth. "You're so damn sexy when you talk about burning our enemies."

"I'd marry you in this hospital room if I had to," August declared with a resolute tone and a steely gaze. "Do you still want to walk her down the aisle, brother?"

"I'll crawl if I must," I declared confidently, pushing the nurse call button as a token of my commitment.

August ran his hand through his hair and glanced at Leo out of the corner of his eye. "I need a best man."

Leo gazed at all of us in turn, gulping audibly. "I've always stood by your side, August. Shouldn't stop now."

I growled and took Christine's hand in mine as the nurse entered the room. It was time to take my Little Monster to her wedding.

Chapter Twenty-Five

I stood with a fierce fire blazing behind me, illuminating the battlefield with its glow. The charred corpses at my feet served as a reminder of our victory over our enemies, while the billowing smoke carried our triumphant cries to the star-filled night sky. I could feel the weight of destiny on my shoulders as I shifted nervously, my gaze sweeping over the soot-covered soldiers and lords that filled the royal gardens.

I welcomed the pressure of fate that brought me to this place and time. I had accepted a crown, but love had brought me to my knees. I wanted her name to be tied to mine forever, and for my title to come from her lips and her soul. She had made me a powerful man, and I was hers and she was mine. There was no other title that could encompass our burning love.

Leo stood beside me, his presence a balm to the anxiousness that coursed through me. He tugged on the immaculate collar of his uniform and waved at his mother, who was sitting in the front row just beside Elizabeth DuPont.

"I always knew you'd marry her one day," he said softly, his voice conveying a combination of wistfulness and wonder.

I couldn't help but smile a little at his words. Turning to him, I looked into his eyes and nodded slowly. "Me too," I replied.

He let out a little chuckle, his lip quirking up at one side. "Just expected it to hurt a little more."

I looked at the crowd once more, then dropped my mouth open in shock when I saw Adonis fast walking toward me. His arm was cradled in a sling as he marched forward, a look of determination on his face. "Augustus!" he snapped, making my spine straighten.

"Adonis, what are you—"

"I taught you how to drive. I followed you to the ends of the earth—"

"Adonis, you're going to get your blood pressure up again," I said, cutting him off.

"You were going to get married without me?" he asked. "I had to race here. I almost didn't make it."

I felt a smidge bad as he huffed at me. "Adonis…"

He walked up to me and placed a hand on my shoulder. "I am so proud of the man you've become." The old man had tears in his eyes as he looked up at me.

"I'm sorry I didn't call. Things have been…hectic," I replied. "I couldn't imagine getting married without you here. You've been more of a father figure than *both* the men who claimed me as their son."

Adonis blinked. "Don't say things like that, Your Majesty. I'm a grown man. It would be humiliating to cry here in front of everyone."

I shook my head and wrapped him in a hug, a broad grin on my face. "I love you, Adonis. Thank you for putting up with my sorry ass all these years."

When I pulled away, he was full-on crying. "It has been my greatest honor, Augustus," he whispered before swiping at his tears and finding a seat on the front row.

The crowd began to stir as my attention gravitated back to the ceremony, and I saw Christine approaching in all her magnificence. Everyone stood to welcome her and my heart swelled. Her arm was locked tightly onto Atticus's, who was pale and unsteady but determined to march her to me. In his own flawed way, he was offering me the chance to share in the love of this woman he'd possessed ever since he first laid eyes on her. Her beauty and strength radiated from her as if it were written on a script, like an exquisite masterpiece waiting for its grand unveiling.

The moment she stepped onto the platform, her eyes were fixed on mine. She looked like an eternal goddess in her red gown, the color of passion. I wanted to take her in my arms and ravage her right then and there. My cock throbbed beneath my trousers as I drank in her beauty shamelessly.

Beside me, Leo gave an approving nod, with a knowing smirk on his lips. We both couldn't help but beam goofily with pride.

The hushed murmurs of the congregation filled the air as the priest spoke. His voice boomed as he uttered the fateful question, "Who gives this bride away?"

Atticus stepped forward from his place in the crowd, standing tall and smirking at me as Christine stepped beside him. His eyes fixed on her, and in the same instant, his lips crashed into hers. He took her with a wild urgency, exploring her mouth hungrily with an intensity that left everyone in the crowd breathless. I could feel the electricity in the air, and I knew this was his way of displaying his unrelenting possessiveness of her. Nothing less could be expected from the brutal asshole. He truly was devoted to Christine.

When they eventually broke apart, Atticus held on to her hand tightly, preventing her from leaving him. I had no intention of taking her from him, but I wanted to make my own mark on our relationship by being part of what would be one of its most important moments yet: Atticus's blessing.

Christine's face flushed a bright red as he pulled away slowly, her lips swollen and her eyes bright. "No one is giving her away today," he said, loud enough for everyone to hear. "Christine decides for herself what she wants. She's my queen. My heart. My Little Monster. My everything."

I cleared my throat, gently raising my arm for prominence. Atticus looked up at me with a fiery glare before slowly releasing his grip on Christine's hand and reluctantly stepping away.

Christine walked toward me with a newfound confidence that filled me with pride and love, taking my proffered hand without hesitation. She smiled up at me with steadfast assurance that showed just how deeply she trusted me to keep her safe and protect our love.

Atticus moved to stand beside Christine. The way we were situated, all four of us were at the altar, with my love and me in the middle.

I stood proudly with my man, Leo, at my side. His presence brought me a peculiar sensation of courage and security. We towered over the priest at the altar, and I could feel Christine's admiration and desire as she looked upon me.

The priest cleared his throat before commencing. "We have gathered here today to witness the union of two souls. A union of love, devotion, and an unbreakable bond." He opened his ancient book and began the ceremony. His words spoke of the courage it took for us to unite, of the irresistible force that pulled us together, and of the passionate love we had for each other that would last for seven lifetimes. He beamed his approval as he continued to read, and I could feel Christine's arms around me in a pulse of warmth as if she wanted to shout out to the universe how happy we were.

The priest spoke of fate, and I looked up at him with a bit of a snort. Fate fucked me so hard; I didn't think I'd have to work for anything in life, but I was wrong. A mother with more secrets than I ever knew. An abusive father that wasn't even my real father, and a biological dad that wasn't much better. I had all my luxuries stripped away. My title. My future. But I never realized that fate gave me more than I ever expected. She gave me the most beautiful woman I'd ever seen in my life, with a spirit that could break through the coldest of hearts. Fate gave me the brother who almost died, only to make me a better man. Fate gave me an unlikely family with my guard. Fate took my hand and led me to Christine.

I tightened my grip on her small, dainty hand as I turned to face the priest. The weight of the crown sitting atop a pillow in his grasp radiated throughout the room. The crown I was soon to inherit.

"Augustus of Aldrich, please speak your oath to the kingdom," the priest said.

My lips curled into a knowing smirk as I looked at her. Sure, there was a formal oath that I was expected to read, but I wanted to take this opportunity to express my own vow.

"I accept the crown that comes with her hand—her beautiful hand that I'm so lucky to hold—because Christine would want me to. There's no way of knowing what life is without her. Her gentle and determined spirit makes me a better man and leader. I solemnly swear to devote my life to Aldrich and support her as she leads this kingdom. I vow to earn the people's trust and lead them with honor and grace. I will protect her from any hardship and love her through everything."

My eyes barely held back the glistening tears of raw emotion as I watched the priest raise his hands, placing my crown onto my head, a weight I hadn't expected to carry so lightly. This new path was no longer a sentence, but a way to show Christine how much I loved her.

Leo handed us both our wedding bands, and I grasped Christine's hand, never wanting to let go.

"Christine Abernathy," I declared with certainty. "I've been in love with you since the moment we first met. And now, here we are."

The electricity between us was tangible, as if we were both daring to take a chance on something that we'd thought impossible for so long. "I vow to love you until the stars burn out and the earth crumbles. I've seen you grow into an awe-inspiring creature, a brilliant being radiating beauty and passion. Every day, I dream of being the man you deserve, the one who can shelter you from harm, your beacon in the shadows of life. That's what I vow to do—fight for your joy and share the life we build together. No matter what comes our way, I will take it head-on, all for love's sake." I put the ring on her finger and smiled. She looked up at me with tears streaking down her face, and she was *beautiful*.

She spoke. "Augustus." I smiled as I looked into her glistening blue eyes. "I love you. You are my reason for breathing. I promise to cherish you and always be there. I love you more than I could ever say. I never thought I'd be this happy. I never thought I'd find someone who looks at my soul and still loves me. Someone who grounds me and reminds me of the parts of my innocence I'd long forgotten. And I'm thankful that fate brought us back together. I promise to take care of you, to love you no matter what, to lead the kingdom with you and honor you always."

She placed the ring on my finger and squeezed my hand. She smiled and I could feel the warmth in her hand as she squeezed it. "I love you."

"I love you," I whispered, squeezing her hand back.

"By the power vested in me by the kingdom of Aldrich, I now pronounce you husband and wife. Official king and queen." People cheered loudly, clapping for us. The priest's voice broke through the noise. "You may kiss the bride."

I bent down and kissed her. Her lips were soft and warm, and I savored the taste of her. When I pulled away, she looked at me with the brightest eyes I'd ever seen. I still had one more gift to give her. One last thing to bring her joy—because that was my ultimate purpose in life now. Make the girl I love happy.

I held her hands and guided them to Leo. The crowd grew quiet with confusion. She looked at me curiously as she grabbed his hands, and Leo swallowed while staring at our girl.

"This is your moment, too, Leo. It's time to step out of the shadows," I whispered.

Leo looked at the crowd, then back at her. Clearing his throat, he then said, "I promise to love you, Christine. I promise to fight for your happiness. I promise to cherish you and make you feel safe. I promise to try to keep that smile on your face for the rest of my life. I promise to nourish the soft parts of you that Augustus loves." She sniffed and he pulled her close. "I promise to lead the kingdom with you—to do my duty and to help you shoulder the burdens of leadership. I promise to never be far away. I promise to fight your demons and stand beside you as you fight. I promise to cherish the parts of your soul Atticus has brought to life. I promise to love you in the dark, and in the light."

Christine was sobbing as Leo spoke. Her sobs grew louder as Leo spoke, as he laid down his oath. "I promise to love you forever."

He kissed her on the forehead, and she looked at him. She squeezed his hand, and I saw her whisper something I couldn't hear. He nodded and smiled.

The crowd cheered for us, and I felt the weight of what we had just done. As Christine and I walked down the aisle, I thought about the promises we had made to each other.

We had promised to love each other unconditionally, forever. We had promised to fight for each other's happiness, no matter what life threw our way. And we had promised to lead Aldrich into a brighter future. It was a lot of responsibility, but one that I knew we could handle together.

Suddenly, a cheer erupted from the crowd. People started throwing roses and lilies in our path, creating a path of petals as we walked toward our future.

We reached the end of the aisle and I paused for a moment to take it all in—the starry sky, the burning fire, our people clapping and cheering us on—and said a silent thank-you for this beautiful beginning that lay ahead of us.

Christine looked up at me with tears in her eyes and smiled as she grabbed my hand tight in hers. Atticus and Leo followed close behind us as we stepped out into our future together as king and queen of Aldrich.

What better way to begin our lives than together.

Chapter Twenty-Six

LEO

The air was thick with the stench of Redview soldiers, drunk on Theodore DuPont's finest wine. Christine and August were at the head of the room, their heads close together as they chattered excitedly over the remnants of the feast. The royal wedding reception was far from the elegant event Nathan had planned. Every detail had been meticulously crafted—no doubt expecting his own enjoyment—and here it lay, wasted, a mere memory on an altar of ashes.

It was so much more than a royal wedding ceremony. The soldiers were celebrating their new queen. It was dirty and raw and perfect.

The room was dimly lit by flickering candles and shrouded in a deep green fabric that hung from the grand chandelier. The platters of meats and cheeses were half-eaten and wilting, covered in a swarm of frenzied flies. People were singing and laughing around them, but Christine and August remained still, eyes focusing on each other while they silently communicated in a language more intimate than words. The tension between them was so palpable that it made the air crackle with anticipation.

I should have been jealous.

But I was so fucking happy.

Because I knew that I had my own claim to Christine's heart as well.

Atticus sat vigilantly, barely keeping his eyes open, at his mother's side. He had a monumental recovery ahead of him, but he wouldn't leave Elizabeth DuPont's side—not even for a moment. His worry was apparent; she had killed her husband earlier today and it had taken its toll.

I was worried about him. There would be plenty of men that would want revenge for killing Theodore, not to mention power seeking individuals that would challenge him. He had a long road ahead to claim his empire, but I knew he was up to the challenge.

Christine was breathtakingly beautiful, and in that

moment, I knew I had to prove to her that I was committed to making things right. I'd made too many mistakes and hurt her gravely, yet here we were. I could feel the hope in the air and silently promised myself that I would never let her down again.

Despite everything I'd done, she still let me back into her life and accepted me in places that no one else could go. I wouldn't ever be perfect, and I'd never be able to erase the horrible things I'd done in the past. But I wanted to show her that we could make one another happy.

A burning passion took over me as I stepped closer and softly kissed her cheek. A faint hint of a smile curved up her lips.

"You alright?" I muttered, my lips brushing against her earlobe.

"It feels too surreal," she whispered. "Can't help but think something will ruin it all."

I glanced toward August, who silently nodded back at me. "Come," I said, offering my hand. The band started playing as she placed her delicate fingers in mine, and I gently pulled her toward me, inhaling the sweet aroma of her vanilla perfume.

"Where are we going?" she questioned, her breath a whisper against my neck.

"Our first dance, baby," I whispered, my fingers

digging into her hips as I guided her to the middle of the room. Every eye in the room followed as I confidently positioned our bodies in the perfect spot. I held her close, so close that I could feel the heat of her body radiating through me and her heart beating rapidly against my chest. A soft smile tugged at her lips.

"How did you know that this is exactly what I wanted to do?"

The intensity of my gaze pierced into hers, and I crushed my lips against hers. Her body melted into mine as I deepened the kiss, wanting—no, needing—to prove to her that this was just the beginning. We pulled apart, my hands still gravitating toward her hips, and the fire in her eyes burning hotter than before.

I could feel the music reverberating in my chest, overwhelming me with its intensity. Drawing Christine closer, I began to move, though admittedly clumsily. I used to be so awkward in the face of her grace and beauty, but now I wanted to push myself and be that man she so deserved.

As I guided us around the room, I heard her humming along with the melody. I was in awe of her and the effect she had on me. My heart raced as my desire to kiss her consumed me, but instead, I whispered into her ear how much I had missed her and how determined I was to never let her go again. Tears filled

Christine's eyes, as if she could feel my love as strongly as I did, and she smiled up at me, pressing herself even closer against my chest.

In that moment, I knew that this was only the beginning. My love for Christine had been reignited, and nothing would be able to separate us again.

My heart was pounding as we moved together, passionately swaying to the music. I was adamant that this time, nothing would get in the way of us being together and making a life. I wanted to forget the past and start afresh. Everything around me seemed perfect —like it should have been all along.

My gaze locked with hers as I spoke in a low whisper, "Come with me." And I grabbed her hand, leading her through the crowd and down the hall. August gave me an approving nod as we passed, and Atticus looked envious—like he wished he could come with us. He'd be in for some serious trouble if he didn't stick to what the doctor told him about *no strenuous activities for six weeks.*

I could feel the tension between us as I pushed open the door and we stepped into the hall, ready to seize our future together.

I shoved us into the secluded sitting room, my heat enveloping her completely. Her curves pushed against my body with a wantonness that I desperately wanted to fulfill.

"Christine," I grunted against her lips, knowing full well that we were taking a chance by being alone together.

"Yes?" she whispered back, her eyes full of anticipation.

"Be quiet," I commanded gruffly, "or your husband and guests will hear you scream."

She nodded before my mouth descended on hers and I plundered her with an aggressive passion that was both desperate and fierce. My hands roamed over her body as my teeth sunk into her soft lips, sending a shiver through her as her moans filled the room. Clothes were quickly torn off in our haste to join our bodies together, and I smiled as I ripped open the bodice of her gown and exposed her breasts to my hungry gaze.

I was overwhelmed by sensations. The satin-smooth feel of her hands as they caressed my face. The softness of her skin brushing against mine. The warmth of her breath on my skin.

I captured her lips, exploring hungrily as I lingered on her every gasp. "Damn, you're stunning," I uttered in reverence.

Her eyes closed as she enjoyed the sensation of my lips on hers, her tongue matching mine in every beautiful curve and arch.

My hand ran its way down her body and slipped

beneath the lace of her panties. She shuddered at my touch, and I moved eagerly, sinking two fingers deep inside her core. She gasped at the sensation, nails digging into my flesh as she arched against my hand. The wetness quickly grew, coating my digits as I moved them with an increasing ferocity. Our eyes locked as I took her, and I admired the way it made her shudder.

I pressed a kiss below her ear and whispered fiercely, "I want to see my cum leaking out of that tight cunt of yours on your wedding night, baby."

My grip on her tightened as I whispered in her ear, "Come for me, baby." I felt her shudder in my arms as my skilled fingers tormented her clit, and a wild scream escaped her lips. She was close, so I increased the pressure, circling around the bundle of nerves. I wanted to hear her moans. I wanted to hear her sounds of pleasure. I wanted to hear her scream my name.

A guttural cry ripped from her throat as I pushed her over the edge and waves of pleasure washed through her body. Her walls constricted around my fingers, milking every last ounce of pleasure from my touch. I savored the moment as I held her close, inhaling her scent and reveling in the satisfaction of knowing that I had given her such pleasure.

"Holy fuck," she breathed against me, clinging to my body as she slowly came back down to reality.

I smiled against her neck and gently kissed it. "You're such a good girl, coming all over my fingers when I tell you to," I said with a satisfied smirk. "Now, I'm going to taste you, baby," I said while walking her over to a chaise lounge in the corner of the room.

My need for her was insatiable. I put her back on it and spread her legs, as my eyes glowed with deep desire at the sight of her dripping pussy. I could smell the sweetness of her arousal, and I wanted to consume every inch of it. With my tongue, I teased and tasted her swollen clit, and she groaned wildly in pleasure. She was so unbelievably delicious and I made sure to savor every moment of this experience. My hands kneaded her skin while my mouth feasted on her flesh. Her body trembled and shook as she gave into me and allowed me to take complete control of her pleasure. I licked harder and faster until finally, she screamed out as another orgasm hit her hard.

I settled heavily on top of her, my hands fisting her long locks as I forced her lips open with my tongue. My chest rubbed against hers, and I felt my cock harden even more with desire. With the tip of my tongue, I explored the depths of her mouth, tasting the sweetness of her as I claimed her.

Her legs opened further to accommodate me, and I seized this opportunity. With ardent intent, I thrust my fingers inside her pulsing core as her hips lashed nearer to me. Her breath hitched in her chest as her mouth opened with wonder and delight. The sweetness of her breath was almost orgasmic in its own right.

"Ahhh…" she sighed out in pleasure, her body shuddering beneath mine with each exquisite movement of my fingers.

I could feel the beginnings of her orgasm grip around me as a feral growl ripped through me. I wanted more. I wanted to feel her come apart beneath me, to make her surrender completely to me and only me.

"Oh, God, Leo," she breathed out. Her arms looped around me possessively as my name rolled off of her tongue like a secret prayer.

I brought my fingers to my lips, and I licked her taste from them, letting my eyes roam all over her body with an intense desire. I wanted her and I wanted her now.

My groan barely escaped my lips as I positioned myself over her. Her eyes grew heavy with anticipation as she felt my naked skin against hers. I gently caressed her cheek, allowing my fingers to slide down to her lips.

Her moans were muffled by the sound of our combined breaths as our lovemaking intensified. She held on to me tightly as I thrust myself inside of her with a deep resolve.

My eyes met hers as I pushed myself farther and farther into her. She tried to contain the sounds of pleasure that were escaping from her mouth, but failed miserably. I let out a loud roar as I buried myself completely inside of her tight walls, conveying the deep love that I had for her.

"I love you, Christine," I groaned before pushing myself even deeper into her.

"I love you too, babe," she responded in a whisper.

I plowed into Christine with a ferocity I had never experienced before. Her sweet wetness clung to my erection as she quickly responded with a throaty groan. She clung to my back with her fragile yet powerful fingers, digging in to keep rhythm with my thrusts. I moved my face away from hers and looked into her eyes. I wanted her to know that I was in control.

"Look at me," I commanded as I drove into her harder, faster, deeper. Her eyes flew open and she shook beneath me as I pounded away into her depths. I wanted to see her surrender as I unleashed the raw energy that was coursing through my veins. "I want to see your face while I take you," I said. With a passionate kiss, I felt her climax come upon us both like a flood of pure pleasure.

My eyes glinted with intent as I drove deep into her, my cock filling her as our hips ground together. I tangled one hand in her hair and pressed my lips roughly against hers, pushing her head even further back into the pillow. My other hand wandered down to her swollen nipple, teasing it before claiming it between my teeth, causing her to moan out loud.

My thrusts grew harder and faster as I felt the steel bands of pleasure tightening around my shaft. My groans of satisfaction mixed with her own as I plundered her body, driving us closer and closer to the edge. With a final guttural roar of pleasure, I surged harder and faster, pushing us both over the edge, our bodies shaking in bliss as explosions of ecstasy ripped through us. I groaned, every muscle in my body tensing as a final shudder ran through me and my hot cum flooded her.

We lay there together, panting and exhausted, but this wasn't what I wanted. I wanted more. I wanted to show her how much I loved her, and I wanted her to experience things she had never imagined.

Once the haze of pleasure had settled, I carefully slid out of her and gently kissed her temple. Then, I carefully scooped her up and carried her over to one of the larger sofas in the sitting room. She snuggled against me happily as I wrapped her in the warmth of my arms. I wanted to hold her like this for the rest of my life.

As I gazed upon the woman that I loved, a paralyzing sense of vulnerability encompassed me. I was certain that I had to tell her my truth.

My chest tightened as I let out a deep sigh. "Christine, I need to share something with you."

Her face tensed as she locked eyes with me, apprehension radiating from her voice, "Okay?"

I inhaled deeply and paused for a second. "I'm sorry for ever doubting you, Christine. I'm sorry for ever doubting the love we share."

She tenderly caressed my cheek. "It's okay," she cooed. "I knew you needed time to adjust."

I shook my head firmly. "When I saw them take you, it all came back. The fear, the dread, the helplessness of that night three years ago. I felt my whole world come crashing down again. But this time, I realized something." I laid my hand protectively on her swollen stomach. "I can't keep running away from it. I need to face it, for us and for our family."

I kissed the palm of her hand. "I realized that I can't live with myself if I lose you. I love you so much, Christine. I love you so fucking much, and I can't lose you. I won't lose you. I've never been one to believe in fate." I paused, looking into her eyes. "But if there was any way to prove that it exists, to prove that we were meant to be, to have a life together and a family together, then I would have to say that you're it."

She started to speak, but I put a finger against her lips to silence her.

"Let me finish," I said. "I promise to fight for you. Always. I promise to never let you leave me. I've learned I like fighting with you."

"Oh?" she asked.

"It usually ends with one of us on top of the other," I teased.

She rolled her eyes. "You're terrible."

I chuckled and continued, "I've also learned that if I fight for you, then you'll fight for me too." I gently nuzzled her neck. "I love you, and I promise to love you forever."

I whispered my love for her, my hands running up and down her curves, as if to imprint her body onto my soul. "I will never let you go," I vowed, my voice a deep, possessive rumble. I pressed my lips to the delicate shell of her ear, making her shudder beneath me.

"I'm so scared I won't be a good father," I admitted, my brow furrowing in worry.

She pulled away and looked into my eyes, her own depths full of warmth and understanding. She traced gentle circles on my skin with a single finger, making me close my eyes in pleasure. "You will be," she promised. "You are strong and capable and brave."

My breath hitched in surprise, humbled by her faith in me. Was she really the only one who believed in me?

"I-I can't promise I won't make mistakes," I stammered, almost ashamed of the weakness of my confession.

She laid a hand on my cheek and smiled up at me tenderly. "But you can promise to learn from them," she said softly.

I nodded slowly, knowing that this was something I could do at least; I could try to learn how to be the best father that I could possibly be—for our little one, but also for her.

"I believe in you," she whispered against my lips, her breath soft and sweet like the dawning of a new day.

Her words were a balm to my worries. I wanted more than anything to make her proud of me as a man and a father.

She kissed me then, like no other kiss before—a kiss that promised me strength, that promised me courage, that promised me undying love.

Epilogue

THREE MONTHS LATER

I held the sonogram, staring adoringly at…well…I wasn't exactly sure *what* I was staring at. A baby, apparently.

A baby *girl*.

"Pink. Everything in this room has to be pink," August said while looking around the nursery.

Leo pinched the bridge of his nose. "I thought you wanted to paint a mural of Christine on the wall?"

"That's only *one wall*, Leo. We have six others that need decorating, too," August scoffed.

Atticus wrapped his arms around me and peered over my shoulder at the sonogram. "She has my nose," he murmured in my ear.

"I don't even know where her nose is," I admitted with a laugh.

He chuckled. "Me neither. But it seemed like the right thing to say."

I let Leo and August bicker about crib safety ratings while I spun around to face him. Atticus was doing a lot better and was moving around more. He even tortured a few of the men still loyal to his dead father, though he needed some help from Eva, who was all too happy to get her hands dirty. She was a bloodthirsty little thing.

"How was work?" I asked.

"Busy. I think I finally have a solid group of men again. A lot of them like the direction of the business since I got a new arms dealer. Lots of cash. Money makes men loyal."

"Nothing is working!" August shouted, making all of us look at him. "This room doesn't have enough natural light. Natural light is very important for babies. And how am I supposed to have a rocking chair for each of us in here if there isn't enough room?"

I released Atticus to walk over to August. "We don't *all* need a rocking chair," I said softly.

His face twisted up. "Yes, we do. We all need a place to sit for bedtime stories."

I knew that August was determined to be a better

father than his own, but it was making him crazy. "We'll figure something out," I promised him.

"Nothing about this castle is good enough for our baby, Christine," he said before crossing his arms over his chest.

I didn't like being in this castle any more than he did, but this was our only option.

Leo cleared his throat. "I think the room is perfect. It's across the hall from us—"

"No," August said. "It's not good enough. Come with me."

August wrapped his hand around my wrist and carefully tugged on my arm, coaxing me to follow him out of the room.

"August. Where are we going?" I asked.

Leo tried to hide his smile behind his hand, and Atticus licked his lips.

August led me into our bedroom and shut the door. Releasing my hand, he moved to my desk and grabbed a scroll I'd never seen before. "Here are the blueprints," he said while spreading it out.

I walked over to him and peered over his shoulder. "What is this?" I asked.

"It's more energy efficient. The architect's design is really something special," August explained excitedly. "It has an atrium, and I already spoke with an award-winning landscaper about the gardens. It isn't as big as this castle; in fact, it's significantly smaller, but it backs up to a lake so—"

"August," I interrupted. "Are these plans for us?"

He spun around to face me with a big grin on his face while Leo and Atticus surrounded me. "This castle has a lot of memories, Christine. Most of them are bad," he said as tears filled my eyes.

Leo spoke up. "Coming back to Aldrich was hard on you. You shouldn't have to live somewhere that traumatizes you."

"You shouldn't have to raise our baby here, either," Atticus added.

August turned back to the plans. "It won't be ready for a few years, but this is where I want our family to be, Christine. This is where we can make our own story."

I looked around the room. "What about here?"

"We can turn it into whatever we want it to be. Yasmin suggested a homeless shelter and training center. We could refurbish everything and make it a place for the people of Aldrich. Maybe put some good back into these walls," Leo said with a smile.

"A castle is expensive, August. We're still recovering from your father's shady investments. The country won't allow for such spending."

August and Atticus exchanged a look. "I happen to have a very good investor," August said.

Atticus pulled me into his side and kissed my temple. "I want you to be happy, Little Monster. We all think this would be good for our family."

I wanted a place where my family could be happy. I just didn't think it would ever happen. "Okay," I told them.

August's eyes went wide. "Really? You're not going to argue with me or ask me a million questions?" he asked.

"No. You are right. I don't like living here, and I don't care how we do it, but let's get out of this castle. Together. With our baby," I said.

Leo and Atticus pulled me into their arms as August squealed.

I knew that the four of us would be happy no matter where we were.

ONE YEAR LATER...

"Is she asleep?" I asked, my voice groggy as August shuffled into the room.

"Nuzzled warm in her crib. You know she loves to fall asleep snuggling her Papa." I grinned at him and stretched out on the mattress. Leo was sitting beside me, and Atticus was pouring over a document at the desk.

"I'm worn out, though," August added. "How do people take care of a baby with just two parents? We need a fucking army."

I chuckled, shaking my head. "That's why we have each other," I said, reaching out to stroke August's arm. He smiled softly and leaned against me for a moment.

Leo slid closer, meeting my gaze with a mischievous glimmer in his eyes. His strong hand found mine and he tugged me closer until I felt the warmth of his body next to mine. August shifted over as well, pressing up against my other side while Atticus watched quietly from across the room. "Since Kate is asleep, why don't we enjoy some of the downtime?"

The air around us suddenly seemed charged with electricity as Leo placed a gentle kiss on my neck. That single touch set off an explosion of arousal within me, sending a tingle down my spine that left me wanting more.

I tilted my head to give Leo better access as his lips slid down my neck, pressing gentle kisses against my collarbone. Beside me, August was doing the same, making me feel like I was the center of their universe. With each kiss, each touch, I felt my heart pounding faster and my lungs struggling to take in enough breath.

"I'm in the mood to worship my queen," Leo growled, sitting up to press a kiss against my lips. The room was filled with the sounds of soft kisses, the rustle of clothing being tossed to the floor, and the murmur of deepening voices.

I felt my body heating up as Leo's lips began a trail down my stomach. I closed my eyes, allowing my mind to fully relax and focus on the sensation of each kiss and touch. Leo's hands felt good sliding over my chest as I closed my eyes.

August's entire body vibrated with desire as he dragged his lips across my neck and collarbone, his erect cock pressing against my hip. I felt myself go wet, my pussy tingling with anticipation as I curved my back.

"I want you all so much," I sighed. "Please."

The men ravenously seized me in their arms, pressing their lips to my cheekbone and neck. Their firm hands roamed my body, awakening a scorching heat between my thighs. I could not contain my moans as they kissed me with greater hunger.

Leo's touches were slowly driving me mad as his hands moved possessively over my hips and waist. Atticus stepped toward us from the desk. His strong hands pulled Leo closer, and their intense kiss sent waves of pleasure through us all.

Atticus's gaze locked with mine as he kissed Leo, his

lips so close I could feel Leo's breathing against my skin. Atticus's chest was bare, his muscles glistening with sweat as they moved.

I gasped, my heart pounding as I felt myself getting even wetter. Leo and Atticus had realized not long ago that it made me hotter to see them kiss, and now they were indulging that hunger in the most exquisite way. It was raw. Potent desire. They did anything they could to make me feel good, including exploring one another in the sanctuary of our bedroom. Their mouths moved against one another, their tongues sliding and colliding, their breaths syncing in a howl of sensation.

"Please," I whispered, my eyes fluttering as I felt Atticus's and Leo's hands moving over my breasts. I gazed up into August's eyes, the look of desire in his gaze making my heart flutter. "Right now."

With that single demand, the men moved. Leo helped me out of my pants and tossed them to the side, his eyes sparkling as he took in the way my body was flushed and glistening with desire. Atticus slowly slipped the thin tank top over my head, my body quivering as I felt the cool air against my breasts.

Slowly, lovingly, the men helped me remove my bra and panties, leaving me naked as they admired me. I felt utterly desirable as their eyes raked over my naked body, and I felt my pussy growing wetter by the second.

Atticus finally crawled on top of me, gently pressing his lips to mine. I moaned into his mouth, my tongue brushing against his as he kissed me. His hands moved over my body, stroking my skin and igniting a fire deep within me.

August and Leo moved closer, their hands exploring my body as they gently kissed me. I felt my legs parting naturally, desperate for the release that I knew would come. Suddenly, Atticus sank down my body and his tongue was on my clit, teasing it out of its hiding place and sending streams of excitement radiating through me.

I exhaled in delight as I felt their tongues flicking across my skin, giving me sensations that had me buzzing with bliss. August sucked on my neck. Leo teased my nipples. Atticus stroked my clit. The men were all working together to satisfy me, each one taking turns licking and caressing my body in ways I never thought possible.

I looked down and saw Leo had moved to the needy place between my thighs to join Atticus kissing my pussy. Their tongues seemed to dance around each other as they pleasured me, creating an erotic symphony that had me trembling and screaming in delight. I felt my body quivering, every touch pushing me closer and closer to the edge of ecstasy. My breath came in ragged gasps as the feeling overwhelmed me until I finally reached my climax, screaming out their names as wave after wave crashed through my body.

"Such a good girl," Atticus praised. "You love it when we kiss your pussy. You grind my face so nicely."

Leo and Atticus moved to the side of my bed, and I climbed over to them.

Goose bumps broke out all over my body, my nipples hardening into delicate peaks as I kissed Leo. I could taste myself on his tongue. "I want to shove my cock down your tight throat, baby," Leo said. "You want to choke on my cum?"

I undid his pants. He panted, grinning as I slipped my hand down his body and over the bulging erection within his boxer briefs. I teased the sensitive tip, stroking his shaft until I felt his body shuddering.

I rose and slid my body downwards, pushing his jeans and underwear down his legs until he kicked them off. My eyes widened as they took in his thick cock and big balls, my pussy aching as I looked at him and thought about just how much pleasure he could give me. I slowly slipped my lips around his shaft, taking him in inch by inch until I had his length down my throat. I closed my eyes as I sucked him, my tongue flicking over his sensitive tip and making him gasp.

"Holy fuck, Christine," Leo groaned, his hands

moving over my hair. "You have no idea how good that feels."

I loved the way he talked to me. He was a soft gentleman around other people, but in the bedroom, he showed me a side of himself that was wild and uninhibited.

I sucked harder, hollowing out my cheeks as I bobbed my head up and down. I could feel him growing even harder in my mouth, the salty taste of his pre-cum already coating my tongue. Saliva pooled in my mouth and I swallowed it, taking him even deeper into the back of my throat until I nearly gagged.

Suddenly, August moved behind me, and I felt his hands on my hips. He knelt down, pressing a kiss to the small of my back before pushing my legs apart and moving closer. He settled underneath me and grabbed my thighs. His tongue flicked against my clit, tracing circles around it before he began thrusting it deep into my slit. "You taste like heaven. I could eat this pussy all day."

I gasped, the sensation of his tongue coupled with Leo's cock in my mouth nearly sending me over the edge. With every movement of their tongues and body parts, I felt myself growing more and more aroused until I was screaming out.

My orgasm came suddenly and ferociously, passion

crashing over me as I rode out the climax until I finally collapsed onto the bed in a panting heap.

The three men moved around me, kissing my skin and stroking me gently. Leo pulled away, spit dripping down my chin as he grinned at the satisfied expression on my face.

Atticus and August moved closer, their intense gazes heating up my body. "You ready, love?" August asked. I nodded eagerly, desire coursing through me as I felt them move behind me. I got up on my knees and spread my legs as wide as they would go. Leo positioned himself under me, pushing his hard cock against my wet pussy as Atticus and August spread my ass cheeks apart.

Leo slid into me slowly, the sensation causing stars to burst behind my eyes. He thrust into me gently at first before increasing his speed until I was screaming once more.

Meanwhile, Atticus and August took turns lubing up and slipping their fingers into my tight asshole. I gasped as they massaged me, bliss radiating through my body with each movement. The sensations built until my entire body was vibrating with ecstasy, and I felt myself cresting over the edge once more.

"I've dreamed about this perfect, tight hole," Atticus

said. We'd been working up to anal, and I was excited to try it.

"Please," I pleaded. "I want you inside me."

Atticus grinned, positioning himself behind me and pushing his shaft against my ass. Slowly, he pushed into me, sliding into my body and filling me with ecstasy. I gasped, my body twitching as he began moving in and out of me while Leo fucked my pussy.

"That feels so good," I sighed, closing my eyes as I savored the feeling. "So good."

"You like that, love?" August teased, watching me fuck them both. I nodded. "We're just getting started."

I gasped as they picked up the pace, my body rocking back and forth as Leo thrust into me. I whimpered as they slammed into me harder and harder, my body shaking as they filled me.

"You're so fucking tight," Atticus purred, his hands moving down to squeeze my ass. I gasped, enjoying the feeling of being completely filled.

Suddenly, August moved closer. His eyes smoldered as he pushed himself into my mouth. I sucked hungrily, my tongue lapping against his cock as I savored the taste of him. He said my name, thrusting harder and faster into my mouth until I was howling.

The three of them thrust into me faster and faster, and I felt my body shaking with euphoria. My pussy clenched around Leo's cock, and I moaned as I realized I was about to come again.

"I'm going to come," Leo roared. "I'm going to come inside your tight little pussy."

Leo's words were my undoing and I screamed out their names as I felt the pleasure wash over me. I trembled and cried out as I rode out the ecstasy, feeling my own streams of cum burst from my pussy, the sensation causing me to come even harder.

August's cock pulsed in my mouth, the salty taste of his seed exploding against my tongue. I sucked and swallowed as I rode out my orgasm.

"Ahhh fuck," Atticus rasped. "I'm coming, Christine."

My eyes widened as I felt his seed surge into my body. He grunted, his hands gripping my hips tightly as he emptied himself into me. I felt like I was about to collapse as the three of them lost control and began coming at the same time.

"Christine," Atticus sighed. "Christine."

"I can't take it," Leo said. "I can't hold it anymore."

I felt Leo explode, his hot cum spilling into my pussy and coating my walls. I could feel him filling me up, the thrill and sensation driving me wild.

August and Atticus groaned, filling my mouth and ass with their hot cum until I was overflowing with heat.

I trembled, my body shaking and shuddering as the heat flowed within me. I could feel their cum spilling out of me, my holes dripping with cum and their juices.

"Christine," Atticus groaned. "That was fucking incredible."

I gasped, my chest heaving with exertion. I could feel their release coating my thighs, a slow stream of cum sticking to my body and trickling down to puddle on the bed.

Leo and Atticus pulled out of me, and I collapsed on the bed. We lay there in an exhausted pile, our bodies entangled and glistening with sweat. My pussy still ached from the intense fucking, and I tried to catch my breath.

"That was amazing," I whispered, feeling Leo pull me against his chest. I closed my eyes, savoring the feeling of being completely spent and sated.

"You did so well, Little Monster," Atticus murmured, stroking my hair. "Your ass took my cock so nicely."

"I feel incredible," I said. "I'm not sure I'll ever want to leave this bed."

"Then we'll just have to make sure you don't have to," August said, squeezing my breasts.

I had them all. Forever.

Long live the Bloody Queen and her men.

Acknowledgments

It is with sincere gratitude that I recognize all those that helped me bring this story to life.

Helayna Trask

Amanda Anderson

Katie Friend

Lauren Campbell

Rita Rees

Claire Jones

Meggan Cook

As always, a heartfelt thank you to my family for their unending support. I'd also like to thank Quincy Mayes, for being my fantastic assistant and friend. Special thanks to Heather Maher and Amanda Avendano for letting me read the first chapter of this book to them at Book Bonanza. Their excitement and encouragement pushed me to continue. And lastly, thank you to Brittany Franks and Christine Estevez, who work hard to get my books out in the world.

About the Author

Coralee June is an *USA Today* bestselling romance writer who enjoys engaging projects and developing real, raw, and relatable characters. She is an English major from Texas State University and has had an intense interest in literature since her youth. She currently resides with her husband and three children in Dallas, Texas, where she enjoys long walks through the ice-cream aisle at her local grocery store.

WWW.AUTHORCORALEEJUNE.COM

@authorcoraleejune

www.ingramcontent.com/pod-product-compliance
Lightning Source LLC
Chambersburg PA
CBHW030059310726
48970CB00004B/1068